THE WOMAN IN THE FRAME

JJ MARSH

PREWETT
BIELMANN

The Woman in the Frame

Cover design: JD Smith

Published by Prewett Bielmann Ltd.

All enquiries to admin@jjmarshauthor.com

First printing, 2020

ISBN 978-3-9525191-9-6

To my godfather, Robert Prewett, whose interest in our family
history led me to Mallorca

Chapter 1

It was a strange sensation to put on shoes after two days of going barefoot. She decided against applying make-up because it reminded her of the usual dreary routine at home. Instead, she slicked Vaseline over her eyebrows and on her lips. Her husband was a big fan of the natural look. Facing herself in the mirror, she could see why. Her skin glowed, her eyes shone and her hair seemed grateful for a rest from daily blow dries.

Tanya put on a petrol-coloured cotton maxi dress and added the silver earrings Gabriel had bought her that morning in Port de Sóller. She was ready to meet their hosts and prepared to be on her best behaviour. With a last spray of scent, she wandered out onto the veranda where the man of her dreams was waiting, one ankle crossed over his knee, gazing out at the extraordinary view of sandstone buildings descending in circles down the hill. On the table sat two glasses of Aperol spritz, the orangey liquid the colour of a Caribbean sunset.

On hearing her footsteps, he looked over his shoulder with a smile. Her heart swelled and she wondered if she would ever get used to living with a man overjoyed by her mere existence.

"You look lovely," he said. "Then again, you always do."

"Thanks. I didn't want to overdo it, you know. I packed a proper evening dress and high heels, but it feels inappropriate for a casual dinner with bohemian artists. The thing is, I'm a tiny bit nervous. Maybe a drink would help. When do we have to leave?"

He passed her aperitif across the table and reached out to take her hand. "When we're ready. It's around a twenty-minute walk to their place, I reckon. They said to turn up any time after eight. Relax, it'll be just like having dinner with my mum. They're a pair of arty old hippies, so absolutely no reason to be nervous."

She sank into the chair and picked up a glass, asking herself what she had done to deserve such luck. "Your mum is not a celebrated artist who can flog her latest creation for a seven-figure sum. Which is one of the many reasons I adore her."

They drank in comfortable silence, listening to the cicadas' natural accompaniment to the evening symphony of birdsong. At ten to eight, Gabriel took the empty glasses into the kitchen, picked up the bottle of wine they had bought as a gift and took Tanya's hand.

The walk took under twenty minutes, despite Tanya dragging her heels to gaze into gardens, cafés, restaurants and other people's homes. A little over a quarter of an hour after they left their tiny cottage, they wandered up a slightly posher road towards the white walls of a villa. Nothing about the entrance identified the owner as one of Europe's most revered artists. Large metal gates were closed but nothing else suggested that this particular compound contained anyone special. Gabriel pressed the buzzer and the gates swung open.

Dogs barked as they drew closer to the building and Gabriel dropped to his haunches, greeting the two tatty-looking Irish wolfhounds on their own level. A woman appeared at the kitchen door, glass in hand, calling the animals.

"Harris, get down! Heel, Balfour!" she called. "Fear not, they look dangerous but they're nothing more than noisy and daft. Welcome, Gabriel and his lovely bride! Come over here and let me see you both. It's too romantic for words."

The dogs herded them towards the main house and the smell of grilling fish. Ophelia Moffatt came down the path to greet them, her kaftan wafting around her body like an Indian dancer's veils. She kissed Gabriel on both cheeks and rested her hands on Tanya's shoulders.

"I'm Ophelia, but you can call me Philly. Everyone does, the disrespectful bastards. Tanya, I am delighted to meet you. May I offer my most sincere congratulations? I'm brimming with joy at you darling people and this young man is radiating love like a Ready Brek kid. How are you finding the cottage? It's on the rustic side, that much I know, but we did our best to make it worthy of a honeymoon suite. Let's go in and have a snifter. My Long Island iced tea is getting warm." She slugged the remainder of her drink and Tanya managed to get a word in.

"Pleased to meet you too! The cottage is just perfect. We're really grateful. It's incredibly kind of you to lend us your cottage as a wedding present. I hardly ever get to travel, so this is more of a treat than you can imagine."

Philly clutched Tanya's arm and peered past her to look at Gabriel. "I adore her already. I may cry before the night is done. Harris, put that down, you filthy beast! Come along, my dears, before that useless man buggers up the fish."

On the patio stood a portly grey-haired man wearing an apron and brandishing a pair of barbecue tongs at the wolfhounds. "Here you are!" He dropped the tongs onto the table and opened his arms. "Gabriel Shaw, let me look at you. Heavens above, my godson, a married man! I feel ancient. First things first, introduce me to your beautiful bride." He embraced Gabriel with real affection and Tanya found she was smiling.

"You don't look ancient," said Gabriel. "You look better than ever. Hoagy, this is Tanya, my wonderful wife. Tanya, meet my godfather, Alexander Moffatt, known to his friends as Hoagy."

Tanya held out a hand which he took and lifted to his lips. "Charmed, Tanya, quite charmed to meet you, dear girl. I'm so sorry I couldn't attend your wedding, but I don't travel, you see. I'm doing my best to become a hermit. Tonight we'll celebrate the occasion all over again with cava and plenty of it! Philly, bring these people an aperitif and you may as well top mine up whilst you're there. Have a seat, Tanya, I need to keep an eye on the fish."

"It's lovely to meet you, Mr Moffatt. Thank you so much for the use of your cottage."

"Hoagy, please. It's only solicitors who call me Mr Moffatt. Gabriel, tell me all about your mother. Is she well? Is she happy you married such a delightful woman?"

As the two men conversed beside the barbeque, Philly placed a tray of glasses on the table and sat opposite Tanya. "Chin, chin, my dear," she said, raising her Long Island iced tea. "We're family now. I hear you have a little boy. How old is he?"

"Seven. His name is Luke. Along with my dad, he was sort of best man at the wedding. He made a speech and everything." To her astonishment, her eyes prickled with tears. She had seen Luke only yesterday morning and spoken to him that afternoon, but still.

"You miss him," said Philly, her eyes soft. "I understand. When my husband left me and my daughter, we became each other's entire worlds. Never spending a day apart until the custody agreement. He took her every other weekend and those forty-eight hours were absolute torture."

Tanya pinched the bridge of her nose. "That's it. Most of the time I worry about how much he needs me, but sometimes I think it's the other way around."

Philly took a long draught of her cocktail. "All the times you pick up their toys, their shoes and dream of having some time to yourself. Then when it happens?"

"I know! Don't get me wrong, I'm deliriously happy to be alone with Gabe. I love the freedom, the lack of responsibility and I know Luke's being spoilt rotten by the rest of the family.

It's just, you know, not being able to kiss him good night, smell his hair, I ..."

Philly passed her a tissue and Tanya patted the corner of her eyes, sniffing.

"Hellfire and damnation, woman, you've already made her cry?" Hoagy boomed. "What the devil did you put in her drink?"

In a second, Gabriel was by her side. "Tanya? Are you OK?"

"She's fine! Tanya and I are bonding over shared experiences, that is all. Unlike the testicularly challenged, women find it perfectly acceptable to express emotion. Gabriel, here's your aperitif. As for you, you interfering old bugger, just concentrate on not burning the bloody fish."

"The fish is nearing perfection, light of my life, star in my firmament. Fetch the salad and the bread, give Romy a call and let's eat! Pass my glass before you go, would you?"

Tanya gave Gabriel a reassuring smile and squeezed his hand. "I was telling her about Luke, that's all," she murmured. "Just hit me how much I miss him."

"Me too." Gabriel bent to kiss her lightly on the lips.

Philly shooed the dogs out of the way and placed a wooden bowl the size of a coracle in the centre of the table. The salad, fresh and colourful, was enough to feed a party of ten. She pulled a baguette from the crook of her arm and a bottle of salad dressing from her pocket.

"We thought cava to start unless you prefer wine? Harris? Harris! Where's Romy? Where's Romy? Go fetch! Fetch Romy!" The wolfhound paced away into the garden. "Good dog! So? Fizz all round? Gabriel, would you open these for me, darling boy?" She produced two bottles of unlabelled wine.

Tanya was watching Gabriel uncork the cava so didn't see the new arrival until she was halfway across the lawn. Like a dancer, she moved with feather-light grace, brushing past shrubs and beneath overhanging branches, the dog following in her footsteps. Her white dress was thin and floaty as tissue paper and her feet were bare. Flame-coloured hair fell in waves around her face as she picked her way up the patio steps.

Hoagy stopped in the midst of placing a platter piled high with fish on the table to stare at the girl with open admiration.

Philly tipped her head at the new arrival. "Romy, come say hello to our guests. This is Gabriel, Hoagy's godson and this is Tanya, his brand new wife. Tanya, Gabriel, this is Romy."

Her large blue eyes glossed over them both. She waggled a pale hand, like a child being told to wave goodbye. "Hello, Gabriel. Hello, Tanya."

Tanya waved back. "Hello. Nice to meet you." She was the most startlingly beautiful girl, with a heart-shaped face and golden skin, and such fabulous red hair she could have walked out of a shampoo commercial.

"Hello, Ronnie," said Gabriel, half out of his chair, hand extended.

The girl didn't look at him, picking at her fingernails. "Romy. Short for Rosemary." Her voice lifted at the end of each phrase, as if she was asking a question.

Philly looked up from the glass she was pouring. "Dig in, one and all. Romy, are you going to sit down or stand there making the place look untidy? Out of the way, Balfour."

Romy slid into a chair, stroking the dog's head. "He says he's hungry."

"He's always bloody hungry. Tanya, help yourself to salad. Now then, a toast. To Gabriel and Tanya, may their lives together be filled with love and happiness!"

Everyone raised their glasses and repeated Philly's words, clinking their flutes together in the centre. Hoagy drained his glass in one and smacked his lips together.

"Thirsty work, grilling fish. Philly, I'll take a refill when you're ready. *Buen provecho!*"

"*Buen provecho*," they replied and began to eat.

The fish was perfect, charred and crispy on the outside, but flaky and sweet on the inside. The salad was a delicious, crunchy balance with warm bread as a crusty accompaniment. Fresh, simple food, beautifully cooked, Tanya's favourite kind. She complimented Hoagy on his cookery skills.

"Most kind of you to say so. Yet even as I snatch the compliment with both hands, it's hard to go wrong with ingredients as divine as sea bass caught this morning. Ha! Gabriel, do you remember that time I took you mackerel fishing off the coast at Dawlish?" He grinned at Tanya. "He was only ten years old or so. Poor lad got sick as a dog, while I was up at the bow, throwing myself into the adventure as if I was Hemingway." He roared with laughter, one hand on his stomach, the other holding his fork.

Less Hemingway and more Henry VIII, thought Tanya. His face, so familiar from Sunday supplement profiles, had a photogenic quality. The deep-set eyes radiated light, which switched from sparkle to laser as the conversation switched from fishing trips to forestry work, rival artists, politics and the merits of Spanish cava versus French champagne. It wasn't hard to see why so many women had fallen for his charms. At least a decade younger than her husband, Philly joined in the debate, offering unvarnished opinions and much dry wit. Tanya liked them both enormously.

Reluctant to exclude anyone, Tanya tried to draw Romy into the conversation. The girl ate nothing Philly had put onto her plate, just tearing off bits of bread to feed the dog.

"Not hungry?" she asked, while Gabriel was trying to get Hoagy to tell a particular story from his youth. The girl looked up at her, blinking in surprise.

"I am hungry, actually. I've had nothing but two bowls of Coco Pops all day. But I don't eat fish. It disgusts me."

It seems bizarre that Philly would serve her daughter fish if she had made the choice not to eat it. "Oh, I see. Are you a vegan? Gabriel and I are trying to eat more plant-based food. It just seems a shame not to eat fish when you're on Mallorca. It's so fresh."

Romy reached out a hand and touched Tanya's earring. "They're pretty. How much did they cost?"

Tanya was taken aback. "I don't know. They were a present."

Something attracted the dog's attention and he bounded down the drive, barking and cavorting with his canine companion. Romy grabbed hold of the cava bottle and topped up her glass until the bubbles flowed over the rim. She bent her head and sucked up the overspill from the tablecloth.

"Romy! Not in front of our guests, please!" Philly said, handing her a napkin.

"I'm hungry," whined Romy, dropping the napkin onto her plate of uneaten food. "When are we having dessert?"

Hoagy tore off a lump of baguette and pushed the salad bowl towards the girl. "Eat some greens and have some bread. But don't feed any more to those damned curs. Why don't you try a piece of this fish? I promise you it's a trigeminal delight." He stabbed a piece of fish with his fork and lifted it towards her plate.

She recoiled and pushed his hand away, her bottom lip sticking out like a sulky child. It was difficult to assess the girl's age, but she had to be in her mid-twenties. Tanya could not understand why they treated her like a truculent teenager. Romy arched back in her chair, clasping her hands behind her head and tilted her face towards the emerging stars. It was impossible not to notice her breasts, pushing at the flimsy material of her dress, nipples pointing skyward. For a moment, no one spoke until Philly broke the moment.

"That reminds me, for dessert we have rum babas. Unless anyone prefers cheese?"

Gabriel and Tanya stifled embarrassed laughter while Hoagy clapped cupped palms together in applause, summoning both dogs. Apparently unaware of Philly's wisecrack, Romy dropped her elbows on the table and lifted a beseeching face as if she were Oliver Twist.

"Rum baba for me, please. Is there any ice cream?" She gave Philly a winsome smile and then seemed to see Gabriel for the first time. "Did Hoagy say you are his godson? He's never mentioned you before. Keeping you a secret, I see."

As Philly gathered plates, Tanya stood up to give her a hand. The gesture was driven mostly by good manners, wishing to be a well-behaved guest and partly to escape from the embarrassingly obvious flirtation aimed at her husband.

In the kitchen, she helped load the dishwasher and put the remaining salad in the fridge. She opted for cheese rather than a rum baba. She had never been one for a pudding.

"In that case, you dear sweet thing, I'll join you and we will have a glass of port. We'll leave the sticky sweet stuff to the men. I wouldn't mind betting Romy will eat at least three desserts, so they won't go to waste." She rummaged around in the fridge. "I have Reblochon, Danish Blue and unless that greedy swine has filched it, a slab of Manchego somewhere. Grab a couple of figs and a pear from the fruit bowl, and we shall dine like queens."

Tanya obeyed, placing the fruit on the tray. "You and your daughter don't look alike. Same with me and my son. It's as if my genes aren't represented at all, at least in the physical sense."

"My daughter? Oh, you mean Romy! Didn't Gabriel explain? No, probably not, things have changed since he was last here. My daughter lives in Houston these days and I rarely see her. No, don't sympathise, that's a good thing. She grew up to be a thoroughly unpleasant human being whose sole motivation is judging other people. As you say, one's genes aren't represented at all. Don't tell me that old sot has drunk all the port!" She swanned through a brickwork arch into another room.

Tanya didn't press the point, concerned she had touched on a sensitive area, but when Philly breezed back from the living room with a bottle of port in each hand, she continued her explanation.

"Moral is, only reproduce with the bland. Seeing as Gabriel is extraordinarily handsome, I'd say my advice won't wash with you, dearest girl. No, Romy is not related. Either to myself or Hoagy, which is a damn good thing. Her role is rather different. She's his muse." She placed five desserts on the tray and crossed her eyes at Tanya. "I know. Could we be any more eighteenth-century? But he only paints when he's inspired by an individual. They tend to be females in their twenties, nubile, acquiescent and easily impressed. Romy is the latest in a long line, although the first with Pre-Raphaelite hair. Shall we go rescue your husband? It's far too late for mine."

On the walk back to the cottage, Gabriel's arm around her shoulders, hers around his waist, they said little, digesting the evening and enjoying the warm breeze blowing in from the sea. At one corner, the vista opened up towards the valley and they stopped to soak in the landscape.

Gabriel's voice rumbled into her ear. "There's something special about this place. I don't how to describe it but it feels good for the soul. Am I being too esoteric?" His arms wrapped around her waist and his stubbled chin rested on her shoulder.

She inhaled the scent of honeysuckle and bougainvillea and basil, wafting on the night air. "It is special. Nothing like I expected. My image was sun, sea, sand and some other stuff beginning with S. This is different, but in a really good way. Tonight was so much fun."

"They loved you. Who wouldn't? You were so natural and friendly and fitted right in. I could see he was impressed with your comments on his work. So much more than a pretty face."

Tanya's mind flipped back to the studio visit. While Romy was eating her third dessert and hassling Philly for a glass of port, Hoagy had taken his guests to the inner sanctum, allowing them a preview of his work in progress. Accompanied by the two hairy hounds, they wandered to the end of the garden to the studio, a two-storey stone outbuilding. Inside, canvases leaned against every wall.

Hoagy shut the dogs outside and dialled up the lights to display his work. The focus on his model's body was hard to overlook. Hoagy painted Romy as she performed her yoga routines, naked. The poses themselves were elegant, graceful and artistic, but exposed the young woman in a way that made Tanya uncomfortable. Not just the personal areas of her body, but the sense of being a voyeur at a private ritual. She hid her awkwardness by asking questions about sketches and motion, how to transfer the fluidity of movement onto a canvas.

He answered in detail, his voice growing more voluble and passionate as he described his method. Upstairs, he showed them Romy's room, a futon in the centre and windows on each side where she practised each morning. Hoagy captured the magic and took it downstairs to convey it to canvas.

"Yeah, his paintings are striking. I can see why he's such a big deal in the art world." She paused, hesitant to express any criticism. Then she reminded herself this was Gabriel, her husband, and there should be no secrets. "The whole muse thing, though. Don't you find that a bit weird?"

He kissed her neck and they began walking down the hill. "Weird, freaky, and if I can get all millennial for a second, TMI."

A delighted laugh escaped her. "TMI? Too right. I just met the girl so I'd prefer a longer acquaintance before being exposed to her undercarriage." She intertwined her fingers in his. "The paintings themselves were pretty kinky, but the set-up is what really messes with my head. She lives above his studio, he paints her naked, she has dinner with them both and he toddles off to bed with his wife? Sorry, but WTF?"

"WTAF." Gabriel unlocked the door to their tiny cottage and kicked off his shoes.

In the kitchen, Tanya stashed the Tupperware full of leftover

11

fish in the fridge. Philly had insisted they take it as they left. "Do you want a nightcap?" she called.

"Herbal tea for me. My stomach is swilling with alcohol. You know, Hoagy's always been this way. Philly is his third wife and I reckon she might last the distance. She can handle the whole 'muse' narrative. Heather always says Hoagy found a way to make infidelity not only acceptable but lucrative."

"Was your mum ever one of his lovers?" Tanya asked, filling a pan to boil water. "Oh my God, you're not his illegitimate son, are you?"

Gabriel stretched out on the sofa, yawning like an overfed lion. "Nope. Heather was going through her lesbian phase when she and Hoagy were at The Slade. He and my mother were close but in that you-really-get-on-my-tits-but-I'm-looking-out-for-you kind of way. Hoagy had already hit the big time when Heather got pregnant with me. He sent her a five-figure cheque, with a note saying 'This is your freedom to decide'. So she decided. She chose to go through with the pregnancy and made him my godfather. That's it."

"A very decent man. Even if he does paint his lovers' bits and sell them for obscene amounts of cash. Here's your tea. Gabe?"

He opened his eyes. "What?"

"Did you fancy her? I mean, I'd understand if you did. Romy is one of those catwalk creatures you cannot believe exist. Luminous, glowing and all the other words they put on the packaging of face creams. She's got the body of a teenager, the hair of a goddess and thanks to Hoagy's pictures, you've seen what's under the hood. If I was a bloke, I think I'd fancy the arse off her. I could tell she wanted to jump your bones."

He sat up to sip his tea. "I've seen what's 'under the hood'? 'Jump my bones'? Where do you come up with these expressions? Tanya, I made myself clear when we tied the knot. In my eyes, there's only ever been one woman I wanted. Cobweb or Mustardseed or whatever she calls herself holds no interest

whatsoever. Does that answer your question? Come here."
Tanya forgot all about her tea.

Chapter 2

Gabriel slept soundly, his lips parting occasionally to puff out an exhalation. Rather than wake him, Tanya crept out of bed and threw on last night's dress to go to the bakery. When he woke up, she would have fresh bread, coffee and orange juice on the table. She slid her feet into sandals and made a decision. Drop a note of thanks into the Moffatts from her and Gabriel, then return to the cottage via the little bakery. She put the fish in foil, washed the Tupperware, wrote a warm appreciative letter and left the cottage in glorious morning sunshine.

The route was not exactly as she remembered and she took at least two wrong turns before she found herself on the right road. A ginger cat sashayed across her path and she stopped to give it a stroke, its tail quivering like an aerial. A woman's voice called her name. She turned, shielding her eyes with her hand. Cycling up the hill was Philly, wearing leggings and a flowery shirt. The wolfhounds paced alongside, triggering the cat to scarper. Philly cruised to a halt before Tanya, her face glowing with exertion and the basket on her bike filled with groceries.

"Good morning, dear girl! You're up and about early."

"Good morning, Philly. Yes, I'm on my way to the bakery, but thought I'd leave a thank-you note in your post-box along with your Tupperware. I didn't want to disturb you. Hello, doggies." The wolfhounds greeted her with wagging tails and wet noses.

"Come on in and have a coffee. Hoagy won't be up for another hour. He was utterly plastered when he went to bed. Or are you in a hurry to get back to your brand-new husband? I remember how one can't keep one's hands off them, at least in the early days."

Tanya blushed, recalling their passion of the previous night. "A coffee would be lovely. If you'll take me as I am, still wearing last night's dress."

"Par for the course, my dear. I would be wearing the same kaftan but the dratted thing gets caught in the pedals when I'm on my bike. Very forgiving garments, you know, kaftans." She let out a whistle. "Harris, Balfour, home!"

They strolled up the lane together, chatting as comfortably as if they'd known each other far longer than twelve hours. The house was silent, but all traces of last night's party were gone. Table, kitchen, patio, everything was pristine.

Philly made a cafetière of coffee, warmed some milk and scooped up three cups. The two women returned to the same seats they had occupied the night before, soaking up the morning sunshine. The dogs left a trail of drops across the patio after lapping from their water bowl, and lay in the shade of a rhododendron bush.

"Your home is lovely," said Tanya. "Deià is lovely as a whole, but your house is the loveliest I've seen. Sorry, I do know more adjectives than lovely but it's early and I've not had sufficient caffeine."

Philly laughed, lifting her face to the sky. "When you grasp the best possible word to describe a place, use it. It *is* lovely, all of it. Here is ancient magic. Drink your coffee and open all your senses. You'll see what I mean."

The coffee was rich and creamy, filling Tanya with a sense of well-being. She gazed out at the garden, listening to the sounds of bees around the blooms, sensing the sun on her face and inhaling the aroma of proper strong coffee. One of the dogs sat up to stare at Philly, his hairy eyebrows doing a convincing impression of a stern head teacher. He whined and paced towards the patio, sitting right in front of her chair.

"What is it, Harris? You've had your breakfast and we were enjoying a moment. What is wrong with you, you foolish mutt?"

The wolfhound whined again and lifted a paw to scrape Philly's leg.

"Oh, I see. Romy and I usually have coffee together in the mornings. All right then, Harris, go and get her. Where's Romy? Go fetch Romy."

The dog slunk inside the house, his tail curling under his body, followed by the other large beast. Both kept their heads low as if they'd been reprimanded.

Philly gave a startled owlish look at Tanya. "How peculiar! I'll just pop over to the studio and check all is well. Back in a jiffy." She strode over the lawn and disappeared from view.

In her absence, Tanya cradled her coffee cup and stared up at the sky. Acres of uninterrupted blue with nothing to disturb its uniformity but the occasional vapour trail. The tranquillity of the morning was shattered by a sudden scream.

Tanya jolted in alarm, spilling coffee on her dress. She ran across the grass to the studio and saw Philly at the top of the stone steps, both hands over her mouth, staring through the open door.

"Philly? What is it?"

Instead of an answer, Philly repeated, "Oh my God, oh my God, oh my God," over and over again into her cupped hands.

Tanya bounded up the steps and reached out a hand to the woman's shoulder, following her sightline. A gasp escaped her and she recoiled in shock, her back pressed up against the railing. Inside the room, lit by morning sunshine was a scene of such absolute horror Tanya could not process what she was seeing as real. Romy's body spilled off the futon, her throat gaping open and her Titian hair soaked in blood. In the pool of

17

deep red that spread across the floor, one arm lay limp. The girl's lifeless blue eyes stared at the ceiling. Beside Tanya, Philly crumpled to her knees and made a high-pitched keening sound. Someone should do something. Trembling uncontrollably, Tanya realised that someone would have to be her.

"We have to call the police. Let's get back to the house."

Philly's eyes flooded with tears, shaking her head in disbelief, unable to wrench her eyes from the macabre scene.

"Here, lean on me." She eased the older woman to her feet and with some difficulty, the two shaking women managed to get down the stone steps and across the garden. Once back on the patio, Philly stared at Tanya, uncomprehending.

"She's dead."

"Yes, she is. Can you call the police?" Tanya's voice was unsteady.

"The police?"

"Yes. Call the police and tell them it's an emergency. You have to report a murder."

When Tanya finished giving her statement and stumbled out of the police station into the midday sun, Gabriel was waiting. All Tanya's barely controlled panic and worry bubbled up and overflowed. She fell into his arms, weeping tears of relief and delayed shock.

He held her tightly until she was able to speak. "Are you OK?" he asked, stroking her hair.

"I am, but what about Philly? The police detective wouldn't let me see her. Or Hoagy. They were both in such a state this morning. They shouldn't be dealing with this alone."

"Don't worry about Hoagy. They released him around an hour ago and I insisted on driving him back to our cottage. He can't go home as the forensic people are still crawling all over the villa. I sent you a text in case you came out while I was gone."

"Oh, I haven't even checked my phone. Why are they keeping

her if they let him go?"

Gabriel shrugged, a helpless gesture. "The police know who to call when she is released, so why don't we go back to the cottage and wait?"

Tanya hesitated, reluctant to return to the station but uncomfortable at leaving Philly alone. "Should I ask them to pass on a message?"

"I already did. My Spanish is a bit rusty but I was able to give them my number and explain we are their guests. They called me to get Hoagy and again to collect you. When they let Philly out, we'll be the first to know. Come on, you must be hungry."

Tanya wiped her eyes and took his hand as they set off down the road. "No, food is the last thing on my mind. But I am desperate to get out of this dress, have a shower and clean my teeth."

They drove to the cottage in silence, which Tanya appreciated more than Gabriel could possibly know. It took all her mental strength to focus on the present and blot out the last few hours of reliving and retelling the same horrific moments of that morning. Silence was the balm she needed. A ginger cat watched them from a windowsill, reminding her of the one she was stroking when Philly called her name. To Tanya, that seemed like several days ago.

At the cottage, Hoagy was asleep in a chair on the veranda, his chin resting on his chest. Gabriel closed the door so as not to wake him and began making sautéed potatoes to go with yesterday's fish. Tanya got into the shower. She scrubbed and lathered and let the water cleanse her. If only she could do the same for her mind. She dressed in clean clothes, dried her hair and told herself she was fully restored. Until she opened the bedroom door and saw Gabriel's face. Her breath caught and her mind ran through all of her terrors before he could speak: Luke hurt in an accident, Dad had a heart attack, someone assaulted Marianne, an ex-con kidnapped Beatrice, Gabriel's house burned down ...

"The police are keeping Philly in overnight. Tomorrow they plan to charge her with murder."

Both their heads rotated to look at the sleeping form on the chair outside.

Oblivious of his wife's predicament, Hoagy continued to doze.

Chapter 3

Beatrice checked off the next item on her list and allowed herself a moment of satisfaction. She had made breakfast, taken Luke to school, put the washing on, bought the shopping, made the dessert for the evening's dinner party and done a spot of matchmaking. Quite the overachiever. She checked the clock and saw it was almost one o'clock. She made two cheese, onion and salad cream sandwiches, and took one outside for Matthew, who was trying to fix the lawnmower. Huggy Bear, who had been asleep under the table, sat up, her nose twitching.

"Any luck?" she asked, placing his plate on the garden table.

"Think it might be the spark plugs. I'll pop into town after lunch and buy some new ones." He looked at the table and his face fell. "Oh, just a sandwich today? I have been gardening all morning and I walked the dog."

"Tinkering about is more like it. Yes, sandwiches for lunch because we've got a lot to do. I'm going to eat mine while I check my emails. Multitasking, you see. If you're still hungry after that, have an apple. Don't go ferreting about in the kitchen for cake because we're having a three-course dinner later."

"Three courses?" Matthew's expression brightened.

"Yes, I've already made the summer pudding. After this, I'll crack on with the starters. Potted crab, I thought. Main course will be baked salmon with a green vegetable medley and baby spuds."

"Ooh, I'm very partial to potted crab. Do you need a hand at all?"

"No, thank you. Your contribution is mowing the lawn and organising the wines. Something fizzy to start and then a light-ish white with the meal, I suggest. Who's going to fetch Luke from school?"

"I should be able to manage that, presuming I can get this blasted machine to work."

Beatrice left him to his sandwich and took hers into the study. Part of her hoped there would be no new cases to investigate for a while, as the summer so far had been very busy. Plus she wanted a week off to look after Luke while Tanya was on honeymoon. Her inbox contained one enquiry about proving a husband's infidelity. She groaned. So many suspicious spouses out there. Still, they earned her enough to afford an assistant, so she wrote back asking for more detail.

Admin done, she went into the kitchen to start work on the crab. She was chopping shallots when the telephone rang.

"Beatrice Stubbs speaking?"

"Hello, Beatrice, it's Tanya. Something horrible has happened and we need your help."

Two hours later, Matthew returned from town with spark plugs and Luke. The boy burst into the kitchen with his usual clatter to be welcomed with equally noisy enthusiasm by Huggy Bear. The two rolled about on the floor, beside themselves with delight. From the rocking-chair in the corner, Dumpling gave them a baleful, yellow-eyed stare.

"How was school?" asked Beatrice.

"All right. Mrs Shaw gave us a surprise maths test which everyone said wasn't fair, but she did it anyway and when we got our marks back, I got seven out of ten. Mark Newell got ten! But he's always top in maths."

"Seven's pretty good. Now remember we're having guests for dinner at eight o'clock. So I want you to do your homework, have some tea and then say hello when people arrive. Then you can have an hour of TV before bed. I will come and check you've cleaned your teeth and washed your face. Do you want a snack now to keep you going?"

"Yes, please. Can I have a slice of cake?"

Beatrice cut a slab of carrot cake and handed it to the boy. "What homework have you got?"

"Can't remember," Luke mumbled, his mouth full.

"Well, go and check. Can't let standards slip just because your mum's not here. Take that into the dining room and you can use the table in there. Matthew, I need a word."

Luke picked up his school bag and went off into the hallway.

Matthew, who was pinching crumbs from the cake tin, looked at her in anticipation.

"Is it about the lawn? Because I'll do that the minute I've had a cup of tea."

"Never mind the lawn. Tanya called with some rather unpleasant news."

Matthew sat at the kitchen table, his brow corrugated. "Is she all right?"

Beatrice explained in as much detail as she knew and told him Tanya's request. "I did tell her that I really don't think I could do a better job than the Mallorcan police. Her view is that they have got what they consider to be a likely suspect and have stopped looking for anyone else."

"What a dreadful thing to happen! And a rotten start to Tanya and Gabriel's honeymoon. I'm surprised it's not all over the papers. He's terribly famous in the art world."

Beatrice cut him a small slice of cake and poured them both some tea. "It only happened last night. The thing is, if I were to go, that would mean leaving you with the sole responsibility for Luke. Unless we can get Marianne to help."

Matthew sipped his tea. "Much as I love both my darling girls, Marianne is not the most responsible when it comes to her nephew. I'm also realising that my age is making certain things more of a challenge, one of which is coping with a seven-year-old's energy. If you really want to go, Old Thing, could we not travel as a threesome? That would be gate-crashing Tanya's honeymoon, which is not ideal, but at least we'd all be together."

"What about Luke's school?"

"Ah. I hadn't thought of that." Matthew chewed on his carrot cake. "Write him a sick note?"

Beatrice gave him a stern look. "That would be most irresponsible. Oh, I don't know what to do. I told her I'd call her back this evening after speaking to you, but I really don't think this is practical. She's probably in shock and grasping at straws. After dinner, I'll give her a ring and offer some remote advice. I can't be doing with another last-minute dash to an airport. Right, time to get on."

"Very well. I'll replace those plugs and mow the lawn." Matthew yawned.

"Never mind the lawn. Why not put the wine in to chill and have forty winks? Our guests won't mind a bit of overgrown grass. Go check your grandson is doing what he should be and then get your head down in the conservatory."

"Why, that sounds like a marvellous plan." He kissed her, washed up his mug and wandered away in the direction of the dining room.

Beatrice pushed Tanya's horror story out of her mind and concentrated on the evening ahead. First job, persuade Luke that potted crab and salad was exactly what he wanted for tea.

Chapter 4

By ten to eight that evening, the table was set, candles lit, glasses sparkling and divine fishy smells wafted from the oven. Beatrice, Matthew and even Luke had changed, ready to receive their guests. Luke placed small pots of nibbles on the garden table while beside him, Matthew prepared the cava.

Marianne arrived early, bringing two bottles of English sparkling wine and a huge smile. Beatrice opened the door to her and gave her a quick hug.

"Am I the first? I wanted to be early so I could talk to you before the others arrive. Here, these are for you." She thrust the bottles at Beatrice and opened her mouth to continue but the phone rang.

"Put those in the fridge. Your father's in the garden."

Beatrice picked up the phone, convinced her plans were about to fall to pieces. If the caller was DS Perowne, cancelling because of work, the evening would be a major disappointment. No date for Marianne, odd numbers at the dinner table but Luke would definitely enjoy another portion of potted crab.

"Beatrice Stubbs speaking?"

"Beatrice, it's Gabriel. I know Tanya's already asked you, but I wanted to say it would make a huge difference if you could come. My godfather has gone to pieces. We all know Philly would never be capable of murder, but I found out today, the main detective has personal reasons for pinning this on her. We need professional assistance. Hoagy, I mean, Alexander Moffatt, is willing to pay your fee and all expenses."

"That's very generous, Gabriel, but ..." She dropped her voice. "I don't want to leave Matthew alone in charge of Luke. He's getting a bit scatty in his old age."

"Pam can look after Luke. She's his grandmother and babysits him all the time. Why don't you bring Matthew with you? Some sea air might do him good. Just don't leave Luke with Marianne. She means well but, you know."

The doorbell rang. "Yes, I know. Look, we have guests this evening, but I'll talk to Matthew and see what we can do. Take care of each other. Love to you both."

On the doorstep stood DS Perowne, carrying a bottle of wine and a bunch of flowers. "Hello, Ms Stubbs. Thanks for inviting me. I brought you these."

Beatrice beamed. The flowers and the wine were all very well, but the man himself was even more handsome than she remembered. "Thank you so much! Now you must call me Beatrice. Ms Stubbs makes me feel like I'm at work. Come in."

"Thank you, Beatrice. My name is Jago. Yeah, I know. What can I say? I have very traditional parents from Kernow. Here, I've been to Upton St Nicholas for the parade, but I didn't realize how pretty the whole village is. Nice place to live."

She escorted him out through the conservatory. "It really is. Where are you based?" she asked, as if she didn't know. She'd done all her research, as a good matchmaker should.

"Crediton now, which is nice enough, but I do miss Saltash."

"I'm not surprised. Gorgeous part of the world. Ah, here they are. Jago, I'd like you to meet my partner, Matthew Bailey, and his daughter, Marianne. This young man is Luke, whose mum is away on honeymoon this week. Everyone, let me introduce Jago Perowne. He's the detective sergeant who worked with me on that Hollybridge case."

Huggy Bear began barking at the sound of the doorbell.

"That'll be Adrian and Will. Matthew, give this man a drink." She dumped the wine and flowers in the kitchen and hurried to open the door.

There they were, looking urbane, stylish and utterly adorable. Her ex-neighbour and his husband were two of the finest looking men she knew and she loved them both dearly.

"A sight for sore eyes!" She embraced them both and accepted more wine and flowers. "You don't need to bring us presents, you know that. How's the holiday going?"

"Brilliantly. We went to Padstow today. Devon and Cornwall are just packed with delights," Will answered, his scent a mixture of spice and lemons.

Adrian peered over her shoulder. "Is he here? How are they getting on?" he whispered.

"He's just arrived. They're in the garden. Come on, let's join them. Adrian, don't be judgemental, OK?"

"Me? As if. Ooh, something smells appetising. That wine, by the way, was handpicked by an expert as the best choice for all kinds of fish or summery ..."

Will interrupted with a cheer. "Yay, the man of the moment!" He crouched to catch the small boy barrelling across the hall.

"Did you go surfing in Newquay? Mum says I can go with Gabriel when they get home. Was it good? My friend Richie has been twice and says it's epic! Hello, Adrian!"

Adrian reached out a palm to high-five Luke and followed Beatrice outside, leaving Luke and Will discussing waves.

Introductions performed, Beatrice allowed the conversation to flow and kept Jago Perowne in her peripheral vision. He chatted to Matthew about the area, spoke to Marianne about her job and talked shop with Will. She sidled over and shared, in the vaguest of terms, what had happened to Tanya and Gabriel.

"The thing is, they want me to go over there to investigate. I'm not sure it's a good idea. I don't speak Spanish, I'm unfamiliar with the circumstances and I really was looking forward to staying home, having some quality time with Luke."

Jago lifted his shoulders to his ears. "Tricky situation. Can't see the local force welcoming you with open arms, Beatrice. Sounds to me like they need a lawyer, not a PI."

"I agree," said Will. "No disrespect, but what can you do? If they're charging this woman with murder, she needs an excellent counsel, not a well-meaning friend of a friend. And what about Luke?"

"You're right, both of you. I think the situation has rattled them and they're calling the only person they think can help. I did wonder about Matthew and me flying over, not so much in an official capacity, but to offer emotional support. I think a few days by the sea would do him good. As for Luke, he can always stay with his grandmother, Pam."

"NO!" Luke's voice came from behind her. "I'm staying with you! You promised, Beatrice! You promised Mum you'd look after me!" His eyes filled with tears and he ran inside the house, chased by Huggy Bear.

She apologised to the guests and followed in the boy's footsteps. She found him in the living room, curled up on the sofa, crying into the Border Terrier's fur. She sat beside him but did not attempt to touch. She waited till the storm subsided and spoke.

"I'm very sorry, Luke. I should not have been talking about you while you were present. That is appalling behaviour on my part. You caught the end of a conversation. The fact is, your mum and Gabriel asked me to fly out to Mallorca to help them out of a pickle. I was just talking about the options. Option A, we could all go. I'd investigate while your mum, Gabriel and Granddad looked after you. Option B, you stay here with Granddad while I go to work. Option C, you spend a few days with your Grandma Pam while we sort things out."

Luke shook his head and raised his face from the dog's coat.

"I don't want to stay with Grandma Pam! She's always cross with me and never listens and makes new rules and I hate it there. If you and Granddad are going to Mallorca to see Mum, why can't I come?"

She gave him an honest response. "Because you should be at school. The other problem is the case itself. It's not very nice and I don't want you listening to us talk about nasty events when you should be learning the capital of Norway in your geography lesson."

"I already know the capital of Norway. It's Oslo and that's not the sort of thing we learn in geography. What about Huggy Bear? What about Dumpling? You can't leave them alone either. OK, then. Option B. I'll go to school and stay here with them and Granddad."

"The thing is, Luke, he's getting older and sometimes he can't keep up with you."

"There is an Option D," said Will, from the doorway. "If you wanted to take Matthew for a few days in the sun to support Tanya, we'd be happy to look after Luke. Adrian and I are spending the whole week in Devon anyway. We could cancel the room at The Angel and move in here. We'd also feed the animals and make sure Luke does his homework. While he's at school, we could still travel around the county. You know we'll take good care of him."

Luke released Huggy Bear and looked at Beatrice, grin wide and fists already clenched in triumph. "Say yes, please say yes, Beatrice. I really, really, really don't want to go to Grandma Pam's. Please?"

"Let's go and ask your grandfather."

Luke shot out of the door and into the hallway.

Beatrice flicked a glance at Will. "Does Adrian think that's a good idea?"

Will didn't meet her eyes. "He'll love it. It will be fun."

At nine o'clock, Matthew took an overexcited Luke up to bed, while Beatrice cleared the starters away. Adrian got up to help her as Jago, Marianne and Will were deep in conversation.

She drained the peas, broad beans, asparagus and mangetout, her mind whirring with questions. Once Adrian had stacked the plates in the dishwasher, she tipped the veg onto a serving plate and withdrew the salmon from the oven.

"Can you get the tartare sauce from the fridge? Top shelf. One question, did Will check with you before offering your services as babysitter?" she asked.

Adrian found the sauce and placed the butter next to the baby potatoes. "No, but he knows I don't mind. Luke's a nice kid. To be totally honest, if a few days' childminding cures Will of his broody phase, I'm all in. Do you have any mint for these spuds?"

"On the windowsill. I didn't know he was broody. He would make a lovely dad."

Adrian tore off a few leaves and scattered them over the dish. "Perhaps he would, but not with me. You know how I feel about having children. Shall we take this lot in before it gets cold?"

The meal was going swimmingly of its own accord, for which Beatrice was thankful. Distracted, she was not playing hostess as well as she should. Will and Jago had a good deal in common and Marianne was listening attentively. On her other side, Adrian and Matthew pontificated about the wine Matthew had chosen. Her mind wandered to the murdered girl and what reason could possibly propel someone to commit such a brutal act.

"Beatrice?" Marianne nudged her. "You're miles away, aren't you? I asked you whether Theo was going to Mallorca with you."

"I'm sorry. My mind's already on this case. No, I shouldn't think my assistant will be necessary. Although his language skills might come in handy."

"Everything about your assistant is handy," said Jago. "He's smart, holds his nerve and can take care of himself. When you helped us out with that romance fraudster, I asked him if he'd thought about joining the force."

Beatrice raised her eyebrows. "Trying to poach my staff, DS Perowne? No, I can't really see Theo as a copper. He's too much of a free spirit. You and Will know as well as I do what a grind it can be."

"True enough." Jago grinned. "So how come you continued investigating even after you retired? Haven't you seen enough of the shady side of humanity?"

"I think I'd been doing it so long, I forgot how to do anything else. Did I hear you say you were going for promotion to inspector?"

"Are you?" said Marianne. "Having heard all about the job from Beatrice, that sounds like a real challenge."

"But Beatrice was in London with the Met. That really is a challenge. Things are a bit quieter down here."

The conversation moved on to relative differences in police forces and other joys of country living, enabling Beatrice to steer the conversation away from romance fraudsters for Marianne's benefit. Jago's admiration of Theo concerned Beatrice a tad. She watched him as Matthew cleared the plates and brought in the summer pudding. Had she called it wrong and that eligible young bachelor was more interested in men?

Matthew topped up everyone's glasses and Beatrice seized her moment. "Perhaps you should only have half a glass, my love. Don't forget you promised to drive Marianne back to Crediton later."

As if she'd pressed a button, DS Jago Perowne picked up his cue. "You live in Crediton, Marianne? Me too. I can give you a lift, if you like? I've only had one glass, promise."

"Oh? Well, if you don't mind, it would save Dad having to go out. Thank you."

As Marianne and Jago smiled at each other, Adrian side-eyed Beatrice and dropped his arm beneath the table to give her a low-five.

Matthew filled his glass. "That's very kind of you, Jago. Perhaps just a half a glass more for a toast to the chef? A delightful meal, I must say. To Beatrice!"

She chinked her glass with each guest in turn, giving Marianne a meaningful look. The girl was glowing.

Huggy Bear hopped onto the sofa to snuggle up between Matthew and Will. Beatrice put her feet up on the pouffe and watched as Adrian poured four glasses of white port.

"Definitely not. Sorry, Beatrice, but your gaydar is nowhere near as refined as mine. Jago Perowne is straight. Where you do deserve credit is for bringing those two together. He's a really likeable man and my money says they'll be on a date by this weekend."

Will stroked Huggy Bear who rolled over for a tummy rub. "Adrian's right, even if he does use old queen terms like 'gaydar'. You have far better taste in boyfriends for Marianne than she does herself. That one has potential. Did you like him, Matthew?"

"Tremendously. A decent sort. I was also impressed with the way he spoke to Luke. The measure of a man is how he treats children, animals and waiters. That chap scored highly on all three counts."

Adrian handed him a glass of port. "Waiters?"

"You know what I mean. His manners were excellent. On which note, thank you for the port and the offer to stay with Luke. I have no fears for him whatsoever. He will adore having two energetic sorts as carers. My concern is for your holiday. Can you really enjoy the break you planned while minding the little person?"

To Beatrice's surprise, Adrian answered. "Yes, we can. Day trips, visiting moors and beaches and restaurants can all be done during the day. Then we'll collect him from school, cook or go out to eat and relax in this blissful cottage. You're doing us the favour."

Beatrice sipped her port, feeling sleepy. "That's not true. I wouldn't be able to dash off ..." She stopped as her phone beeped. Reaching for her glasses, she read the message and beamed.

"It's Marianne. She says Jago invited her for dinner at Chez Bruno on Saturday!"

Adrian put down his glass and lifted his arms to the sky, receiving imaginary applause. "What did I say?"

Beatrice clasped her hands together, hunched her shoulders to her ears and indulged herself in feeling very smug indeed.

Chapter 5

The long night of bad dreams merged into dawn and with the light, Tanya eventually fell into a deep sleep. When she awoke, it took her a moment to realise where she was. Gone were the stone walls and wooden beams of their little cottage. Instead, she found herself in a white room with French windows and a chaise longue opposite the bed. The events of the previous day came back to her like a stinging slap.

When the police had given permission for Hoagy to return to the villa yesterday evening, Gabriel was reluctant to leave him alone. They decided to accompany him home, make sure he ate something and offered to stay the night. It was the only thing to do; he was in such a dreadful state. He seemed completely incapable of functioning without Philly. He wandered from room to room as if looking for something then sat with his head in his hands. His studio was cordoned off and the police had warned them to go nowhere near that area.

Tanya managed to make him eat a bowl of soup, for which he thanked her with tears in his eyes. Just before nine o'clock, he said his goodnights and went to bed. Gabriel took the opportunity to call Beatrice, adding his persuasive ability to Tanya's request.

She rolled over to gaze at her husband, who was still asleep, despite the brightness of the day. Some honeymoon this was turning out to be. With a sigh, she got out of bed and found her phone. A message from Beatrice.

```
    Booked flight into Palma airport
  arriving 12.30 local time. Am bringing
your father. Will and Adrian moving in to
  stay with Luke. Can you collect us? Bx
```

"Oh, thank God," she breathed.

Gabriel's voice came from the bed. "Good news?"

"Yes." She showed him the text.

His sleepy eyes blinked and focused on the screen. "He'll love that. Luke worships the ground Will walks on."

"So sweet of them. I'll jump in the shower then start on breakfast. Will you call the police to see if there's any news?"

"Sure. Listen, Tan, I'm really sorry about all this. We should have nothing on our minds but each other. When this is all over, we'll have another honeymoon, OK?"

She stroked his face. "I'll hold you to that, Mr Shaw. Anyway, this is not your fault. I'm actually glad we're here because I don't know how Hoagy would manage on his own. The most important thing now is to get Philly home. And find out who committed such a foul act." Scenes from her nightmare flashed into her conscious mind. "That poor girl."

When she got downstairs, Hoagy and Gabriel were sitting on the patio, drinking coffee and eating toast. Gabriel was dressed but Hoagy was in dressing-gown and slippers. He still had the haunted look around his eyes, but he gave her a weak smile as she joined them.

"Good morning, lovely girl. Not quite the honeymoon you imagined, eh? How did you sleep?"

"Well, thank you," she lied. "It's a comfortable room. How about you? Were you able to get some rest?"

He stared into his coffee cup and his attempt at bonhomie evaporated. "Do you know something? I hope you won't judge

36

me for what I'm about to say. The fact of the matter is this: I wish I had been the one to find her. You will think that very odd, I'm sure. But it is the truth. When someone is taken so abruptly, it's incredibly hard to believe you'll never see them again. If I'd seen her, I might be able to accept her death as a reality. The other reason I wish it had been me is that had I been first on the scene, I would be the one in a police cell, suspected of her murder, not my darling, precious Ophelia." His voice cracked and he placed his hands over his eyes.

Tanya stood beside him and held his heaving shoulders, shooting a worried glance at Gabriel.

"I'll try the police again. Hoagy, is there anyone else we can call? Friends, neighbours, someone you trust?"

Hoagy's head jerked up and he wiped his eyes with the sleeve of his dressing-gown. "My God! Raf! We must contact Raf. He'll know what to do. Why didn't I think of that earlier?" He got to his feet. "My agent, Raf Beaufort, in London. Enormously clever man, wields immense influence here. I'll telephone him this minute."

Tanya poured herself a coffee and listened to the two separate conversations; Hoagy in the house, Gabe on his mobile. This was the exact same spot she had been sitting yesterday morning. Her gaze drifted across the lawn, unable to prevent her mind from conjuring up an image. The doorway framing that bright white room, where the only colours in the picture were two slashes of red.

"They're going to let her go!" Gabe interrupted. "Philly will be released without charges at eleven o'clock!" He ran inside to tell Hoagy.

Not necessarily religious by nature, Tanya pressed her palms together and thanked the universe. The thought crossed her mind to tell Beatrice to postpone her trip, but she opted to leave the status quo unchanged. The thought of seeing Beatrice and Matthew in a few hours almost brought her to tears, but this time, of joy.

Palma Airport was only forty-five minutes away, but Tanya calculated an hour for safety. Gabriel and Hoagy left to collect Philly at half past ten and Tanya busied herself with cleaning the villa. She wanted everything to be perfect for when the lady of the house returned. She sat waiting for the sound of Hoagy's diesel-fuelled estate, watching the minutes tick away until she had to leave. As a distraction, she had a WhatsApp conversation with Marianne. Beatrice's less-than-subtle attempt to hook her sister up had gone well.

> He's smart, got a great job, good table manners and he's not exactly sexy, but nice. I could do with some nice. But inviting me to Chez Bruno for a first date?!? Classy!

Tanya gave an enthusiastic reply although her heart was not in it. Marianne had not once asked about Tanya or Gabriel or their scary situation. She replaced the phone and looked around the garden. Someone had come in here, armed with a serious weapon, with the intention of taking a young woman's life. What if the perpetrator was still watching the villa? What if he hadn't finished? She stood up, angry at her own mental processes, and checked her watch. She had to leave so would miss Philly's homecoming. With a loud expletive, she got into their hire car and departed for the airport.

The first thing Beatrice wanted to know was the reason for Philly's release. Before they'd even left the arrivals terminal, she quizzed Tanya for answers. There were none.

"Gabriel spoke to the police, not me. I don't know if he even asked why. I guess they realised she's just not capable of that kind of thing. I mean, whoever did that has to be pretty strong because ..." She stopped and bent over, breathing deeply, refusing to vomit all over the airport concourse.

"Tanya?" Matthew ran a soothing hand down her back. "Are you all right?"

Tanya pushed herself upright and swallowed. "Sorry. Thought I was about to heave for a moment. First time I've ever seen a murder victim. First time I've ever seen a dead body. I suppose it's easier for a detective. You get hardened to it."

"Have a sip of water," said Beatrice, offering her bottle. "Some people do get hardened to it. Some don't. It sounds to me like this was rather nasty, so not surprised you're shaken. When you get home, it might be an idea to see a counsellor."

They left the airport and drove north out of the city. With Matthew in the passenger seat and Beatrice in the back, Tanya replied to all her passengers' questions with her focus on the road.

"How do you find Alexander Moffatt?" asked Matthew. "I have to say, in all the interviews I've seen with the chap, he comes across as rather genial."

"Yes, genial is a good description. He's really friendly and welcoming and he's known Gabriel since he was born. I get the impression he needs a woman in his life."

"I assume you mean that in the practical sense," said Beatrice. "Or were you referring to the other woman, or as he would have it 'muse'?"

"I was talking about the domestic arrangement. He seems completely helpless without his wife." Tanya shrugged. "But I admit I don't really understand the muse business. Gabriel and I were talking about it last night and both of us found the set-up very weird."

Matthew nodded, scratching his chin. "Indeed. However, he's always been a little eccentric. The muse concept is integral to his work, to my knowledge. Of course it was that dancer woman who made him famous, but before that he painted nudes, especially young ones, doing the daily chores, reclining on the bed, putting on make-up."

"Yes, I know. Which I also find weird. I don't know about you, Beatrice, but I don't tend to do the hoovering, the ironing or the washing up in the buff."

Beatrice snorted with laughter. "Nor me. It's not very practical, particularly the ironing."

Tanya smiled into the rear-view mirror. "I'm very pleased to see you both, you know. There may not be a case for you to investigate after all, but I am glad you're here."

Matthew reached across to pat her shoulder. "I'm glad we are here too. Even if you don't need us, it's reassuring to be present in case you do. And if it turns out we are superfluous to requirements, we are perfectly capable of entertaining ourselves, exploring fish restaurants, walking on the beach and relishing a spontaneous mini break. Aren't we, Old Thing?"

The sea came into view and they all released an appreciative sigh.

"Exactly," said Beatrice. "Although my curiosity is piqued by this particular case. I do hope the police will be friendly. It's always a tricky sort of dance as a private investigator working with the law. Could you drop me at the police station first? Matthew can unpack without me."

"The police have been really nice to Gabriel, keeping him informed, so in your shoes, I'd be feeling pretty optimistic. Let's be honest, Beatrice, most police officers love you."

Chapter 6

Not all police officers loved Beatrice Stubbs. Some found her an irritant and a pain in the neck. Detective Pedro Quintana belonged in the latter category. Communication was complicated by the fact that Beatrice spoke no Spanish and he refused to talk to her in English. An interpreter was press-ganged into translating their hostile conversation in which Beatrice discovered the police would share zero information. Her friendly overtures met with aggressive threats and warnings not to impede their investigation.

Quintana, a stocky sort of man with a thick brush of hair, had a bullish way of speaking so that someone without a reasonable grasp of the language was left in no doubt in terms of the tone. Their conversation lasted no longer than fifteen minutes. Beatrice left the police station, frustrated but not surprised. As usual, the onus was on her to prove herself.

She walked downhill to the cottage Tanya and Gabriel had found for them, turning over what she knew of the crime. With no photographs, witness statements or forensic investigation, the tools at her disposal were limited. She had one advantage over the police. Tanya. With time, tact and an analytical mind, she could extract far more than the blunt instrument of an official interview. She took a deep breath and noticed something unusual. Simply breathing in such a place lifted her spirits.

Somehow the place realigned her, settling her mind and infusing her with the feeling that everything was going to be tickety-boo. A feeling stronger still when she saw the cottage.

The front door of the sandstone building opened directly onto the road, a lilac tree on one side and green-painted shutters at each window. On the windowsill were little multi-coloured ribbons attached to sticks and 'planted' in terracotta pots. Beatrice supposed holiday cottage owners could not be sure all tenants would water real plants so this was the next best thing. She glanced up at the mountain leaning over the town, its presence benevolent and protective.

Inside, one large room contained two sofas and a TV, a dining table and French windows opening onto a terraced garden with a view of the distant sea. Matthew was sitting under the shade of an awning, doing the crossword in the copy of *The Times* he'd picked up at Exeter Airport. To the left stood a little kitchen, not much bigger than a corridor. On the opposite side of the room was another door, presumably to the bedroom and ensuite bathroom. She joined Matthew to take in the blues and greens of the unfolding landscape.

"Ah, there you are, Old Thing. Good job too, as I was getting peckish. How did it go at the cop shop?"

"The detective in charge has as much personality as a gargoyle and is likely to be similar in terms of flexibility. I'm hungry too. Shall we go to a restaurant for lunch and get some provisions for the fridge on the way home?"

"I'd say that's a marvellous plan. There's a tapas bar a little further down the street. I wouldn't say no to a plate of fried whitebait and a slice of tortilla."

"Has Tanya gone back to the Moffatts' villa?"

"Ah yes, meant to say. Gabriel called and apparently the police released the lady of the house about an hour ago. Messed them about a bit and made them wait, but she's home now. We have been invited round for a conference at six o'clock. Gives us plenty of time to grab a bite to eat. What do you think of this place? I'd say it's just the ticket and the air is already having an effect on my appetite."

Beatrice took in the higgledy-piggledy arrangement of houses, the cypress trees, terraced gardens and strip of ocean on the horizon. "It's one of the most beautiful places I've seen. Let's get some lunch. My stomach has been grumbling since we got off the plane."

The tapas bar did indeed offer whitebait and tortilla, Plus *albondigas*, clams with sherry and Serrano ham, and roasted red peppers stuffed with chorizo and cherry tomatoes. Beatrice and Matthew exclaimed over and over again at the deliciousness of the food, trying to remember when they had last enjoyed a meal as much. Next was a trip to the supermarket for some essentials and a rest at the cottage. After two glasses of Tianna Bocchoris, Matthew was ready for a snooze on the bed, while Beatrice studied her map of the town.

Later, as they prepared to wend their way up the hill to meet the Moffatts, Matthew demonstrated all the signs of being nervous. He paced around the living area, his hands behind his back as if he were Prince Philip inspecting a naval officers' parade. He chivvied her to finish her make-up even though they were a good hour before the appointment. When she told him to leave her in peace, he went into the kitchen to make them both a cup of tea. There was an aspect of Matthew's personality which rendered him starstruck by achievers in the artistic field. Musicians, poets, painters and authors all became somehow elevated in his value system, largely above criticism. Normally such a good judge of character and unimpressed by the phenomenon of celebrity, he remained loyal to those whose creations he loved. Even those who had been publicly disgraced.

Matthew had always hero-worshipped Alexander Moffatt and today would meet him under exceptional circumstances. He drank his tea on the veranda, humming to himself, while Beatrice completed her toilette and tipped her tea down the toilet, wishing she had packed proper tea bags. Finally, they left the cottage and ventured out into the afternoon sun.

Tanya's directions were accurate and they found the place without difficulty. The villa's gates were shut, presumably to keep out gawkers when the news broke. Beatrice rang the bell and immediately two large hairy dogs pelted in their direction, barking with gusto.

The first person Beatrice saw was Gabriel, waving from the patio. The intercom buzzed into life and Tanya's voice told them the dogs were harmless and to come in. The gate swung open. The dogs sniffed and swirled around their legs, tails and backsides weaving in welcome. With those two hairy escorts either side, they arrived at the patio, where three people were waiting.

Gabriel embraced them both and made the introductions. "So pleased to see you! I'd like you to meet my godfather, Hoagy and his wife, Philly. Hoagy, Philly, this is my father-in-law Matthew Bailey and his partner, private investigator Beatrice Stubbs."

Both people looked exhausted. Hoagy's face was lined and grey, but Beatrice had nothing to compare it to other than touched-up portraits in Sunday supplements. Whereas Philly was of a type Beatrice knew well. An Englishwoman of the countryside, rosy of cheek and stout of frame. The kind of person who would never faint at the sight of blood and could wrestle cattle if circumstances required. Yet now, her capable demeanour had threadbare patches and her handshake was little more than a quick squeeze. Her manners, though, were solid.

"Beatrice, Matthew, please excuse my assumption of familiarity. Call me Philly, and he only answers to Hoagy. I cannot tell you how grateful we are that you have rushed to our assistance. I don't think anyone could accuse me of overstating the case if I say Tanya and Gabriel have been a godsend. Neither of us could have coped without them and now you fly in to offer us your aid. We are most profoundly grateful."

"Well said, Philly." Hoagy got to his feet to shake their hands. "Welcome to you both. Matthew, please have a seat. Beatrice, I want you to know that I am more than happy to cover your fee and all expenses. You find us out of sorts, but I hope we can enjoy a dinner together once the terrors have subsided. I echo Philly in saying thank you for coming here at such short notice. Sit and let's have a drink. I imagine you have a hundred questions for us."

"Thank you, Hoagy, Philly. I do have a lot of enquiries. Perhaps now I can get the general story, but I might want to speak to you separately."

Philly caught Hoagy's hand and clenched it to her chest. "Whatever you wish, Beatrice, but there are no secrets in this household. You can talk to us together."

Tanya carried a tray of glasses, a bottle of gin, tonic waters and an ice bucket out of the kitchen and placed it on the table between them. "Hello, Dad. What did the police say, Beatrice?"

"Precious little. Basically, they told me to bugger off."

"That would be that monstrous Quintana man, I suppose?" Philly asked. "Tanya, would you be mother? My hands are still on the shaky side. Pluck a lemon off that tree over there, Gabriel. Drinking G&Ts without fresh lemon is unthinkable."

Beatrice answered the question. "Yes, Detective Pedro Quintana. He's an irascible sort of chap, isn't he?"

"That's one word for him," Hoagy replied. "He can't stand us at the best of times, but adding a case like this to his summer workload has tipped him into loathing."

Beatrice pricked up her ears. "Why does he dislike you?"

"Good question. One that is extremely relevant, in my opinion," said Philly. "Let's start at the beginning. But first, the drinks. Cheers, everyone, and thank you for being here."

They clinked glasses and drank, the delicate aroma of gin absolutely appropriate for sitting in this large, fragrant garden.

Philly released a contented moan. "Ah, that hits the spot. So, Quintana. To put things into context, Hoagy's art depends on his muse. Many women have inspired him. You probably know the most famous, Alyssa di Parma, who was the subject of Hoagy's breakthrough series."

Matthew nodded. "Wonderful paintings. One of my first stops whenever I visit the Tate."

"You're very kind," said Hoagy, with modest grace. "Yes, the *Ballerina* pieces enabled me to find my style. At that time I was living in Ravenna and highly influenced by Gian Berto Vanni or Federica Ravizza, blending Impressionism with Surrealism when painting the human body. Only when I saw Alyssa dance did I realise what was missing. Her grace, her energy inspired me to put the beauty of movement onto canvas."

"How long was she your muse?" asked Beatrice, vaguely recalling there was some kind of drama about the end of their relationship.

"Three years. My wife at that time was a very difficult woman. Jean objected to my spending so much time painting one woman's body and gave me an ultimatum. I knew that if Alyssa had to leave, I would no longer be able to paint. I pleaded with her, but she filed for divorce and returned to England. The irony is that Alyssa loved Jean like a mother, so when she left me, Alyssa was heartbroken and could no longer dance. Everything was ruined."

Philly took up the story. "Hoagy spent some time in Biarritz, where he remarried and found other muses, a burlesque dancer, a model and an athlete amongst others. After that marriage failed and the muses ceased to inspire, he moved to Deià. That's where we met. By then Hoagy's fame was such that people were queueing up to offer their services as artist's model. What was the first one's name? Linda? Lena? I don't recall, but she was the girl in the *Beach* series, mostly painted at our own little cove. Then came Nuria Quintana, whose figure is at the centre of *Flamenco*, which earned him a seven-figure sum when he decided to sell. Nuria Quintana is the niece of Detective Pedro Quintana and when his brother died, took over as her father figure. He was horrified and disgusted by her role here, calling Hoagy all kinds of unpleasant names and accusing me of being a pimp!"

Hoagy shook his head sadly. "Soured the relationship, if I'm honest. Nuria had a noble bearing and a pride in her movements, but she only lasted six months. Maybe there was only one painting I could do of her and I'd done it. Maybe it was her uncle's surly attitude, upsetting her and us, but we parted company early last year. She was furious, but he was worse. He hated her being here but when we sent her away, he came round to hurl abuse. It was a very stressful time."

"If he has a personal grievance against you, he's the last person who should be in charge of this murder investigation," said Beatrice. "I would strongly recommend you ask for another investigating officer."

"I did try," said Philly. "He told me there was no one else and asked if I was doubting his professionalism."

"Oh dear. This is going to be awkward." Beatrice sipped at her drink, hesitant to focus these gentle people on the events of two nights ago. "After Nuria, was Romy the next in line?"

"After Nuria," answered Hoagy, "there was no one for a while. I wasn't painting much, but I was working with my agent on a book about my art. It wasn't until September when I saw Romy and Miranda holding a yoga class on the beach that I found my next muse. Her fiery hair, her grace and her innocence caught my imagination. Since then, I've been painting constantly and completed, what is it, Phil? Half a dozen new pieces?"

Philly looked up to the skies in thought. "If you count the one you just finished, that makes seven." She looked at Beatrice and

Matthew. "And every single one of them is extraordinary. We can't show you, of course, as the studio is out of bounds to us until the police permit us to return. But Gabriel and Tanya saw some of his most recent canvases the other night."

Gabriel looked up from his drink. "We did and they are amazing. I don't have the vocabulary to talk about art with any kind of authority but I'm familiar with my godfather's work. I would say these are his best yet. Tanya and I agreed, they're hypnotising. In the paintings we saw, there's something dynamic and maybe even a little bit spiritual. We didn't see seven, though. I counted only four."

"Yes, you're right. We only have four on the premises because Raf took possession of the other three. He's Hoagy's agent and has some kind of system whereby he hints to buyers that those are the only three in the series, pushes up the price and then reveals a few more. He's very good at his job."

Hoagy's head bobbed in agreement. "He'll be here tomorrow. You can meet him. Enormously capable man, Raf, he's handled all my business arrangements for the last thirty-odd years. I honestly don't know where I'd be without him. Matthew, what do you say to another? Just because the rest of them are slackers, there's nothing stopping you and me having a top-up."

Beatrice refused a second drink and wanted to get the facts before her interviewees' memories became impaired by alcohol.

"I'm sorry to ask, but I do need to know exactly what happened after Tanya and Gabriel left you the night before last."

Hoagy gave Philly a helpless look.

"Yes, all right. To be honest, and I promise to be nothing else, Hoagy was drunk and expansive after our guests had gone. After we said goodbye to Tanya and Gabriel, Romy finished her port and went off to bed. The pair of us sat here chatting for another hour, I'd say, as he got progressively louder. Eventually I shut him up and insisted he go to bed. I cleared up, loaded the dishwasher, locked the dogs indoors and went upstairs to join him. Judging by the state of the bathroom, he had managed to clean his teeth and wash his face but had not quite completed the act of undressing. He'd managed to take his shoes and trousers off but then fallen asleep on top of the duvet, snoring like a chainsaw. I performed my ablutions, put on my nightshirt and inserted my earplugs, then got in beside him and fell asleep."

Hoagy held out his hands in an appeal. "Do you know how many years it is since I've seen my godson? It was a celebration! If I had a glass or two too many, who could blame me? I was filled with joy at meeting his lovely bride." He turned to Matthew. "You and I should have a glass of port with a cigar. You did a very good job with that young lady."

Matthew beamed, Tanya blushed and Philly rolled her eyes. Beatrice could sense the atmosphere slipping away from the professional and into the social. She refocused and took out a notebook to add an official note to proceedings.

"Do you always wear earplugs, Philly? Or was that night a one-off?" she asked.

"Always, my dear. Hoagy only ever snores when he's had a glass or two but he won't mind me saying he's always had a glass or two. That night, so had I, and slept deeply and well. The next morning, I woke at a quarter past eight, showered and dressed in clothes suitable for my bicycle. Hoagy was still partly dressed and on top of the duvet. I fed the dogs and had a glass of juice before getting on my bike to cycle to the bakery. I bought fresh bread and went a little further to get some vegetables for lunch. Then we came back up the hill while the morning was still cool and I spotted Tanya standing in the street, stroking a ginger cat."

"We?" Beatrice asked, her pen hovering.

"Me, Harris and Balfour. The dogs," Philly explained. "I take them out with me in the mornings. The great hairy beasts have such long legs I simply can't walk fast enough. So I cycle, they trot beside me and everybody's happy."

Tanya spoke to add her testimony. "I was bringing back her

Tupperware and a note to say thank you. She invited me in for a coffee and I accepted. We were sitting here on the patio, in the sunshine, drinking coffee when one of the dogs started whining."

The late afternoon remained as warm as ever, the blossoms from the garden filling the air with fragrance and the sounds of insects provided a relaxing backdrop. However, the atmosphere on the patio grew several degrees colder. Hoagy hunched over, tucking his hands into his armpits. Gabriel frowned and placed a hand on Tanya's arm. Beatrice waited. From here on in, it had to be Philly's story.

"When I want to summon Romy, I'm usually busy and don't feel like walking over there. So I send Balfour and Harris. She loves the dogs and they love her. Loved, I mean. So I tell them to go fetch. Harris ..."

The lighter of the two hounds lifted his head at the sound of his name.

"Harris knows what to do. He trots over there and up the steps, scratches at the door and whines. She understands that is our equivalent of the dinner gong. Quite often, in the mornings, Romy and I have coffee together on the patio until Hoagy rises. She usually wanders down to the yoga studio or café to see her friends, I make his breakfast and sometime after eleven, she returns and they go to work. That's our routine. Except that morning Harris began whining while Tanya and I were sitting here talking. I told him to go fetch Romy, but his reaction was most out of character. He curled his tail and slunk inside. Balfour too. The sort of behaviour they manifest if they've stolen something from the kitchen bin. Guilty or at least afraid they will be blamed for something." She used a cocktail stick to stir her drink, her face pensive. "How would they know?"

Gabriel lifted his head. "Dogs understand things we don't. It's not simply a better sense of smell. They are more attuned to their environment. From your description, they knew something bad had happened and it would make you angry or upset you." He reached down to stroke the darker one, who lifted its chin for a scratch.

"How though?" asked Philly. "They were locked inside the house all night and woke up happy to see me when I came down to breakfast."

Beatrice interrupted. "When you left, did you close the house behind you? Did you lock the gates? Was anything different to normal?"

Philly shook her head. "The police asked me the same thing. Everything was as I left it the night before. The gates were locked and the house was secure. When I left to go shopping, I didn't lock the house in case Romy came over early for coffee. I cycled down the drive and there's an automatic device which opens and closes the gates attached to my bicycle. I definitely closed the gates behind me, because I always check neither of the dogs is in the way."

The moment of truth could be put off no longer. Beatrice took a deep breath and met Philly's grey eyes. "What did you do when the dogs crept off?"

The woman took a large draught of her gin. "Do you know, I would like a top-up. But we'll need some snacks with that. Hoagy, be a darling and fetch us some nuts, and what about making those toothsome chickpeas you do so well, the ones with coriander. Just a few nibbles, you know. Perhaps your godson might like to give you a hand. Choose some music while you're at it."

He gave her a knowing glance but she maintained the breezy smile and waved her glass at Tanya. Gabriel got up and placed a kiss on Tanya's head.

Once the men had moved into the kitchen, Philly's demeanour changed. She leaned forward, clutched Tanya's hand and recalled the horror of what she had seen.

Chapter 7

Noises came from downstairs. Machines buzzed and whirred, conversation bubbled and a child burst into laughter. Adrian luxuriated in the double bed and gazed out of the window. Matthew and Beatrice's house had a good vibe; cosy, countrified and, apart from the two loud voices downstairs in the kitchen, blissfully quiet.

He sat up and looked across the garden towards the stream, registering the sounds of the front door slamming and the Audi's engine bursting into life. So much greenery and all those patches of colour opening up to the sun did a body good. He pulled on his robe and took advantage of the empty kitchen. On a normal working day at home in London, Will left for work two hours before Adrian. Those two hours were welcome, just to enjoy a leisurely breakfast, read the news and prepare himself for the day. Now they were on holiday with all the time in the world to relax together, Will was forever leaping out of bed as soon as the sun rose and proposing a trip to some cove or beach or West Country hotspot they'd be crazy to miss.

At the foot of the stairs, Huggy Bear danced about his feet, her comic toothy grin making him smile. "Good morning, Miss Bear. I trust you slept well. You seem in fine spirits and why not in this wonderful weather? I do hope you are amenable to taking a small excursion today. Mr Quinn and I plan to visit Dartmoor.

No doubt he'll make a fuss about a canine in his carriage, but a lady like you knows how to comport herself. Shall we share a slice of toast?"

Huggy Bear's tail wagged so fast Adrian wondered if it might fall off. He drank his coffee in peace, read the news, admired the white rosebush growing outside the kitchen – a wedding present for himself and Will which they had entrusted to Beatrice's care – and fed the Border Terrier little crusts of toast. He was washing up and tidying when he heard the Audi pull up on the forecourt.

"You're still not dressed?" asked Will, hands on his hips.

"Rumour has it I'm on holiday. Did Luke get off to school OK?"

"Yeah, no problem. Right, you jump in the shower and let's get out onto the moors. Big hike, pub lunch and back to collect Luke at twenty past three."

"We're looking forward to it." He dropped his gaze to the expectant terrier.

"A dog? In my Audi?" Will's eyes widened.

"You just had a child in your Audi, so why not Miss Huggington Bear? I'll find a nice cosy rug for the back seat and she'll behave beautifully, I'm sure. Give me ten minutes to have a shower. Why don't you send Beatrice a message to see how she's getting on?"

He skipped out of the kitchen before Will could protest. A wild walk on Dartmoor and lunch at a country pub. He was almost as excited as the dog.

So many places on Adrian's bucket list had turned out to be a disappointment. Mostly because they were on everyone else's bucket list. Not this holiday. Everywhere they went turned out to be better than he could have imagined and this was the best yet.

Wilder and more atmospheric than any photograph could convey, Dartmoor laid claim to at least a third of the world's sky.

Ponies grazed in grassy valleys, heather dabbed the coarse scrubland with splotches of colour and winds unchecked by barriers buffeted them in unexpected gusts. Huggy Bear was in her element, racing from tussock to rabbit hole and returning to her guides. Her joy was so all-consuming, Adrian and Will kept bursting into laughter at her eager face.

Naturally, Will had planned the hike to the last detail. After an hour's roaming, they ascended to a plateau where a solitary pub could be seen on a country road. Like a beacon in the distance, The Burrow's lights welcomed hungry travellers, weary from their journey across the bleak and unforgiving wilderness, offering a haven from bogs, pixie lights and the Beast of Bodmin Moor. Adrian reminded himself it was midsummer, twenty past one in the afternoon, he'd been walking for just over an hour and Bodmin was in an entirely different county. In his defence, this landscape lent itself to romanticised history and flights of imagination. Or maybe that was just Adrian.

Will spotted a table outside and went inside to order the special of the day: scallops on summer salad, two portions of fries, two glasses of Chenin Blanc and a bowl of water. Adrian tucked Huggy Bear's lead under his buttock. She lay beneath the bench, apparently worn out by their trek. Instantly Adrian began to worry. She was an old dog, according to Gabriel, and she'd not had the best start in life. Dragging her across a moor might be cruel at her age and while they stuffed their faces, she would have nothing to eat. What was he thinking?

He jumped at the sound of a bark. An Alsatian jerked away in alarm as Huggy Bear attempted to defend her territory, hackles high and teeth bared. Adrian caught her collar.

"Sorry, she's not normally like this. Have a lovely afternoon!" The Alsatian's owners walked off without a reply and Adrian gave the dog a hard stare. "Here am I feeling sorry for you and you attack a dog four times your size? Wind your neck in, sit down and I'll give you some of my chips. Sit now, good girl."

The food, the air and the atmosphere worked its magic. They ate and admired the view, Adrian sneaking chips under the table for the attack dog who had once more assumed the persona of Little Miss Docile.

Will checked his watch. "We have two options. Walk back to the car together. Or I use the opportunity to jog across the moor while you stay here with that overfed dog and have another glass of wine. Either way, we have to make a move soon so we're back in time for Luke."

"Miss Bear and I are quite comfortable where we are, thank you. We're in favour of option two. You wear yourself out running across rough terrain and we'll risk everything on an Antipodean Chardonnay. Do be careful, Will. Have you got your mobile?"

Will laughed and pulled on his jacket. "Who's the cop here?" He kissed Adrian briefly and took off over the road to start his run. His form grew smaller and smaller as he progressed across the undulating rolls of the moor. He became aware of two people staring. Two Hell's Angels types on a table closer to the road were watching him. Both bearded and muscular, they switched their attention from Adrian to Will's diminishing figure and back again. One of the two stood up and came to loom over Adrian, casting a shadow over his empty glass.

Despite a sinking heart and fear for Huggy Bear if he were about to be subjected to a homophobic attack, Adrian attempted a relaxed greeting. "Good afternoon. Lovely weather, isn't it?"

The sun was behind the man, so Adrian couldn't see his eyes.

"Is that your boyfriend?" His voice was deep and might well have made a decent baritone in the Gay Men's Choir.

"No," said Adrian, clasping Huggy Bear's lead tightly. If he was about to get beaten up, enough observers would surely help him out. His priority was making sure the dog wasn't injured. "He's my husband." He jutted his chin, half in challenge, half in defence – *hit me first, don't hurt her.*

The bearded man thrust out a hand. "Congratulations. He's a fine-looking fella. I'm Mac. This," he gestured to the other man in a biker jacket, "is Buster. We've been together for nine years but never tied the knot. Can we sit down, buy you a drink, like?"

"Oh, I see. My name is Adrian. Yes, please do."

Buster knelt and offered his hand to Huggy Bear. "All right, wee fella? What you drinking, Adrian? My round." His grin was so broad Adrian couldn't help but laugh.

"We had white wine with lunch, but what would you recommend? Is that cider?" He pointed at Buster's glass.

"You're not wrong there, but it's the rough stuff. Still got bits ˙ of apple floating about. How about I get you a half, see how you get on?"

"That sounds lovely, yes, please."

When Will drove up half an hour later, Adrian was on his second half of cider and in deep conversation with Mac and Buster. Huggy Bear spotted him first and dashed off towards the road although Buster was supposed to have hold of her lead. Luckily, Will caught her and scooped her into his arms.

"Oh shit, sorry, mate. Took me eye off the ball there. Your dog's a real character, isn't he?"

"No worries. Huggy Bear's a handful all right, but he's a she and she's not our dog. We're looking after her for a friend." He passed Huggy Bear to Adrian and held out a hand. "I'm Will."

"Hello, Will, pleased to meet you. I'm Buster and this is Mac. We're on holiday and we've been introducing your husband to the local cider."

Will shook hands with both men, his smile broad. "You're touring by bike? That must be a brilliant way to see this area."

"The only way!" said Mac, with an expansive gesture at the scenery. "You should come up to the Lakes one of these days. We've lived there all our lives and there's still more to see. Can I buy you a pint, Will?"

"I'd love to but we've got to do the school run to pick up the boy. Thanks anyway."

"He's not *our* boy, you understand," said Adrian, draining his cider and getting to his feet. "Another one we're looking after for a friend. There's also a cat called Dumpling."

Mac nodded his understanding. "Shame you can't stay. It was good to meet you both."

"Bye, Huggy Bear," said Buster.

Will smiled. "Enjoy the rest of your trip. You've got great weather for it."

They said their goodbyes, got into the Audi and Will pressed the button to retract the roof. They waved to the bikers as they drove away.

Adrian's head was a bit floaty and he quite fancied a nap in the conservatory when he got to the cottage. "They were nice, weren't they? When they first came over, my heart was in my mouth, but they turned out to be completely lovely."

Will overtook a motorhome and checked his mirrors. "Yeah, they seemed friendly enough. Why did you make such a thing about Luke not being *our* boy?"

"What?" Adrian yawned. "I didn't make a big thing. Just told the truth, like you did about Huggy Bear. You know what, I think I'm a tiny bit drunk."

Will laughed, glancing sideways. "That rough cider is lethal. Good job I came back when I did, or after another glass you'd have been dancing on the table and singing Scissor Sisters."

"Ooh, yes, let's have some music. Now we have the top down, can we blast out some George Michael?"

"If you like. Only till we get back to the village though. I don't want to rock up outside Luke's school like *Priscilla, Queen of the Desert*."

The Audi streaked over the moor, wind rippling through both Adrian's and Huggy Bear's hair as she sat on his lap, while he and Will joined in the lyrics of 'Faith'. All three of them wore huge toothy grins.

Chapter 8

When Philly, with Tanya's assistance, had finished her account, Beatrice gave them a moment to compose themselves but maintained the pressure. She knew she would be repeating the same questions the police had asked, but in a more relaxed environment and with a trusted interlocutor, Philly might find something under stones already turned. She asked Tanya to help the men with the food and keep them there until she was ready.

"Why did you give Tanya that leftover fish? Why not keep it for yourselves? To your knowledge, has Hoagy ever walked in his sleep? Why isn't the studio locked at night? Surely the most valuable items on this property are stored in there? Why keep the wolfhounds indoors? Aren't they supposed to be guard dogs? Who else has access to this property? Gardeners, cleaners, anyone else? How secure are the walls? Who are your neighbours? If neither you nor Hoagy is responsible, who do you think could commit such an act? More importantly, who would want to? Philly, in your heart of hearts, who do you believe did this?"

Philly listened intently, pressing her fingers to the bridge of her nose.

"It's clear you have a professional background, Beatrice. I feel in capable hands. The reason I gave Tanya the fish was out of kindness. That would have made a nice meal for a couple on a budget. I told her Hoagy never eats leftovers and that Romy won't touch the stuff. The first was a white lie and the second entirely truthful. Hoagy doesn't sleep walk because he's usually drunk. No, he's always drunk. Most nights he can barely manage to get to the bathroom. The studio is locked. Always. Hoagy keeps the code to the keypad to himself and the only people admitted are by invitation. Access to upstairs is via the outdoor stone steps. The two floors operate independently and there is no internal staircase. It's a converted grain store, you see. The dogs are pets. They sound, and perhaps with a squint even look impressive, but they are a pair of softies who sleep on the sofa. We do have a cleaner and two gardeners but they buzz for admittance. No one else has a key. Why would they? We're always here."

She surveyed the wall marking the end of the property. "Our neighbours. That's an interesting question and possibly answers your last point. Our neighbour to the right has offered to buy this property. Bernie Whistler is a British property developer who wants to expand his own estate onto our land. Twice we refused politely, but he has recently become more aggressive and threatening. He's a rather nasty sort, the classic pub bore with unpalatable political opinions. We avoid each other as much as we can. Physically, he is tall and absolutely strong enough to ... commit such an act. It would play neatly into his hands if Hoagy or I went to jail. But to kill Romy? Could he really be that much of a shit?"

Beatrice scribbled her notes, her mind lighting up with possibilities. "Thank you, Philly. Can I ask one last impertinent question?"

"So long as it's pertinent, you can." A vague smile lifted her wary expression.

"Was Romy Hoagy's lover?"

Philly's eyes met Beatrice's. "I wouldn't put it that way. Now if you asked that question the other way around, I could say yes.

Hoagy loved Romy. He was obsessed with her. He loved her with a desperate passion but whether they consummated that relationship, I honestly don't know. Some relationships are stronger than sex. His love for her was all-consuming. Hers for him, I couldn't say."

Beatrice gazed at her and could only wonder at the depth of her pain. Perhaps she'd got used to playing second fiddle.

Philly spoke, her voice low and confidential. "There's something I haven't mentioned to anyone else. Quintana has put me under house arrest. Hoagy won't notice because I rarely go farther than the shops. The police are gathering enough evidence to charge me by the end of this week. We have enough money to pay for lawyers and so on, but I would spend months in custody. Don't think I'm being self-pitying, I'm not. The fact is, Hoagy would be completely unable to look after himself. The only person actively seeking the real perpetrator is you. We must find who killed her in the next three days. Whatever you need, Beatrice, we can pay for it."

Pressure corseted Beatrice's ribcage. "I understand. I promise you I will do everything in my power. My assistant would be useful as he's a Spanish speaker and can help me with interviewees."

"Summon him instantly. Whatever it takes, I mean it. Please keep my predicament to yourself. If Hoagy thought I was at risk, he'd go to pieces. Thank God Raf is due tomorrow. His presence tends to ground Hoagy more than most. Although he too adored Romy. He'll be devastated."

"Perhaps this Raf chap might find time for a little chat with me. Right now, may I take a walk around the grounds to talk to Tanya? The snacks must be ready and I'm sure you could do with another drink."

"Thank you, Beatrice. You restore my faith."

The party reformed on the patio with some divine-smelling food, but Beatrice stuck to her discipline and asked Tanya to accompany her on a tour of the garden. An unsubtle ruse which Tanya understood.

They stepped between two flowery shrubs, avoided the studio and wandered the perimeter wall. Tanya exhaled. "Come on then, I'm ready for my interrogation."

"Very well. I just have a few questions. What time did you wake up? Was Gabriel still asleep?"

Tanya stopped walking, pressed her fingers to her temples, thought for several moments and answered. "I woke up just after eight. Gabriel was fast asleep when I got up. I only meant to go to the bakery, but thought I'd say thank you for dinner with a little note. I decided to bring the Tupperware at the same time."

"Did Philly ask you to return the Tupperware in the morning? Or did Gabriel suggest that?"

"Philly asked me to take the fish because Hoagy won't eat leftovers and nor will Romy. I believed that. The night before, Romy ate none of the main meal, only the desserts. Philly gave us the fish in a Tupperware and didn't even mention bringing it back."

They continued their walk. "I know it was the first time you met the girl, but what was your impression of Romy and her role in the household?"

Tanya shot an apologetic glance at Beatrice. "I have to speak as I find. If I met her at home in Devon, I'd say she's a classic flake. Meeting her here, I'd say she's a typical European dilettante. Funded by wealthy parents, unable to stick to any imagined 'career' and floating around between ski resorts and Mediterranean islands trying to alleviate her own boredom. Her role here, I assume, was as Hoagy's muse and lover, which Philly alluded to on Monday."

"How do you mean, 'alluded to' her role?"

"Romy was openly flirting with Gabe. In the kitchen, when Philly and I were alone, she said something like we should go and rescue my husband as it was too late for hers."

Beatrice thought it over. Gabriel was a startlingly attractive man, so it was not a surprise that a young woman would pay him attention. But to flirt with him in front of his new bride was crass in the extreme. "How did Hoagy react to her behaviour?"

"Hoagy? I didn't really ..." Tanya hesitated, her head tilting from side to side. "He looked sort of sad, like as if his favourite cat was sitting on someone else's lap. But somehow resigned at the same time, as if that's what the cat always did. Does that make any sense?"

"Yes, it does. Let's return to the others. I need to ask Theo to join us and then tomorrow I'm going to visit the bloke next door. I already know I'm going to hate him."

When they turned the corner to the patio, there was some kind of commotion going on. Hoagy was shouting and gesticulating, Philly was on her mobile, the house phone was ringing and Gabriel was frog-marching someone off the grounds, followed by the dogs. Matthew stood in the kitchen doorway, holding a plate of chick peas and looking bewildered.

"What is it?" Tanya asked Matthew. "What happened?"

He seemed relieved to see her. "Journalists. The police must have released the story and there's a pack of them outside the gate. All the phones are ringing off the hook and one cheeky beggar scaled the gate to get a picture. Gabriel is seeing him off."

Tanya broke into a run, heading for Gabriel. Beatrice caught hold of Hoagy's arm and guided him inside. "Stay off the patio. The last thing you need is a long lens photo of you enjoying a G&T with friends after what happened. Matthew, get Philly in here."

The shrill insistence of the telephone frayed her nerves, so she picked up the handset, cancelled the call and left it off the hook. Matthew returned with Gabriel, Tanya and Philly, who was ending her conversation.

"As soon as possible, please. Tomorrow is the earliest you can manage? All right. No, four people. Two on the gates and two in the grounds. That's fine. See you in the morning." She placed the phone on the table. "I've hired a security firm. We need protection from these godawful parasites. How dare they give the press the story without warning us! Put the television on, H, I need to know what the police are saying."

Beatrice seized her opportunity. "Philly, Hoagy, we'll leave you to it. I need to make some calls and make a plan of action. If I were you, I'd stay inside and out of view." She looked at Tanya in enquiry.

"Yes, we'll come with you. If you need anything, Philly, you have my number. Take care and see you in the morning."

They forced their way out through the throng of cameras and found Matthew the most effective at repelling the microphones thrust in their faces. "Oh, do bugger off!" he shouted and the press pack receded a few steps.

Two or three followed at a distance for a few paces but when Gabriel turned, opening his palms with a 'What do you want?' gesture, they returned to haunt the gates to Alexander Moffatt's villa.

"Let's not go home," said Tanya. "Why don't we park ourselves in a nice little restaurant and have something decent to eat? We need to make a battle plan."

Gabriel pulled her close. "So glad you said that. I'm starving and also in need of a beer. I've drunk more gin in the last two days than I would in a normal month."

Once settled in a quiet corner of the garden outside Los Flores, they ordered drinks and relaxed under the canopy of multi-coloured lights. The four of them, so familiar in each other's company, did not need to make small talk. Instead, the absence of idle chatter came as a welcome break from all the frantic conversations. The waiter delivered two beers for Tanya and Gabriel and two glasses of white wine for Matthew and Beatrice.

After the toast, Beatrice made her announcement. "I'm going to ask Theo to fly over. Philly assures me the expense is not a problem and I need his skills in Spanish to conduct the interviews with potential suspects." She chose not to mention the urgency of finding a likely suspect before Philly was arrested and charged. "I just hope he's physically fit. The Finnish escapade took its toll on the poor boy."

"You have suspects?" asked Gabriel, wiping beer foam from his lips.

"I have several people of interest, let's put it that way. Unfortunately, one of them is the detective in charge of this investigation."

"Is there anything we can do to help?" asked Tanya. "Obviously we'll check in at the villa on a daily basis, make sure they're holding up. But our honeymoon has been postponed for now, so we may as well make ourselves useful. Right, Gabe?"

Beatrice softened at the couple opposite, so in love and in harmony. She took a swig of wine to mask her emotions.

"How lovely of you to offer! Yes, there is something you can do. Find out more about Romy's background. Hoagy said he saw her leading a yoga class on the beach with someone called Miranda. Poke about some yoga studios she might have worked at, dig out where she used to live, if she has any family or close bonds on the island. Then I will tackle the acquisitive neighbour." She wrinkled her nose. "Matthew, would you ask a few questions of Hoagy's agent, mostly to gain an impression of the chap? When Theo gets here, we'll interview the ex-muse. It's my only hope of gaining some sympathy from the police."

Matthew had not volunteered to assist, but Beatrice was confident of his support. They each accepted their orders, studied the menu and opted for a family paella and a bottle of Can Catorra. For a couple whose romantic getaway had been diverted, Tanya and Gabriel seemed happy to see them.

"Do you think Theo will manage to get time off work so

soon?" asked Matthew.

"Time off work? He works for me. As to whether he's ready to get on another plane, that's another question." Beatrice tore into a bread roll and dug out her phone. "Let's find out, shall we?"

Chapter 9

Deià boasted rather more yoga facilities than most small towns, which said more about its guests than its inhabitants. A quick online browse showed Tanya that most hotels employed yoga teachers and there were six private businesses, one of which was run by a woman called Miranda Flynn. Beatrice hadn't mentioned the surname of Romy's partner, but that seemed a good place to start. She shared her findings with Gabriel, who was searching the Internet for any detail on Romy's family, other than her ubiquitous brother.

"If I see one more picture of that grinning goon, I will puke," Gabriel grimaced, pointing at an image of Nat Palliser. Tanya observed the racing driver's triumphant grin as he held up a magnum of champagne.

"Yuk. He is nauseating. Look, the yoga practice has a class at eleven this morning. I think I might go and join in, if you don't mind. It's a while since I've done a Downward Facing Dog, but I can remember the basics. I won't ask any questions, just observe and test the mood."

Gabriel reached a hand behind her head and drew her down to kiss him. "In that case, I'll keep searching, make us lunch and maybe this afternoon, we can sneak off to the beach. Should we invite your dad, as Beatrice is busy?"

Tanya sat on the arm of his chair. "Maybe we should. He's

been a bit ..." she trailed off, wondering how to voice her concerns.

He rested his head on her shoulder. "Distracted? I know. I spoke to Will about it on the way home from the Stag Night. He thinks we should keep an eye on him. Although Beatrice doesn't seem to have noticed a change."

"The problem is that Beatrice's attention is usually occupied elsewhere, even when she is physically present. He's said a few things recently that make me think he's getting forgetful. To be honest, I'm glad Will and Adrian are taking care of Luke this week. If he'd been on his own with Dad, I'd be worried."

Gabriel was silent for a moment. "Let's just observe, take notes and hope Beatrice picks up on his behaviour. If not, we'll give her a nudge. You'd better get a move on if you want to get to that yoga class. Do you need a lift?"

"No, it's just a few streets away. See you back here for lunch. I love you."

"I love you too. Don't pull any muscles."

The yoga studio was on the second floor of a building on an ordinary street of small shops and by the time Tanya located it, she was the last to join the group. Five women and three men were already seated cross-legged on mats. The instructor waved her in.

"Hi! Welcome to Nirvana and Vinyasa Practice. Your first time?" A tall woman with blonde hair, she had an American accent and impressive musculature visible under her vest and knee-length lycra shorts.

"Yes, sorry to turn up late. I couldn't find the studio. Um, should I pay you now?"

"Grab yourself a mat and we'll deal with payment later. I'm Miranda. Are you new to yoga?"

Tanya left her shoes and bag outside, and selected a purple mat from a pile at the side of the room. "Not new, exactly, more lapsed. My name's Tanya, I'm here on honeymoon."

"So sweet! Congratu-LA-tions!" Miranda's voice rose and fell in pitch and she initiated a round of applause from her fellow practitioners.

Tanya blushed and muttered her thanks while rolling out her mat. Why the hell she had said that? The last thing she wanted was to draw attention to herself.

The class began and within fifteen minutes, Tanya was bored. Miranda spent far too long, in Tanya's opinion, wittering on New-Age-style about mind, body and spirit. It took half an hour before they actually started doing anything than conscious breathing. She was paying twenty Euros for someone to tell her how to breathe?

A few forward folds, planks, cobras and volcanos later, the class ended with them pulling their mats into a circle, placing their hands together in prayers and saying Namaste to everyone else in the class. In her head, Tanya was already rehearsing the story for Gabriel. The class applauded Miranda and began rolling up their mats. Tanya fetched her bag from the hook and followed her 'teacher', who was reducing the volume of the stereo.

"Can I pay you now, please?" she asked, holding out a twenty-Euro note.

"You sure can!" Miranda accepted the note and slid it into a purse. "How did you find the class? My morning classes are pretty relaxed but we have a Power-Up session every afternoon if you're looking for more of a workout."

Don't ask any questions! Tanya told herself. "My husband and I are going exploring this afternoon, but I might come back tomorrow. That must be such a busy day for you, classes morning and afternoon. No wonder you're in such great shape."

Miranda directed her attention past Tanya's shoulder. "Bye, you guys! See you tomorrow." Her attention snapped back with a false smile. "Thank you! I've been practising for years, so you know, it pays off. It's pretty full on, yeah, but I don't teach all the classes myself. Another practitioner does the Spanish-language sessions and a couple disciplines I don't teach. We also use the space as a spiritual home, a place of worship. If you're looking for a belief system, we welcome enquiring minds."

Tanya was backing away before she finished. "Well, that's very nice. Thanks so much for the yoga class. Very stimulating. Now I'd better go and find my husband. Have a nice afternoon."

Chapter 10

Bernie Whistler had one of those faces which cried out for a slap. Everyone is at the mercy of their genes when it comes to arrangement of features, pleasing or not. Where one can influence the countenance one presents to the world is in one's choice of expression. Bernie Whistler had that shiny smug sneer dearly beloved of toxic politicians. Fundamentally, it said, 'I'm all right, Jack'.

It was clear from the outset that Whistler had only agreed to meet Beatrice in the hope of gaining some gossip. He sent a servant to open the gates while he paced around the pool talking on his mobile. He wore a cotton dressing-gown over Bermuda shorts and leather flip-flops with a designer logo, his florid face shaded from the morning sun by a baseball cap. Beatrice's first instinct was to push him into the pool.

She thanked the greeter boy and assured him she did not need coffee, juice or water, while waiting for Bigmouth to finish shouting into his communication device. She sat quietly at a garden table in the shade of the house, hands in her lap, as if she were at prayer.

Eventually, his yelling fizzled out and came in her direction, one sweaty hand outstretched. "Call me Bernie. You're a private detective? Really? Thought they only existed on the telly. Didn't Miguel get you a drink or nothing?"

"My name is Beatrice Stubbs. I'm not thirsty, thank you. I only have a couple of questions, so I'd rather keep this short and continue with my investigation."

His face darkened.

She compensated. "I have no official jurisdiction so it's kind of you to give me a few moments of your time. I can see you're a busy man." She loathed herself for pandering to his ego, but knew it was the only way to get his cooperation."

He yanked his shorts up and sat heavily on the chair opposite. "Busy don't come close. Twenty-four-seven." He opened his flabby mouth and yelled. "Miguel! Coffee! *Rápido*!" He winked at Beatrice. "Shoulda called him Manuel, innit?"

She gave him a blank stare. "My questions concern your relationship with your neighbours. I understand you had an interest in acquiring their property."

"Not anymore I ain't. Wouldn't touch it with a bargepole after that young girl got murdered. Brutally stabbed to death, is what I heard." He waited for her confirmation which she withheld. "I always said there was something dodgy about him having the missus and his bit on the side in the same house. Turns out I was right. The police let Moffatt and his wife go, though. What's all that about?"

The young man returned with a pot of coffee and two cups on a tray. Whistler ignored him but Beatrice gave him a smile. He returned the gesture and went back to the house.

"The police have told me nothing, Mr Whistler, but my experience as a detective leads me to suppose they do not have enough evidence to charge them. How well do you know your neighbours?"

He poured the coffee. "Sure I can't tempt you?"

"Thank you, no. Your neighbours?"

"Not my kind of people, tell you the truth. He's done very well for himself, in more ways than one, but Gawd knows why. You seen his pictures? My granddaughter paints better than that and she's not yet ten years old. There's a few of those sorts in this area, older arty-farty free lovers who keep banging on about the good old days. Me, I'm part of the newer entrepreneurial wave helping modernise the place and make the most of its assets."

Beatrice made a few notes, her jaw clenched. "Why did you want to purchase their property, if you don't mind my asking?"

"Matter of fact, I do mind. My plans are under wraps, specially now I'm gonna have to find another site. People don't want holiday homes right next to the site of a sordid scandal." He dropped his voice and leaned closer. "They said on the news she was the victim of a frenzied attack, but my lad," he indicated with his thumb over his shoulder, "knows one of the guys at the morgue. He told Miguel she was practically decapitated." He looked at Beatrice, eyebrows raised.

"Best not to believe local gossip. People love to exaggerate. Did you know the victim at all?"

He stirred several lumps of sugar into his coffee, his face sulky. "Seen her a couple of times at Sa Fonda. The place where the celebs hang out? She and her brother come from a posh family and they ain't short of a bob or two. Why the hell she wanted to move in over there and let that old git perve over her, I have no idea."

"Where were you between the hours of ten pm on Monday and eight am on Tuesday?"

"Monday night?" He scratched his chin. "I was having a few drinks at the Hotel Residencia bar. I had a couple too many, matter of fact, and got a taxi back here. That must have been after midnight, but I don't know exactly. When Miguel turned up for work at nine, he found me asleep on the sofa with an untouched bottle of beer on the table."

Beatrice snapped her notebook shut. "Thanks for answering my questions. One last thing, do you have security cameras on your property?"

He frowned. "Yeah, why?"

"Would they be situated in a position to see if anyone accessed the house next door?"

"Nope." He scratched his stomach. "Got one outside the gates, but that's trained on the entrance to this place. Hey, before you go, why did they keep questioning her and not him? Surely he'd be a suspect? Jealous rage if he saw her with another bloke or something? I don't get it."

"Neither do I. Which is why I'm making enquiries. Thanks for your time and have a pleasant day."

He scowled, evidently unused to people not complying with his demands. Whistler turned his attention to his phone and Miguel appeared at her elbow to escort her from the premises. As they walked to the gates, Beatrice tried asking a couple of innocuous questions, but Miguel's English was either unequal to the task or he'd been told to keep his mouth shut. Miguel locked the gate behind her with friendly wave. This was where Theo would have been useful. Beatrice waved and broke into a broad smile. Thankfully, the cavalry was on his way.

The family regrouped for lunch at the café Whistler had mentioned. For some reason, Matthew addressed the waitress in Italian, which led to some confusion at first. She switched to English and they successfully ordered the *Menú del Día*, grilled fish with roasted Mediterranean vegetables. Gabriel had located Romy's yoga practice and Tanya had even attended a class there that morning, in order to get an inside view. Beatrice was impressed and said so.

"Matthew, did you manage to meet Hoagy's agent?"

"Yes, after a fashion. These people are all a bit overwhelming, I find. Raf Beaufort is clearly well-to-do and indebted to his star artist, although Hoagy seems to view their relationship in the opposite light. As Philly mentioned to you, Raf was just as besotted with this Romy person as Hoagy. Tears, sobbing, the works. Whether that's personal emotion or a more cynical economic outlook, I'm in no position to tell. The big news of the day was the studio."

The drinks arrived and conversation stopped until they were alone again.

Matthew continued. "Raf used his influence with the authorities. The man obviously carries considerable weight. The police gave them permission to access the outbuilding, on condition it was only the ground floor. We went inside together and it was the most dreadful scene. Every last painting of the girl had been slashed. The curious thing is that was not the case on Tuesday morning. The police officer who let us in was appalled. He herded us all out and called for a forensic team. It looks like whoever killed the girl returned to destroy her image."

Tanya's hand rested on her clavicle. "When we were asleep in the guest room! Poor Hoagy, poor Philly! To have their home invaded twice with such violent, cruel results!" Her eyes welled with tears.

Gabriel drew Tanya closer. "Wait, though. If someone returned to wreck the paintings, it couldn't possibly have been Philly. On Tuesday night she was in the cells. She's in the clear, right, Beatrice?"

She interlaced her fingers and thought. "No, she's not. She came home on Wednesday afternoon. No one checked the studio after the police left. It's easy to assume the killer returned on Tuesday, but it could just as easily have been Wednesday. And the painting slasher might be an entirely different person. If you wanted to implicate Philly in both crimes, you'd make sure she was at home, with access to the studio for at least one night. Then discover the ruined paintings the day after. You know, I'm growing increasingly concerned that poor woman is being framed."

No one spoke for several moments and the waitress placed the food in front of a silent, dour group of four.

"Thank you," Beatrice remembered her manners. "Let's eat

and then I'll walk up to the villa and find out a bit more. Who's going to the airport to collect Theo?"

"No one," Gabriel replied. "I offered but he said he'd hire a car. He said it makes sense to have two vehicles. He has a point. So we're free this afternoon, if you need us to do anything?"

"No, I don't. Why don't you go exploring? Take the car and go off to a beach somewhere. You are on honeymoon, after all."

Tanya squeezed some mayonnaise onto her plate. "Actually, I wouldn't mind a swim. We could go a bit further afield this time and find a bigger beach. Deià's cove is beautiful, but it gets pretty crowded. Would you like to come with us, Dad? See a bit of the island? Cap de Formentor is supposed to have fabulous views."

Matthew blinked. "Wouldn't you prefer to be on your own? I shouldn't like to be a gooseberry."

Gabriel poured more wine for them all. "Matthew, we'd love to have your company. It would be ideal if Beatrice could come too but I understand she's got to work. Come with us. We can drive along the north of the island and go beach-hopping."

"That sounds jolly marvellous. Unless you need me to do anything here, Old Thing?"

"No, I can handle the other English-speaking interviewees so there's not much more to be done until Theo arrives. You go and enjoy yourself. Whole roasted garlic has the most divine flavour, don't you think?"

She ensured Matthew had his cap and sun cream before he left and put on her own straw hat to walk up the hill to the villa. The mid-afternoon sun was fierce. She pondered the same question which had nagged her from the moment she got Tanya's phone call.

Motive.

The police clearly thought they could pin jealousy on Philly. The destruction of the paintings only fostered that theory. But the paintings were the source of her and Hoagy's income. As for

Hoagy himself, she was unsure. Could he have suffered an attack of jealous rage after she flirted with Gabriel, killed the girl and destroyed his own paintings of her to erase the memory? Tanya had made light of the flirtation, but who knows what was going on internally? He did have the only code to access the studio, after all.

Whistler, the neighbour, didn't look muscular enough to climb over the wall and stab a young healthy woman, but he was certainly the sort of man who could hire someone to do the job. Beatrice didn't believe the bluster about scandalous gossip devaluing the land. If he managed to get them out and purchase the property, he'd raze the place and build apartments. The story of the previous owners would be nothing more than a footnote in history.

She was itching to meet the previous muse, niece of Detective Quintana, but that would have to wait for Theo's translation skills. If the woman would even talk to them.

Outside the villa, a couple of journalists hung about, smoking. They made a half-hearted attempt at asking Beatrice questions but she waved them away with a flap of her hand. Years of experience had made her an expert in ignoring members of the press. She pushed the buzzer at the gates. When she announced her presence, the gates swung open but the dogs did not come barking down the drive. She waited till the entrance had completely closed to ensure no photographers sneaked in after her and trudged towards the house.

The patio was empty and Philly came to greet her at the kitchen door. "Hello there, Beatrice. We're taking your advice, you see, and staying indoors. Are those wretched tabloid hacks still out there? Bastards. Come and meet Raf. I've told him all about you." She led the way into the cool tiled living area. "Did Matthew tell you about the studio? I've had to give Hoagy a Valium, whereas Raf is self-medicating with a bottle of Mahou. Don't worry, it's only beer."

The two men sat on white sofas, the dogs flat out at their feet. Philly made the introductions and poured Beatrice a glass of lemonade.

Raf Beaumont stood to shake her hand. He was exceptionally tall, towering over her at well over six feet. He wore a linen suit which appeared to have been chewed by a cow. His thick white hair flopped over his face, he sported a bristly white moustache and wore wire-rimmed round glasses. He looked like an older version of Dirk Bogarde in *Death in Venice.*

"Delighted to meet you, Beatrice. We're very fortunate to have someone of your calibre aboard. I want you to know, as I have told H. and Philly, that should the police re-arrest this fine woman, I shall fly in my own lawyers to defend her. These damned local bully-boys will not get away with pinning a heinous crime on an innocent Ophelia."

Beatrice glanced at Philly, checking whether the secret was out.

She gave a resigned shrug. "They asked me to go in today for a second round of questioning. Raf insists I refuse until I have legal representation. Which will be tomorrow."

Beatrice assessed Raf. "That's a very generous gesture. A top legal team will be exactly what this situation demands. I hope to throw open other lines of enquiry to occupy police minds, but I fear the situation in the studio may give them further reason to suspect the lady of the house."

"Beatrice! You can't think I would destroy my husband's art?"

"Of course I don't think that. If I believed you were the perpetrator, do you think I would have accepted this job? No, I am wholly convinced of your innocence. The problem is that you don't have a solid steel alibi for either event. Other than being asleep in bed. Philly, I'm just trying to think like the police, who are seeking the simplest explanation to wrap this case up fast."

Raf sat down next to Hoagy, who hadn't looked up from his

hands since Beatrice had entered the room, and drained his beer. "Is there anything we can do?" he asked.

"Now that you mention it, there is. Am I right in thinking only one door opened by keypad provides access to the studio?"

Raf stood up and wandered into the kitchen as he spoke. "Yes. Hoagy changes the code regularly and only he knows the combination. Not me, not Philly and certainly not Romy. Security is tight because there is always the threat of theft." He opened the fridge and withdrew another bottle of beer. "You couldn't sell a Moffatt on the open market, but there are plenty of private collectors who would pay over the odds to have an unseen original."

It was interesting to note the level of familiarity Raf Beaufort demonstrated with Hoagy and Philly's home. Opening your host's fridge was unthinkably rude, at least in Europe, unless you were close family. Raf was evidently part of the inner circle.

"I see. Hoagy? Can I ask when you last changed the code to the studio door?"

He looked at her with a vague expression. "Not for a while. I can't remember. I try to do it every month, but I may have missed one."

"Not since March, if memory serves, old boy," Raf interjected.

Beatrice made a note. "And the only security is a sturdy door and the keypad entry? No cameras?"

"Yes, we do have cameras," said Philly. "But only on the front gates. The police took the footage from Monday, Tuesday and Wednesday nights. If they still suspect me, it stands to reason there's no sign of anybody else coming in or out."

"Right. Could you and I have a little wander round the garden? Out of sight of the photographers, obviously."

Philly got to her feet. "Keep an eye on him," she said to Raf and escorted Beatrice out of a back door, facing away from the road.

"Let's meander through the shrubs for a bit and then I'd like to get a look at the studio. From a distance, of course. I have some questions about Romy. What do you know of her background? Her friends? How did she earn her income before coming to live here?"

There was a little bench against the garden wall, cluttered with cushions and rugs, in the shade of a magnolia tree. Philly stood on it to peer over the wall, then beckoned Beatrice to join her. "My reading corner. Just checking Bernie the Barbarian is not lurking the other side. Now let me see. Rosemary Palliser, daughter of Maxwell and Santa Palliser, sister of Gregory and Nathaniel, better known as Greg and Nat. You've likely heard of Nat Palliser? Formula One driver?"

Beatrice shook her head.

"No? Well, he's hugely successful and as obnoxious as they come. Lives in Monaco most of the time and turns up here once or twice a year to show off. Their parents have a home outside Port de Sóller, but rarely use it because they're tax exiles in Bermuda. Their children have the run of the place. Romy never 'earned her income' because she has no need. Her parents provided her and her brother with an allowance. As for intimates, she was seeing a swimmer called Juan Carlos for a while, but broke it off when she moved in here. Silly girl. He was fit as a butcher's dog."

"Was he upset? Do you know his surname?"

"His surname is Mendez and I have no idea how he took being dumped. I only saw him the once. Her friends are a loose circle of similar people, drifting from season to season and occasionally starting a life-coach business or idly dabbling in some form of art. I'm only aware of one you could call close. Miranda Flynn and Romy set up 'Nirvana', a yoga practice in the town around two years ago. They sometimes held dawn classes on the beach, which is where Hoagy spotted her." Her face grew wistful for a moment and then her eyes focused on Beatrice.

"Ah, here's a thing. Romy's business partner and Romy's younger brother Greg are an item, romantically speaking. There was quite a falling-out when Romy dropped all her classes to become a life model here."

Beatrice scribbled notes as Philly flowed on.

"Her brother Greg is a classic drifter. What hasn't he tried? Bar owner, manager of a band, restaurateur, literary novelist and then he went on some kind of retreat and now he's started a church. Cult, more like. He calls it 'The One Truth', invites all these esoteric preachers to speak and charges an absolute fortune to hear them spout arrant nonsense, while running his own 'healing' sessions. He even sells online course at a premium. When Romy dropped the yoga business, he stepped in with financial backing and started teaching spirituality. What never ceases to amaze me is that people actually pay for this hogwash. There's no accounting for gullibility."

Beatrice closed her notebook. "Those two will be my next port of call. Philly, please try not to worry too much. You'll have a lawyer with you tomorrow, I'm pulling out all the stops to find the person who did this and my assistant arrives today. We're all behind you."

"You are a marvel. I know you're doing a wonderful job, as is Raf. I'm in safe hands, I know. But what about Hoagy?"

Beatrice had no answer to that. Instead, she asked to see the entrance to the studio. It faced away from the entrance to the property, hidden by large bushes of camellia and rhododendrons. Hoagy could walk from the back door of the house to his atelier without being seen, if he wished. The steps to Romy's apartment were on the other side of the two-storey outbuilding. It reminded Beatrice of those weather vanes. One goes in on the left and the other comes out on the right.

If anyone were to spy on Hoagy pressing the numbers on his keypad, they would have to be quite literally in the hedge, which backed up against a wall. She scanned the area, observing nothing more than hedge, grass, cypress tree and an abundance of fragrant flowers.

"Who's on the other side? You have the Whistler man to the north and east, the road to the south and what's to the west, the other side of this wall?"

"An old Spanish lady from Madrid, Señora Navarro. She's rarely seen outside and pays a local couple to tend the house and garden. We have almost no contact."

Beatrice made up her mind to visit the old woman with Theo at her side and ask permission to study the garden wall. There had to be another way in that someone could use at will. If there wasn't, Philly's situation looked very bad indeed.

Chapter 11

For the second day in a row, Will harried them through a coffee and dessert, impatient to get back to Upton St Nicholas. Adrian dallied on purpose, to remind Will of the reason they were in Dartmouth. Mornings were lovely. Relaxed breakfasts and trips to absorb the glory of the countryside. But as the clock ticked towards three, Will became agitated.

Adrian announced he was visiting the bathroom and spent an extra few minutes in a stall, with no good reason. The imposition on their lifestyles would eventually get through to Will, and his romantic concept of fatherhood would be exposed for the fantasy it was. Huggy Bear and Dumpling could be left alone for a few hours, enabling him and his husband to continue visiting the places they'd earmarked when planning their holiday. The one restriction on their freedom was taking Luke to school, picking Luke up from school and entertaining Luke in the evenings. Yet Will showed no sign of tiring.

When Adrian returned upstairs, their table was empty and Will was waiting in the doorway, car keys in hand.

"I paid the bill. Come on, let's go. It'll take us a good hour to Luke's school and I don't want to be late. Maybe I should drop you off at the supermarket to get some veg for tonight. I also need more fruit to put in his lunchbox."

Adrian waved a thank you to the waiting staff and followed

Will out into the sunshine. "What a beautiful location. I could spend all day sitting by this river. People living in the countryside don't know how lucky they are. I mean it, every single day we walk out in this gorgeous greenery makes me feel better. Do you feel that too?"

Will glanced at his watch. "This holiday is certainly doing me good. Where are you going? The car is this way."

As they belted themselves into the Audi and left the picturesque town of Dartmouth, Adrian raised a point of concern. "I know things have been a bit hectic and not exactly according to plan, but we have a dinner reservation on Friday night, booked two months ago. That was my birthday treat for you and I really don't want to lose it. Somehow or another, we need to find a babysitter."

"Or take him with us."

Adrian shook his head with some emphasis. "No, we can't. Kids are not allowed, I checked online. Can't we rope in either Marianne or Luke's Grandma Pam for the occasion? It's just for a few hours, to give us one evening to ourselves."

Will drove faster, accelerating to the point Adrian sensed was borderline unsafe. He still had not responded.

"Will, slow down a little, please. Even if we are a few minutes late, the school will keep him in until we arrive. You haven't answered my question." He withdrew his phone from his pocket. "I'll call Marianne, and ask if she's free on Friday."

"No, not Marianne." Will's gaze remained on the road but he shot a sideways glance at Adrian. "At the Stag Night, Gabriel made a very gentle joke about Marianne and her lack of responsibility when it comes to her nephew. Even Matthew laughed. Marianne won't want to babysit and we already know Luke doesn't like staying with his grandmother."

Embers glowed in Adrian's gut and he clenched his teeth. Why should these people's preferences supersede his? Why shouldn't Luke spend a few hours in a sub-optimal situation so that Will and Adrian could enjoy a five-star birthday dinner? Why did Will rate Adrian's needs as secondary to the whims of a seven-year-old? For several miles, he was unable to speak, the pressure on his molars almost painful.

"You're right though," said Will. "We can't lose that reservation. When I dropped Luke off at school this morning, I bumped into Susie."

Adrian's lower jaw jutted forward as if he were Huggy Bear. He detested this whole 'mums at the school gate' bullshit and grew irritated beyond belief at Will's assumption he should remember each mummy's name. He'd be suggesting play dates next.

"Who the fuck is Susie?"

Will shot him a puzzled glance. "The landlady of The Angel, who served us breakfast every morning for the last week? Ring any bells?"

"Oh, that Susie." Even though he liked the landlady, Adrian's temper was not yet calmed. "And the significance of that would be?"

"Yeah, that Susie. Her daughter is home for the Midsummer Solstice."

Adrian crossed his eyes. "Shit. I knew I should have packed my Druid robes."

"Do you want to drop the attitude?" Will's voice dropped a register, signalling danger. "As I was saying, Susie's daughter Frankie used to be Luke's babysitter. You must remember her. She was here around the time of our wedding. Anyway, Luke loves her to bits and she might well be free on Friday night. Shall we ask her?"

Frankie. An image floated across Adrian's vision: a beautiful heart-shaped face framed by straight black hair, a wide laughing mouth and obsidian eyes. His lips lifted at the thought of her animated face and how her life force reminded him of Catinca.

"Yes, that's a great idea. The perfect solution all round. So we can still go to El Pescador for your birthday?"

Will reached a hand across the gearstick to squeeze Adrian's thigh. "After waiting this long, I think we really should."

All his snark melted away and Adrian's gaze ranged over the hedgerows, conjuring up the menu and that fabulous wine list.

Will cruised to a halt outside the pub, Adrian jumped out and Will sped off towards the school. Several tables outside the pub were occupied and someone called his name. The two bikers he'd met the day before were sitting in the sunshine, their bikes parked right in front.

He waved and went over to say hello. "If it isn't the Cider Bikers! Hello, Buster, hi, Mac. I was fit for nothing after having two halves of that rough stuff yesterday."

Mac laughed. "We can't tempt you again then?"

"No, not with cider. But let me buy you a drink, unless you're in a hurry?"

"We're not going anywhere today," said Buster. "We had a long ride out to Seaton this morning and booked ourselves a room here for tonight. Thanks, mine's a pint of Bulmer's." He drained his glass and held it out to Adrian.

"Cheers, mate. I'll have a pint of Tanglefoot," said Mac.

Adrian took their glasses and went inside for refills. The interior of the pub was dark in comparison to the brilliant sunshine outside and his eyes took a moment to adjust. Behind the bar, Susie was serving an elderly man in a flat cap. She looked over at him with a smile.

"Hello, stranger. Where's that handsome husband of yours?"

"Doing the school run. How are you?"

"Busy. We've got the Midsummer Solstice this weekend, so we're rushed off our feet. What can I get you?"

Adrian ordered the drinks and asked about Frankie. "Will said she was home and I wondered if we could bribe her into babysitting on Friday night. I booked us a table at El Pescador months ago, you see."

"Ooh, lucky you. I haven't been there for donkey's years. Are you sitting outside? I'll give her a shout."

"Thanks, Susie. Can you add a drink for her too? By the way, your hair looks nice."

"You are a charmer. She'll have the same as you. White wine. That's nine pounds fifty, please."

Adrian paid and took the drinks outside on a tray, careful not to spill any. He asked Mac and Buster about their ride and was hearing all about the joys of Seaton beaches when Frankie came to stand by the table. She was even prettier than Adrian remembered in a summery blue dress which matched the sky.

"Hello, Adrian. Mum says you're looking for a babysitter. Hello!" she said, nodding at the bikers with a smile.

"Frankie! Come and join us. I got you a glass of wine. This is Buster and this is Mac, from Cumbria. They're touring Devon, just like Will and me but in a slightly more rock 'n' roll way than our middle-class Audi. Gentlemen, this is Frankie, whose mum runs the place."

"Yes, we met earlier. I'll be the one cooking your breakfast in the morning. Cheers, Adrian."

She sat beside him on the wooden bench and raised her glass. "Here's to midsummer!"

"To midsummer!" they toasted.

"When is the solstice?" asked Adrian.

"Saturday. There's a party on the green. Are you going to come? You can bring Luke. Kids are always welcome."

"Most probably. What about you two?" he asked Mac.

"No, we're off again tomorrow. Heading Glastonbury way. What do you do when you're not helping your mum out, Frankie?"

"I run an art gallery in Bath. Have you seen the city? It's really lovely."

The conversation continued as if these three had known each

other decades. Adrian sipped his wine and gave them all a benevolent smile. With some surprise, he acknowledged that he liked the country life, knowing the locals and appreciating the proximity to nature. Maybe the dream was closer than he thought. Move to a smaller city, sell the flat and buy a cottage, Will could get a transfer, Adrian could set up a wine shop and finally adopt a Schnauzer.

"... honeymoon?" asked Frankie.

"Sorry, I missed that. Daydreaming about living here permanently. What about a honeymoon?"

"I said when is Tanya back from her honeymoon?"

"Sunday was the original plan, but what with her finding a murder victim, they may have to stay longer."

"Finding a murder victim! What?"

Adrian told them the whole story and Frankie was beside herself at discovering Gabriel's connection with Alexander Moffatt. Buster bought another round and they devised several theories about who would want to kill an artist's muse. Mac told a story about Robert Graves, who also lived in Deià, quoting some of his poetry. Frankie insisted on buying them all a drink on condition that Mac recited more. They were each taking turns to recall a poem from childhood when a small hairy bundle dashed up and placed her paws on Adrian's legs.

"It's Huggy Bear!" exclaimed Buster. "Come here, mate!"

Adrian lifted his head to see Luke charging in his direction, Will strolling behind.

"Frankie!" Luke opened his arms like a mendacious fisherman and Frankie rose to give him a hug. In the general welcome for boy, dog and man, Mac going to get them all drinks and Will reacquainting himself with Frankie, Adrian didn't think to check his husband's mood. Probably because he'd consumed three glasses of Chardonnay.

Well-mannered as ever, Will engaged the bikers by asking questions about their travels, expressed his thanks to Frankie for agreeing to babysit and bought another round. By this time, Adrian was aware he really needed something to eat and asked for a packet of crisps. Will cast him a disdainful look and when he returned with the tray of beverages, there were no crisps.

He left the party to go to the bathroom and bumped into the door jamb, which knocked him sideways into the opposite wall. He faced facts. He was drunk as a skunk and should go home. When he'd finished in the bathroom, he washed his hands and face, hoping it might sober him up. Then he went to ask Susie for two bags of crisps. By that time Gordon was behind the bar, and he chastised Adrian for buying four individual glasses of wine.

"Buy a bottle next time, man! Why waste your money! Here's my cheapest Chardonnay, and I'll give you the cork too, in case you want to take the rest home. What flavour crisps do you want?"

"Salt and vinegar. Can I get a pint of cider and that beer, what's it called? Frangipani or something?"

"Sure. I'll get one of the guys to bring it out to you. Cash or card?"

Adrian paid and made his way outside with a little extra caution to find Will on his feet, Huggy Bear's lead in hand.

"Here he is! Great to see you again, Mac, Buster. Have fun in Glastonbury. See you tomorrow, Frankie. Is half six OK? Brilliant, thank you so much. Come on, Luke, dinner's ready. Adrian?"

"I just bought another round." His voice was not as distinct as usual.

Will's upbeat smile didn't change. "All the more for Frankie. Let's go."

There was no point in arguing. Adrian said his goodbyes, exchanged numbers with Buster and Mac, then allowed Luke to drag him away in the direction of Beatrice's cottage. By the set of Will's back, he knew he was in trouble.

They ate pasta with some red sauce at the kitchen table, Luke entertaining them with a long story about a prank his class had played on their headmaster. The minute dinner was over, Will asked Adrian to clear up while he got Luke prepared for the next day. Luke came to kiss him goodnight and he hugged the boy warmly.

"Sleep well, Little Monster."

"Sleep well, Monster Munch." Luke grinned at Adrian's mock outrage and scuttled out of the kitchen, giggling.

He listened to them creaking about upstairs, asking and answering questions about books, gym kit and permission slips. There was a lot of laughter. Adrian checked his phone. No news from Beatrice but a message from Catinca.

```
Got interview for well massive
commission! B-list sleb is getting married
- can't say Who but that's no typo %)! Can
I use your wedding photos for portfolio?
You having fun playing Daddies? Miss you
two. Catinca xoxoxox
```

He was smiling as he wrote a reply.

```
Use whatever you want. Good luck!
Country life is so me. Daddy so not. Miss
you too. Ax
```

He heard Will wish Luke goodnight and wondered if there was anything decent on television. When he looked up, Will was standing in the doorway, looking at the dirty plates and messy table.

"Oh, yes, sorry. I was supposed to clean up. I'll do it now." He rubbed his hands together, as if he meant business.

"Don't bother. I'll clear up, prepare Luke's breakfast and lunchbox, feed the animals and put the dishwasher on. Why don't you go watch TV?"

His dismissive tone stung. "I was just replying to Catinca. She asked if she could use our wedding photos for her portfolio. She has a celebrity client!"

Will kept his back to him as he scraped leftovers into the bin. "What did you say in reply?"

"I said use whatever you want. Listen to this, she gave me a clue as to who it is."

Will exhaled sharply. "You gave permission for her to use our wedding photographs without consulting me?"

"Why not?" Adrian lifted his shoulders. "It's Catinca. What *is* the matter with you today?"

"With me?" Will paced across the kitchen like a panther and gripped the arms of Adrian's chair. "You don't seem to give a shit about the responsibilities we took on. Yesterday you got pissed with two strangers. Today you didn't go to the supermarket as I asked you and spent the afternoon in the pub. I'm taking care of Luke and the animals and the house while you're behaving like you're on holiday."

Adrian glared at Will and looked pointedly at his hands, still gripping the chair and trapping Adrian. Will moved away.

Adrian got to his feet and yelled. "I AM on holiday!"

With a splayed left palm, Will shut him up. "There is a child in bed, trying to get some sleep. I won't let you upset him with one of your tantrums. We agreed to step in while Beatrice ..."

"No, we didn't." Adrian hissed. "You did. What the hell do you mean, 'one of my tantrums'? Don't patronise me, William Quinn, because I'm not having it. Obviously I wanted to support Beatrice and accepted our holiday wouldn't be quite as we'd planned. What I didn't expect was you turning into Mary fucking Poppins and lecturing me about what I can and can't do while we look after a friend's kid. I'm not auditioning for the role of Perfect Dad. Are you?"

Will stared at him. "Maybe you should go to bed and sleep it off."

"You're sending me to my room? Seriously? Go to hell!"

Adrian picked up his jacket.

"You are not going out." Will's whisper was midway between a question and an order.

"Get it right, Pops. If you want to play Happy Families, I think you'll find your line is 'You're not going out *dressed like that*'. Yes, I'm going out. And in the spirit of Happy Families, don't wait up."

He closed the front door gently behind him, so as not to wake Luke. This situation wasn't the kid's fault. The blame lay one hundred percent with Will. He strode out of the driveway and headed down the lane towards The Angel.

Chapter 12

Nirvana was not easy to find. Beatrice walked past it three times before resorting to the Get Directions feature on her phone. Eventually she realised the little door beside the greengrocer had a nameplate. Nirvana – Yoga and Pilates Studio. She opened the door and ascended the stairs. At the top, a door bearing the same information as the plate below opened into an anteroom with coat hooks and shelves. Beyond was a large airy room with Venetian blinds throwing horizontal patterns across the wooden floor. She spotted two pairs of shoes lined up by the door and took off her trainers.

"Hello? Anyone at home?"

At the other end of the room, a blonde head popped round the door. "Can I help? Church doesn't start till six today."

"Yes, I'm sorry to disturb you. My name is Beatrice Stubbs. I'm a private investigator looking into the unexpected death of your colleague, Romy Palliser. You must be Miranda Flynn."

The woman came out from behind the door, closing it behind her. She moved with a dancer's grace across the floor, her hand outstretched. "Pleased to meet you. I'll do anything I can to help. We're all in shock at what happened." Her grip was strong and her expression grave. She wasn't attractive in an obvious way, but she exuded a certain confidence Beatrice could imagine being effective when she was teaching.

"That's understandable. I just wanted to find out a few things about Romy as a person. You operated this business together?"

"Past tense is correct. When Romy took up the role of however-you-want-to-describe-it with the Moffatts, she quit teaching and pulled out of the whole operation. I had to find another investor as well as a new yogi to handle her classes. I don't mind admitting we had a major fight over that." She sniffed. "I hadn't got around to apologizing before she died. I regret it now. It seems so petty."

"What about Romy's family? You and her brother are an item, I hear."

Her face softened. "Greg and I have been dating for over a year. I'm crazy about him. He lives out at their parents' house because they're usually in Bermuda. They're flying in tomorrow because of what happened. He's a bit younger than me, so I wasn't sure we had much of a future, but just recently, we decided to move in together."

"Congratulations. What does Greg do for a living?"

"He's had a few different jobs, but only since we've been together has he learned his true calling. He founded a church, called 'The One Truth'. It's based on humanist teachings and the power of meditation. We have meetings three times a week, here, and he already has a following of thousands of people around the world. A lot of people who come here on holiday convert to the faith and he holds online courses or even one-to-one consultations so they can maintain their discipline. He's amazing."

Beatrice bit her lip. Her experience of new religions had not been positive. But more of immediate interest was how forthcoming and well-rehearsed this woman's answers were. "How interesting. But can one make money out of founding a church?"

"Oh yes. He makes most of his money through his courses. Greg's such an inspiring speaker, you should hear him. His flock tend to be pretty wealthy and what he charges for his consultations contributes to the church fund so that he can continue to spread the word. He'll be here in around half an hour to prepare for this evening's meeting. He can tell you more about it then. He's very open about what he does."

"And what about you? Are you part of the church?"

"Absolutely. I've never really felt the need for faith before but you know what? Now I don't know where I'd be without it. I grew up in Boston in a typically Calvinist kind of family where church was something to be endured. Greg has opened my eyes to what was missing from my world outlook. You can attend a meeting if you want. It could change your life."

"I'll think about that. Do you make a decent living from yoga teaching?"

She shrugged, her blue eyes downcast. "I get by. Yoga and Pilates classes are one string to my bow but I'm also a qualified masseuse, so I work in the hotel spa two days a week. Hot stones, deep tissue, aromatherapy, Reiki and Alexander technique, I can turn my hand to most kinds of therapy."

"What was Romy's role in your business?"

A shadow crossed her face. "We were supposed to be partners, renting this space and taking turns to run classes. But when she bailed on me, I had all these people signed up for her Hot Yoga sessions and no one to teach them. She had a different kind of training to me. No way could I teach her stuff."

"Do you know if Romy had any enemies? Someone with a grudge against her?"

The blonde head shook. "She was Miss Popularity. Men all desired her and women wanted to befriend her. Redheads have a reputation for passion, but that was something she lacked completely. She never made any enemies because she just wouldn't argue. I don't think I've ever met someone who avoided conflict of any kind. Even her ex-boyfriend speaks well of her. The only person I can think of who can't stand her doesn't really know her. The girl who was Alexander Moffatt's previous inspiration was pretty vicious about her replacement, but to my knowledge, they hadn't even spoken."

"Her ex-boyfriend. What would his name be and why did they split up?"

"Juan Carlos Mendez. He lives in Port de Sóller. I can find his number for you, if you like. I don't know why they split, but I assume it was to do with her role at the Moffatts. It was a bizarro set-up, everyone thought so. How his wife can tolerate that amazes me. Having an affair is one thing, but to move her into your home? A step too far, in my opinion."

"You seem very confident the relationship was sexual."

The woman raised her eyebrows. "Have you seen those paintings of his muses?"

Beatrice chose not to mention what had happened to Hoagy's artwork. "No, I haven't. I confess I'm not particularly a fan. What did you ..."

The door to the studio opened and a young strawberry-blond man stood framed in the doorway. Beatrice's first impression was of a convalescent. His skin seemed papery and white, his eyes hollow and cheekbones sharp. Despite the weather, he was dressed in corduroy trousers and a fisherman's sweater. He knelt to unlace his brogues and gave her a beatific smile.

"Well, well! Somebody is keen."

"Greg, this is Beatrice Stubbs, a private investigator. She's not here about the church, but about Romy."

He froze in the act of shucking off his shoes. "A private investigator? Sorry? Who hired you to investigate my sister's death?" He pulled himself up to his full height and gave her a cold glare.

"Alexander Moffatt, actually. He and his wife are concerned that the police are not treating this case with the professionalism it deserves and asked if I could help. I would just like to say I'm extremely sorry for your loss. You and your family have my most sincere condolences."

"Thank you." He flicked a glance at Miranda. "We agreed that when talking to the police we would do so together, Rand."

Miranda pouted. "But she's not the police."

Beatrice studied him and his public school looks. His body language was affectedly casual, hands in the pockets of his cords as if he were strolling along the banks of the River Cam. "As Ms Flynn states, I'm not police and have no authority to command you to speak to me. Although I would have thought it was in your interests to find who killed your sister. Personally, I'm quite happy to speak to you together or separately. I would also like to understand a little more about your church."

It was a pathetically obvious attempt at getting him onside but to her astonishment, it appeared to work.

"If you are genuinely interested in our faith, the best way of understanding the tenets upon which our belief system is based, you should stay for the service. Talk to my congregation, engage with my guided meditation and keep an open mind. If you still want to speak to me afterwards, I'll be happy to talk to you, as I would any other member of my flock. The first attendance is free, although any donations to the cause are always welcome. Now I need to take a few moments to prepare myself. There's a little coffee shop directly opposite so why don't you go get yourself a drink and come back in twenty minutes?" In his socks, he padded across to the door Miranda had emerged from and disappeared.

Beatrice hitched a handbag onto her shoulder. She gave Miranda a smile, trying to convey both apology and understanding in one expression. "How long do these meetings last? Just because my assistant is due to arrive shortly."

Miranda's focus was on the closed door at the other end of the room. "Um, around two hours, maybe more if people have questions. I have to go now."

Beatrice puffed out a deep breath. Two hours? "In that case, I won't be able to stay. Perhaps you could just tell me where you were on Monday night and Tuesday morning?"

"Greg and I were at my apartment. It's upstairs, on the floor above this. After my last class, we went down to Sa Fonda and had a few drinks. It's a good place to go celeb spotting but on Monday, it was half empty and dull. We came home and had an early night. The next morning, we got up around nine and went to the café over the road for some breakfast."

"Thank you. You have a very good memory for detail. I appreciate your talking to me. Here's my card. Perhaps you could send me the ex-boyfriend's number."

"Yes, of course. Excuse me, I must go help Greg." She covered the length of the room in four long strides.

Beatrice replaced her shoes and went back out into the street, considering the two people she had just met. Flaky? Certainly. Murderers? They were rather peculiar, so it wouldn't hurt to check out their backgrounds. She rooted about in her handbag, found her phone and called Theo.

At ten past six, Beatrice was thanking her lucky stars. Instead of listening to some half-baked guru dispensing wisdom to a group of gullible and wealthy supplicants, she was on a hotel terrace with a martini and a panorama of the sea, waiting for her assistant. Tanya, Gabriel and Matthew were en route from the northernmost peak of the island and the plan was to gather for dinner and collaborate on a strategy. An instinct made her turn and she shielded her eyes from the sun as Theo loped across the terrace, his grin wide.

She stood to embrace him and assessed how he looked. Their most recent case in Finland had taken its toll, but here he was, glowing with health and apparently ready for action.

"Theo, my saviour! I really can't thank you enough for dashing to the airport while you were supposed to take a week's recuperation. Are you truly recovered or do we need to do a fit-for-purpose test à la James Bond?"

"My pleasure, M." He sank into the chair opposite, his eyes warm and shirt loud. "As for martinis, I'll have mine stirred."

She signalled to the waiter to bring a second martini and gave all her attention to the man opposite. As did half the occupants of the terrace. Beatrice had encountered many beautiful people in her time, but Theo brought something else. He commanded attention simply by being. Beatrice wondered if he could teach her that essence and dismissed the thought in an instant.

"Nice shirt. Let me guess, an original Radu."

"Wild, isn't it? She let me keep one after I did a modelling shoot for her. From her 'Artiste' collection. This design is called 'Luxe, Calme et Volupté' from the Matisse range. Can you believe I'm sitting here in Deià wearing designer clothes and about to drink a martini? Wait, I forgot my shades." He slipped on a pair of Ray-Bans and Beatrice chortled in delight.

"I'd better get out the way or risk getting trampled by all your admirers. Whereas I caught the sun pottering around the streets and the only thing that makes me stand out is my red hooter. Are you ready to talk business?"

The waiter placed Theo's cocktail on the table along with a small bowl of nuts.

"I am now. Cheers! So what have you got so far?"

She brought him up to speed with a mixture of facts, opinion and impressions. Theo listened, asked questions and took notes. She studied his face as he re-read his own handwriting. His black plaits had been redone since their Finnish case, his skin showed hardly any bruises or scratches from his cave rescue and his eyes were as bright as ever. But some sort of shadow hung over him.

"Theo, are you truly ready to return to the fray? Do you still want this job now you've seen how ugly it can get? Be honest, that's all I ask."

His gaze remained on the paper in front of him as he nodded

his head. "I still want this job because I think I'm going to be good at it." He looked up. "Eventually."

"You've worked with me on fewer than half a dozen cases and I can already tell you're good at it. I trust you completely. The one thing I know from my time at the Met is the fact that dealing with suspicion, infidelity, fraud, corruption, jealousy, murder and abuse can get under your skin. You're going to need some armour."

"Yeah, I know." He pressed his forefingers to his temples. "I'm working on it. This place helps. There's something in the air, you know?" His gesture encompassed the view of green hills, the distant beach and acres of Madonna-blue sky. "Whoa! It's the happy couple!"

He stood up to embrace Tanya, whose hair was shower damp and her skin sun-kissed. Gabriel stood behind her, his face wreathed in smiles. Beatrice looked past them to Matthew who had bent to address a retriever beneath the table of another guest. He gave the impression of being relaxed and in fine spirits. She went to greet him.

"Did you have a nice afternoon, my love?" she asked, reaching up to kiss his cheek.

"It was quite out of the ordinary, I must say. This is a part of the world I had quite overlooked and wish I had not. You and I must go to the coast, Old Thing. Your jaw will drop, it's that spectacular." He smiled at the retriever's owners. "*Kalispera*. You see, it's fine to bring dogs here. Huggy Bear would love this place."

Beatrice snorted with laughter. "We're in Spain, Matthew, where people speak Spanish. Not Italian, not Greek, but Spanish. As for dogs, Huggy Bear is in safe hands with Adrian and Will. I bet they're having the best time playing Three Men and a Border Terrier. Come along now, let's order some food. I'm ravenous."

"Same here. Oh, there's Theo! Hello, young man! What a

wonderful shirt!"

Chapter 13

On Friday morning, Beatrice awoke early, keen to get on with the job. She was painfully aware of how little time remained and the lack of evidence she had procured. She left Matthew asleep and wondered if it was impolite to call Philly at this hour. While she was pondering, she spotted a text message from Theo.

`Called Juan Carlos (the ex boyfriend) last night - got an appt to talk to him at 10.00. He speaks English, BTW. I'm going for a run. Pick you up at 8.30 to tackle that Quintana woman in Sóller's tourist office?`

She just finished reading when another message came through, this time from Philly herself. She and Raf's lawyer would be attending an interview at the police station at two o'clock that afternoon. Beatrice made herself a coffee and some toast, then sat on the veranda to make a list of possible suspects, their motives and where relevant, their alibis.

Philly Moffatt: Jealous of her husband's obsession with the girl. Asleep in bed with Hoagy.

Hoagy Moffatt: Jealous of the girl's attraction to Gabriel and possibly other male visitors? Raf, for example? Asleep in bed with Philly.

Bernie Whistler: Trying to frame the Moffatts. Drunk on his own sofa.

Miranda Flynn: Revenge for Romy's walking out on their business. (But why would she wreck the paintings?) In bed with Greg.

Greg Palliser: What reason would he have to kill his sister? In bed with Miranda.

Nuria Quintana: Retaliation at being ditched for another muse. Alibi?

Juan Carlos Mendez: Revenge for being dumped. Alibi?

Raf Beaufort: In love with Romy, jealous of Hoagy? But Hoagy's work was his cash cow, so why destroy his muse and his art? In London.

Neighbour/gardener/housekeeper???

The list was feeble, she knew it. If she weren't convinced of their innocence, she would say that the most likely explanation on paper was that Hoagy and Philly had killed her together. It was all very unsatisfactory, but she had to keep turning stones. For Philly's sake. She left a note for Matthew, picked up her bag and went outside to wait for Theo. It was another wonderful day, the air filled with scents of herbs and the sound of seagulls screeching. In some ways, she wished she could forget this case and spend the day exploring the coast with Matthew.

Just then, Theo pulled up in a Mercedes A-class and Beatrice sighed. She had work to do.

Just as Philly had said, Nuria Quintana now worked at the tourist information office in the centre of Sóller. Beatrice waited outside, looking through the window. The second Theo opened the door, Nuria shot him a curious glance, before returning her attention to the elderly couple at the desk. As agreed, Beatrice entered a couple of minutes later to potter about looking at leaflets and maps, as if Theo were a complete stranger. Nuria was speaking rapid Spanish to the pensioners, while Theo waited patiently until she had finished explaining the route to somewhere or other with lots of hand gestures. Looking at the map of Sóller on the wall, Beatrice refocused her eyes to look at the ex-muse's reflection. She was striking, all long eyelashes, black hair and an olive complexion, as she pointed towards the street. It occurred to Beatrice that if Nuria worked in the tourist office, she must surely speak English. Apparently so did Romy's ex, Juan Carlos. So Beatrice had dragged Theo here under false pretences. She shook her head at herself. Oh well, he was bound to come in handy.

The silver-haired tourists finally departed with much *gracias* and *buenos días*. Theo stepped up with his most charming smile. He addressed her in Spanish and Beatrice watched her body language. She listened to his words with interest at first, but when he said the words 'Romy Palliser', her face shut down. She shrugged and folded her arms, with a hostile expression. Theo tried again, his voice soothing and persuasive.

She snorted like a bull and rattled off into a long speech, the tone of which was accusatory. Beatrice managed to catch a few words but could make nothing coherent of the whole. Theo asked a few more questions and her replies were less confrontational. He thanked her and left the little office, ignoring Beatrice completely. With her handful of leaflets advertising local attractions, Beatrice approached the desk with a pleasant smile.

"Good morning. Do you speak English?"

"A little," said the girl, smiling back. "How can I help?"

Beatrice made up some rubbish about hearing of a craft brewery she'd like to visit. The girl was animated and offered several suggestions, of which Beatrice heard almost nothing, fixated as she was on making an assessment of the young woman's strength. Her hands fluttered like those of a Kabuki dancer, elegant with long nails manicured with ruby-coloured polish. Two hikers came in, so Beatrice complimented her on her English and expressed her thanks.

She left the small building and went in search of her assistant, who was waiting outside a nearby café.

"I ordered you a latte and a horseshoe," he said, dunking his teabag up and down in his glass of hot water.

"A horseshoe?" she asked, picking up the pink and white iced biscuit from the plate. "What a good idea. It will bring us luck. So, what did she say?"

"In a nutshell, she wouldn't go near the Moffatt place if wild bulls dragged her. Romy's killer is obvious. Her ex-business partner Miranda is a psychotic violent bitch who should be under arrest. On Monday night, Nuria herself was at Sa Fonda bar till two in the morning and spent the night at her sister's. Did you see the sword?"

Beatrice had a mouthful of biscuit so simply frowned and shook her head.

"There's a lintel above the desk with a ceremonial sword attached to it, a bit like a scimitar. It would make a pretty effective murder weapon. The thing is, she's the detective in charge's niece, so how are we going to suggest testing it?"

Beatrice thought about it. By now, Nuria would have called her uncle, Detective Pedro Quintana, and alerted him to their presence. Taking advantage of Theo's Spanish, Beatrice intended to share her meagre findings. If he still refused to communicate, she would address his superior. Or rather get Theo to do it.

"What reason did she give for calling Miranda a violent psychotic bitch?"

"She said to ask her. Which I fully intend to do."

She beamed at him. "I knew you would come in useful. Right, let's go and find Juan Carlos Mendez. After that, we'll tackle the cops. Be warned, I'm not expecting a warm welcome from either."

Theo dropped five Euros on the table. "No shit?"

Where Juan Carlos was concerned, Beatrice was wrong. His mother answered the door at his address and told Theo he was at the beach. She then called her son on his mobile and asked him to identify himself to the detectives when they arrived. Sure enough, as Beatrice and Theo came down the wooden walkway from the car park, a young man in swimming trunks broke away from a group waving an arm above his head. Unlike the grief-wracked ex-lover Beatrice had imagined, this man was tanned, smiley and possessed the most extraordinary body. Why on earth would Romy leave someone this drop-dead gorgeous to shut herself away with Hoagy?

"Hi! I'm Juan Carlos Mendez. My mother said you wanted to talk to me."

They shook hands and Beatrice pretended that interviewing a near-naked wet sex god in Speedos was all in a day's work. "Thank you so much for taking the time to answer our questions, Mr Mendez."

"No problem. Call me Juan Carlos. You wanna come under one of the beach umbrellas? It's hot out here."

They followed his broad shoulders and tiny bottom as he led the way to one of those thatched palm umbrella type of affairs, which Beatrice always suspected harboured legions of insects.

Beatrice flipped open her notebook, somewhat relieved that Juan Carlos's swimmer's torso was partially concealed by the shelf table around the umbrella's trunk.

"It's about Romy, right? I guessed sooner or later someone would want to talk to me."

Theo spoke. "You need to understand, Juan Carlos, that we're not police. You are under no obligation to speak to us."

"I know. My mother said you're private investigators. I had a feeling the Pallisers would employ someone other than the local police to find out who killed their daughter. It's OK. I'm cool with it. I have nothing to hide."

Neither Beatrice nor Theo corrected his assumption of who was paying their fee. Juan Carlos's hair was so sleek and his face so smooth, Beatrice pictured him as a mannequin, a plastic ideal of perfection. But this young man was only too real.

"Do you mean to say you have not yet been interviewed by the police?" she asked.

He shook his head with emphasis. "No. Nothing. I figured they already know who did it, because otherwise they'd be chasing me. Angry ex-boyfriend out for revenge, I can already imagine the newspapers. For the record, I didn't kill Romy."

"Is it all right if we ask you some rather personal questions?" Beatrice asked. "We're trying to piece together a picture of Romy's world, her friends, family, career, that sort of thing."

"I'll tell you whatever you need to know. Like I said, I have nothing to hide. Romy and I dated for around six, seven months. She was a pretty girl and I liked her energy. Plus it was the first time I'd been with a redhead. We hung out with some of her friends, but that scene, it's kinda weird. Her brother and his church, the Deià rich kids, her business partner, they made me uncomfortable. Romy was sexy and we had some good times, but our fling was pretty much over before she got offered the artist gig. What happened to her is horrible and shocking and tragic because she was so young. But I'm not broken-hearted. We were done." He lifted his shoulders and opened his palms, as if to indicate there was nothing more to say.

Theo rested a cheek on his fist. "I appreciate your honesty. Can you tell me where you were the night she died?"

"Yeah, sure. I was in a hotel in Valencia. I competed in a swimming competition over the weekend and the flight home on Monday was cancelled. Me and my coach stayed an extra night in Valencia and flew home on Tuesday morning." His gaze switched between them. "What else do you want to know?"

Beatrice quelled an impulse to ask if she could touch his biceps and took another direction.

"Who do you think would want to kill her, Juan Carlos? Who hated her that much?"

He opened his palms. "I just don't know. That whole crowd

are pretty weird. Her brothers are both up their own butts and Miranda is a freak. I never met the artist or his wife, so I can't say. Romy and her family are typical of a type. Arrogant, self-confident and careless of other people's feelings. Maybe she made an enemy of someone, I really don't know. Our relationship, if you can call it that, was meeting a couple of times a week for sex. Sorry to be basic, but it's the truth. I didn't like her friends, she didn't like mine. When she said she wanted to end things, I had a moment of bruised ego, which lasted one whole second until I remembered Concha." He glanced over his shoulder at the group of friends he had left. "One door closes, another one opens, right?"

Hot and flustered, Beatrice asked a question to cover her embarrassment. "Do you know Detective Pedro Quintana, or his niece Nuria? She was Mr Moffatt's previous ... inspiration."

He thought for a second. "Don't think so. I mean, I saw the detective guy on the news, but that's about it."

"Where'd you get your accent?" Theo wore a broad grin. "You sound like you come from San Francisco, not Port de Sóller."

"Not far off, man! I went to college in Seattle on a swimming scholarship. Awesome, but I can't tell you how much I missed the sun."

"You're a lucky guy. Nice to meet you, Juan Carlos. Have a great afternoon."

Juan Carlos shook hands and Beatrice hesitated about giving him one of her business cards. Where on earth would he put it?

"Yes, very nice to meet you and if you think of anything else that might help, do please get in touch. Theo is staying at Hotel Residencia and you can reach him there."

He gave them a double thumbs-up and hared away across the sand. Beatrice watched him go and then turned to see Theo's grin grow broader still.

"What a very well-mannered young man. Shall we go? We have time for a spot of lunch before we bother the police."

"Yeah, let's find a restaurant. I'd say you're ready for a portion of beefsteak."

"Shut up now," she said, aware of his shoulders shaking with suppressed laughter.

Chapter 14

Bright light shone in Adrian's eyes when his eyes flew open at a sudden bang. His head throbbed as if someone was using a blender on his brain, his eyes were dry and crusty and his neck was stiff after sleeping all night on Beatrice and Matthew's Chesterfield. The Audi's engine purred into life and crunched its way down the drive. Will was taking Luke to school. Adrian sat up gingerly, his stomach threatening to hurl up its contents. The living room door was closed. Thankfully, Luke had not witnessed the drunken mess on the sofa.

He shoved the blanket off his legs and wondered where it had come from. Last night was a blurred mess of images but he was confident he would not have known where to locate a blanket in this house. He dragged himself upstairs, dropped his clothes in a pile and stepped into the shower. When he got out, he could hear noises in the kitchen and Will's voice addressing the dog. In the mirror, bloodshot eyes and rough stubble greeted him. The urge to vomit was more manageable now, but had not left entirely.

Shaved, dressed and prepared to apologise, Adrian descended to the kitchen, where Will was cooking bacon and listening to the news. Just before he entered the room, Adrian tried his memory one more time. What had happened last night? His memory shot back the same jump-cut footage he had seen when first opening his eyes. A bar, some faces, whisky and a fireplace. A plate of chips and laughter. So much laughter. His abdomen contracted as if in reminder. Whose faces? Not Mac and Buster, not Frankie, not Susie. The man with a moustache who knew his name. How had he got back to the cottage? A moment's panic seized him and he went into the living room to find his phone, wallet and keys in a neat pile on the sideboard. It was time to face Will.

"Good morning." Huggy Bear dashed across the tiles to meet him, her back end waggling like a duck.

"Morning," Will replied. "I thought a full English might be the best way to deal with your hangover. Coffee or tea?"

There was no point in trying to deny it. "Tea, please. A full English is the perfect thing to settle my stomach. I feel like shit."

To his credit, Will did not push the point and simply made a pot of tea. He returned to the Aga and before Adrian had even added milk to his mug, Will presented two plates of bacon, eggs, tomatoes, mushrooms, sausage and beans. The toaster did its jack-in-the-box ejection and Will handed him a slice of toast.

"There, that should soak up whatever you consumed last night." He sliced into a sausage.

Adrian's appetite appeared from nowhere, as if it was running late. He tucked into the food like somebody might snatch it away from him. He hadn't eaten since ... when had he last eaten? Yesterday lunchtime in Dartmouth? Although there was that vague memory of chips.

"Thank you for cooking. Exactly what I needed. Did Luke get off to school OK?"

Will watched him eat. "Yeah, after a far healthier breakfast than this. He had fruit salad and oh, who gives a shit? Look, I'm sorry. I've been having fun playing at parenting and falling into the classic trap of judging others. It was unnecessary and unfair to have a go at you. The choice to babysit Luke was mine, for selfish reasons and I apologise for that. You've been tolerant and patient and I've been a bit of a git."

Adrian put down his knife and fork, more out of concern for his digestive system than anything else, but he made it look as if he were devoting all his attention to his husband. There was a lot to unpack in what he'd just said but now was not the time.

"Thank you. I'm sorry for having a hissy fit and stomping off. So are my head and digestive organs. Why don't we just forget about this for now, go for a walk and enjoy dinner tonight ... together." He avoided using terms such as 'on our own', just in case it kicked off another row. "Tomorrow we could go to the beach, take Huggy Bear and Luke, play cricket or croquet or build sandcastles and make the most of our last day."

Will tilted his head, his expression puzzled. "Our last day? What do you mean?"

"Tanya and Gabriel are flying home on Sunday. Even if Beatrice has to stay in Mallorca, the day after tomorrow, Luke goes home to his mum and we drive to London ready for work on Monday. Back to reality."

Will nodded slowly and bit into his bacon, his expression distant.

Adrian watched him, curious as to how that could possibly have come as a surprise. He picked up his cutlery to tackle his breakfast again. "What's on the agenda today? I wouldn't mind sticking close to home for a change. Maybe get out into the fresh air and enjoy the local scenery. Or did you have plans?"

"Maybe we should split up."

"Sorry?" Adrian's fork hovered in mid-air, carrying a mouthful of baked beans.

"Today, I mean. Do our own things. I'd like to go surfing again, maybe near Barnstaple, but I know you're not keen. You could stick around here and maybe collect Luke if I'm not back in time. You know where the school is, don't you?"

Adrian ate his beans, thinking. After yesterday, he decided, some time apart would probably benefit their relationship.

"That sounds like a good plan. Huggy Bear and I will walk around the village and then read in the garden. I'll collect Luke, no problem. Meet you back here to get ready for our gastronomic treat tonight. Are we driving or shall we treat ourselves to a taxi home? I've been studying the wine list."

Will dabbed up the breakfast juices with some toast, shaking his head. "How you can think about alcohol after last night is unbelievable. Right, you're obviously going to take another two hours to eat that, so I'm going to grab my wetsuit and head off. See you later. Do not forget Luke."

He placed his plate next to the sink, bent to kiss Adrian's cheek and left without another word. Adrian listened to him rummaging around upstairs and waited till he went out of the front door. The Audi crunched across the gravel and Adrian judged it safe to feed Huggy Bear the rest of his sausage. He took a rasher of bacon over to Dumpling, which was warmly received. He scraped the rest into the bin and poured himself more tea.

"Well, now, Miss Bear. 'Tis just the two of us today. Whither shall we wander?"

The woods behind Upton St Nicholas didn't look especially large and paths were clearly marked. Adrian and the terrier set off with no particular route in mind, just appreciating all the glories of a forest in summertime. Huggy Bear led the way and Adrian simply followed. They wandered through patches of shade into pools of sunlight, along a brook, and came across some sort of birdwatcher's hut on stilts. The dog had a good sniff around while Adrian eyed the structure with idle curiosity until he realised what he was looking at. This was the precise spot where his husband had almost lost his life the day before their wedding. A wave of emotion broke and he physically recalled the incapacitating fear of losing Will. And now look at the two of them. Bitching at each other and arguing over nothing. He vowed to be extra nice to his husband tonight.

Huggy Bear scampered towards him, her tail wagging and teeth jutting out, as if she was politely asking him to get a shift on. She took off down an overgrown track leading to some rough steps which descended towards a pond. The village spread out on the other side, with distant sounds of cars, voices and church bells. Adrian sat on a bench to absorb the simple beauty of the English countryside. The pond was like watching a David Attenborough programme, if you paid attention. Water-skaters, a family of coots, a pair of mallards, some yellow butterflies and iridescent dragonflies all went about their business. Adrian reached for his phone to capture the moment and realised he couldn't. So he sat and observed, the dog at his feet.

Out of the blue, three muddy beasts streaked past them and launched themselves into the water. Huggy Bear began barking furiously and Adrian scrambled to put her on the lead. He had no idea if those dogs might be dangerous.

"Adrian, hello!" Heather Shaw, Gabriel's mother, came in his direction, wearing an ombré sundress and a floppy straw hat. At the ankles, the dress was deep green, lightening to a pale blue at the very top. It gave Heather the appearance of emerging from the earth like Mother Nature herself.

"Did they soak you? I'm so sorry. They are a pack of gallumphing great oafs."

In the pond, three mismatched dogs swam in circles. Adrian released Huggy Bear who rushed to greet Heather.

"No, they just gave me a bit of a fright. How are you, Heather? Have you heard any news from Gabriel?" He was careful not to mention the murder, in case she didn't know.

She flopped on the bench beside him. "Isn't it ghastly? Beatrice is a total brick for dashing off to help them. I hear you're taking care of Luke. That's awfully good of you, but what a horrible thing to happen, and on their honeymoon! Worst of all, Tanya saw the murder victim's body. I said to them, and I will insist when they get back, she must have counselling."

"She saw the body? I didn't know that. Poor Tanya, that must be traumatic. You're absolutely right, she will need counselling. That sort of thing could give you PTSD." The dogs emerged from the water, one after another, each following the same pattern of a huge shake, spattering droplets high into the air.

"God knows how Hoagy will come back from all this. It wouldn't surprise me if it puts an end to his whole career." She turned to Adrian, her eyes wide. "Do you suppose that could have been the motive? Professional envy? But what kind of psychopath would murder a rival's muse?"

The three dogs, all different sizes and none of them a breed Adrian recognised, inspected Huggy Bear. While Adrian grew nervous, the Border Terrier didn't mind, giving as good as she got.

"I cannot imagine anyone would be so vile," Adrian replied. "Like you, I'm glad Beatrice is there with them. She has her moments, but generally speaking, PI Stubbs applies logic and common sense. Are all these your dogs, Heather?"

"For now, yes." She fanned herself with her hat. "I'm a foster carer for a local animal rescue charity. A sort of halfway house, if you like. Both Huggy Bear and Dumpling used to live with me, until Beatrice took them home. Some of these creatures need to learn domesticity before finding a forever family. I don't suppose you and Will in are the market for a dog, cat or guinea pig?"

Adrian considered Will's urge to take care of Beatrice's animals and his role-playing as substitute Daddy with Luke. Perhaps a creature would distract him from his broody phase. "That is a strong possibility. Shall we walk back towards the village together and you can tell me more?"

True to her word, Frankie turned up at half past six on the dot. Luke was ecstatic to see her. When Will began the list of instructions, Frankie crossed her eyes.

"I got this, Will, don't worry. I've been his babysitter since he was born." She looked down at Luke. "Even through the nappy stage." She wafted a hand under her nose.

"Frankie!" Luke protested, but he was laughing.

"OK, you have our numbers and we'll be back by eleven. Have fun, you two!"

"Have fun, you two too!"

The pair of them stood on the doorstep, waving at the taxi until it turned the corner, Will and Adrian twisting to look out of the rear window to wave back.

El Pescador was only a twenty-minute journey from Upton St Nicholas. In the back of the cab, Adrian and Will were silent, occupied with their own thoughts. Will, Adrian was quite sure, was envisaging every possible disaster that could befall Frankie and Luke before they returned. For his own part, Adrian was rehearsing various ways of pitching the adoption of a rescue dog to his husband. With occasional diversions towards El Pescador's menu. Thankfully, their taxi driver was a monosyllabic sort of chap and the drive passed peacefully until they arrived at the legendary restaurant.

The reception was everything one would hope for from an establishment of its status. This was a delayed birthday present for DS William Quinn, so Adrian had made a particular effort. Months before, when securing one of the elusive reservations, he had included the request of a birthday cake and a bottle of champagne. Something subtle and discreet but an acknowledgement of Will's special day. Welcomed by name, escorted to the table, offered leather-bound menus and an aperitif, they could see they were in the hands of experts.

The tasting menu began with the *amuse-bouche*: local prawns skewered with cucumber and a soy sauce dip, mackerel pâté served in a savoury cone like an ice-cream, fermented vegetables in a white dish the size of an espresso saucer, and tiny blini topped with a dab of sour cream and two different kinds of caviar. The wine waiter explained the accompaniment was an

English sparkling wine from the Torquay area. Will's grin lit up the table as they toasted his belated birthday.

Five courses later, Adrian had still not managed to bring up the subject of adopting a rescue dog. They were too busy appreciating the food, the wine and the ambience. Will enthused over the freshness of the produce, Adrian raved over the wine pairings and made notes in his booklet. The waiter removed their empty plates after torched hake with braised fennel and nettle cream.

"Did you enjoy your main course?" he asked.

"Divine!" Adrian exclaimed. "That white Burgundy is a thing of beauty."

"That was so good," Will agreed. "Goes right into the top ten of best meals ever. Can we have a little break before dessert?"

"Of course. I'll give you ten minutes or so."

It was the moment to broach the subject, Adrian knew. "I didn't ask how the surfing went, what with all the rushing around to get ready. You look really stylish, you know. How many times have I said you could wear a Tom Ford like a pro?"

"Thank you. It's so comfortable, I don't feel like I'm wearing a suit. Or maybe the ones I wear for work are just crap. Surfing was so much fun. It does my mind good just to focus on the board, the waves, my balance and working with nature. We've been to some incredible places together, but this holiday will stick in my mind."

"Me too. This afternoon I sat with Huggy Bear just watching pond life and loving it. Oh, by the way, I met Gabriel's mum, Heather."

He watched Will carefully as he described the encounter, keeping his tone light and chatty.

"... because I had no idea about Huggy Bear's past. She's never mentioned it. Then Heather asked if we might be in the market for a rescue dog. Obviously, I wouldn't dream of saying yes without your consent, but the idea appeals to me. What do you think? Wouldn't you love a scruffy little pup we could take to the park at weekends?"

Will's face softened. "Yeah, I would. But dogs aren't just for weekends. How would we ..."

The lights dimmed and two waiters approached. One held a cheesecake, Will's favourite dessert, and the other carried a bottle of champagne and an ice bucket.

Adrian could have kissed them for their timing. "Happy birthday, Mr Quinn!"

Their taxi was waiting for them when they emerged, full of excellent food and in a celebratory mood. This driver was far more talkative and wanted to know all about the restaurant, the prices and dress code. Adrian let Will do the chatty stuff, quietly confident that he had won the first round in the Can-We-Get-A-Dog competition. He had all the answers to Will's inevitable questions. He'd get up early and walk the new arrival. After breakfast, he'd take the dog to work with him. He'd take full responsibility for training, registering with a vet and all the other things dog owners do, including picking up poop. He could handle this, he knew it.

The taxi stopped on the driveway and Will asked the driver to wait and take Frankie home. He tipped the guy, who wished him happy birthday again, while Adrian unlocked the front door. As if she'd overheard their conversation, Huggy Bear was first to the door, dancing and weaving between their legs, overjoyed to see them.

Frankie came into the hallway, her bag in her hand. "You're early! How was it?"

"Indescribably delicious. What a birthday treat!" Will replied. "How's the wee man?"

"Good as gold. We watched some YouTube videos which made us both laugh; he went to bed about half an hour after the specified time and I've not heard a peep since. As birthday dinners go, Will, on a scale of one to ten?"

"Ten, easy. You have to go there at least once, Frankie. It's unforgettable. OK, here's your money and the cab is outside waiting to take you home. Thank you for letting us have our night out."

She hugged them both and Will walked outside with her to thank the taxi driver, Huggy Bear on their heels. He was such a decent man.

Adrian relaxed on the Chesterfield, waiting for his husband, too full and content to think about making them a pot of herbal tea. Dumpling slept on Matthew's chair, ignoring him completely. Man and dog returned. Will stood in the doorway, his eyes intense.

"Thank you for an amazing birthday treat. I loved it. Maybe tomorrow we can discuss the practicalities of dog ownership in a London flat, but I am ready to take on a canine dependant. Do you want tea or shall we add the cherry to the birthday cake?"

Adrian stretched out an arm, Will pulled him to his feet, and they looked into each other's eyes.

"Happy birthday, DS Quinn. I love you so much." He kissed his husband, his emotions high. "Let's go to bed. Miss Bear, are you coming? Goodnight, Dumpling, sleep well." As the three of them made their way upstairs, Adrian put in a request. "I know one can't pick and choose, but I've always fancied a Schnauzer."

Chapter 15

The waiting room at the police station was dark and dusty, the shutters closed to keep out the heat of the afternoon. Strips of sunlight patterned the flagstone floor and dusty motes danced in the air while Beatrice and Theo waited and waited and waited. She did her best not to fidget, but the wooden bench was uncomfortable and Theo had gone into one of his Zen-like trances. On top of that, she had left her water bottle in the car. It was exceptionally rude to leave them sitting here for forty-five minutes, especially as they had made an appointment.

Eventually, a young woman in uniform opened the door to their right and asked them to come through. She showed them to an interview room – Beatrice guessed it was probably the only one they had – and stood against the wall. Quintana took his time to make his entrance, naturally. Sure enough, several minutes later the bullish little man barged his way into the room with a sheaf of papers in a grey folder. He glared at his visitors, but when his colleague introduced them by name, he shook their hands.

He sat and placed his palms flat on the desk in front of him, as if he were about to charge, then barked a question in Spanish. Beatrice couldn't understand much but she did hear the words 'Nuria' and '*porque*', which she knew meant 'why'. He knew they had spoken to his niece, as predicted. Judging by his intonation, he was just as aggressive and uncooperative as when Beatrice first met the man.

In contrast, Theo spoke slowly and his body language projected humility. He spoke in short sentences, employing lots of pauses and at one point turning to glance at Beatrice. Quintana flicked his gaze in her direction and back to Theo's face. It was all very frustrating to be excluded but Beatrice forced herself to remain calm and let Theo play this the way he knew best.

While she listened to their conversation, observed the gestures and tried to pick out any recognisable word in the flood of fluent Spanish, she noticed there was another source of information she could use. The uniformed officer whose hands were folded in front of her stomach was listening to the discussion, her interest matching Beatrice's. Her facial expressions were subtle and restrained, but with the right level of attention, one could deduce a great deal from the way she reacted.

At Theo's first questions, her head turned towards him, her eyes widening just a touch. She was impressed and she instantly glanced at her boss to see if he felt the same. Quintana gave little away but his response was significant on two counts. He toned down the belligerence in his voice and dropped his volume to more of a conversational manner than a drill sergeant. The young woman's eyebrows lifted a fraction and the corners of her mouth slid upwards.

At one point, Theo asked a question and Quintana flipped open the file in front of him. He ran his finger down the page, checked some information and replied. Theo made a note and asked a follow-up question, to which Quintana simply shrugged.

"Detective Quintana has kindly agreed to share some police information with us. The coroner believes time of death occurred between three and five am. Also, the CCTV footage of the gates shows no one coming in or out between the time Tanya and Gabriel left the previous evening and when Philly went out with the dogs the following morning. This is why Detective Quintana believes the killer was a member of the household."

Beatrice made a face intended to convey she understood. "That makes sense. Please thank him very much and would you let him know everything we have discovered?" She knew perfectly well Quintana could understand enough English so as not to need a translation, but maintained the pretence for the sake of politeness.

The conversation lasted over half an hour and Quintana grew increasingly more thoughtful and less combative. He shook their hands again as they left and handed Theo his card. Once out in the sunshine, they wandered up the hill towards the scene of the crime. Theo related everything the detective said and shared his own interpretation of the man's words.

"He's willing to talk to us and share a limited amount of information. My impression is, he needs all the help he can get. His usual beat involves parking tickets and handling drunken tourists. But now there's an organised gang of pickpockets operating in the town and an upsurge in drug dealing. The last thing he wants is a murder case which blurs the lines between his personal and professional life."

"Did you ask him about that? About whether he should be in charge of a murder case when his niece is a potential suspect?" Beatrice was slightly out of breath as they crested the hill towards the villa.

"Yeah. He told me the same as he told Philly. There is no one else. OK, how do we play it with Señora Navarro? Just ask about the CCTV and if she saw anything on Monday night?"

"Yes, exactly. I'd also like to have a tour of her grounds. Make it sound like I'm an avid gardener and admire her property enormously. Here we are, you press the buzzer."

"No, you press the buzzer and I'll do the talking off camera. How likely is an elderly lady to open the gate to a strange black bloke?"

As it turned out, no one answered the intercom and the mechanism began to creak. Neither spoke as the gates swung open and they walked up to the entrance of the villa. A very glamorous older lady met them at the door, with a scarf around her head and painted-on eyebrows. She wore a printed silk shirt and high-waisted trousers, like somebody in a 1970s Martini advert. Her voice was husky and smoke-raddled as she greeted them.

Theo turned on his smile and charm as he presented his business card. The woman eyed it and handed it back suspiciously. His gestures indicated he was introducing Beatrice, so she did the same and offered her card. The woman shook her head in irritation and said something to Theo with an exasperated hand gesture.

"She hasn't got her glasses, she thinks we are fraudsters and we can't come in."

"We are already in. Ask if she knows what happened next door. Use first names to show her we are part of the inner circle. Tell her what the police said about the footage. It means the murderer came from either Whistler's property or hers. Stress we want to help her and protect her from the press pack out there."

"What press pack? They have all gone."

Beatrice huffed through her nostrils. "Just tell her."

Theo launched into his Spanish explanation and Beatrice looked around the grounds, paying particular attention to the wall adjoining the Moffatts' property. The gardens were well kept and along the side wall were a series of olive trees and other shrubs, creating a natural green frieze along the base of the edifice. Due to the geographical unevenness typical of Deià, Señora Navarro's property was around two metres lower than the Moffatts' grounds. Likewise, the Moffatts' place was two metres lower than Bernie Whistler's. The three houses were built on three consecutive descending steps. The implication of this was that the wall separating Señora Navarro's property from that of the neighbours was considerably higher on her side. On observing the boundary wall while wandering the Moffatt gardens with Philly, Beatrice would have guessed one could easily leap over the whitewashed stone and into Señora Navarro's garden. From this angle, however, she could see one could easily break a leg attempting such a drop. As for access to the scene of the murder from this place, one would need some climbing equipment, or a bunk up at the very least.

The woman was explaining something to Theo involving lots of hand gestures and pointing at the gates, punctuated by occasional clutching of the silky bow at her throat.

"Her staff members come in and out via the little doorway in the gates. That's always unlocked and it's only when she needs to admit cars or strangers like us that she uses the buzzer. She thanks you for your compliments on her garden and says you can have a look around, if you like. I'll stay here and see what else I find out."

Beatrice gave a little curtsey of thanks and wandered across the lawn towards the wall. She inspected the olive trees, sniffed at the bushes and noted the space between the carefully planted foliage and the wall itself. There was a corridor, in effect, running behind the shrubbery. Presumably for the gardener's ease of maintenance. She walked the length of the wall, grateful for the shade, inhaling all the aromas of a Balearic Island in full bloom. Once she reached the end, she turned and retraced her steps, this time noticing a wrought iron handle just above her head. She stopped and examined it. It was not attached to any door, just embedded in the white concrete and at a strange height for a door handle. With a glance around to ensure she was not being observed, Beatrice tugged at the iron to see what would happen. Nothing budged, apart from a few flakes of whitewash coming away on her hands. If it wasn't a handle, what was its purpose? She looked up and saw a second handle about an arm's length above the first. Not handles, but rungs. The lower part of the wall was covered in ivy. Beatrice dropped to a crouch and calculated. If you wanted to reach the first, you would need to stand on something about knee height. She patted ivy leaves, feeling her way up and down directly beneath the wrought iron rung.

It took her five seconds to find it. Without hesitation she placed her foot on the ivy-camouflaged step and reached up for the first rung. Logically, there had to be something halfway between the two, either to the left or the right which would enable someone to climb the wall. She ran her left arm in an arc across the whitewash but found nothing to help her ascend. She turned her attention towards the right and saw it instantly. Her mistake had been to start with her right foot and right hand. Had she started with her left, another foothold protruded on her right hand side, as did another handhold halfway above. She switched sides and began climbing. Within thirty seconds, she found herself peering over the wall and through the hedge at Hoagy Moffatt's studio.

Señora Navarro knew nothing about the ladder up the garden wall. She assured Theo she'd never seen it and certainly wouldn't dream of climbing it. Beatrice could believe that. Glamorous as the elderly lady was, she seemed fragile and nervous. She took them around to the kitchen garden, where an old man in a beret was working in a lean-to greenhouse. He looked blank at Theo's questions but willingly followed them to the wall to see the ladder for himself. He shook his head, shrugging his shoulders to his ears and swore, on the bodies of several saints according to Theo, that he'd never noticed it in his life.

Expressing profuse thanks to the lady of the house and her gardener, Beatrice and Theo left through the gates.

"While we're here, let's pop next door. I want to introduce

you to the Moffatts, seeing as they're paying your wages. Just don't tell them anything about the case. I want to know for sure before giving them false hope."

Before either of them could press the buzzer, the gates swung open and Bernie Whistler emerged. He threw Beatrice a look. "You still here? Made any progress?"

Beatrice gave him a sweet smile. "Hello, Mr Whistler. I'd love to stop and chat but we're in a terrific hurry. Bye for now."

She walked through the gates, but didn't miss his look of curiosity when regarding Theo.

"Beatrice! And this must be your marvellous assistant! Theo, I am delighted to meet you!"

"You too, Ophelia. What a beautiful name." Theo gave her a winning smile as he scratched one of the wolfhound's ears.

Philly became practically girlish in Theo's company. "How fabulous that you're fluent in Spanish! I can muddle my way through the daily basics but I'd never be able to interrogate a suspect. Can I get you a drink?"

"Thanks, but we really must get on." Beatrice jumped in. "What was Whistler doing here?"

Philly scrunched up her face in disgust. "He came to make us a proposal. Hoagy's having a nap so Whistler had to deal with me. According to him, the property is now tainted and unsaleable, due to recent events, so he was prepared to up his bid and take it off our hands. He told me it was an offer we couldn't refuse. He was quite put out when I refused it."

"Well done you. Give my best to Hoagy. We'd better go."

"Oh, there's not even time to give me a tiny little update?"

"I'd rather not. We're not sure of the facts yet ourselves."

"You know best, my dear. Lovely to meet you, Theo. You simply must come round to dinner one evening."

"Thanks, I'd like that."

The pair of them beamed at each other and it took all of Beatrice's firmness to drag him away. They said their goodbyes and walked down the hill to Beatrice's cottage. Once again, Gabriel and Tanya had invited Matthew to join them on their explorations of the island, so the place was empty. The private investigation team sat in the garden with a jug of water and discussed the implications of their visit to Señora Navarro.

Beatrice stated the facts. "That door in the gate is always open. She has no security cameras. Someone could slip through that doorway and up behind the shrubs to the ladder, hop over the wall, commit some horrific murder and descend the way they came. Señora Navarro's sight is not the best or she wouldn't need glasses. The chances of her spotting a night-time visitor sneaking through her grounds are pretty much nil."

"True. Neither the gardener nor the housekeeper live on site. Señora Navarro has no interest in her neighbours and I believed the gardener when he said he'd never seen that ladder. It's pretty hard to spot, as most of the rungs have been whitewashed. Still, we should maybe inform Detective Quintana, just to show willing."

Beatrice tapped her index finger to her lips. It helped her to think. "Good idea. Why don't you do that and show him the photographs I snapped on my phone. Meanwhile, I will try and find out who lived in that house before her. It's a funny angle to attack this, if you think about it. We're looking at opportunity, rather than motive. The other thing that bothers me is the escape plan. Whatever weapon the killer used was a sizeable blade and after the event, it would have been covered in blood. How come that whitewashed wall shows not a single speck? The police really should do a forensic examination of the site. I'll leave the persuasive language to you."

Theo ran his finger around the rim of his glass. "Two conversations in one day with Detective Quintana. Lucky me."

The obvious place to start when finding previous owners of particular properties was with the local council. However, when

Beatrice checked the opening hours, she discovered the office was only open from nine till twelve and three to six each day. It was now 17.25. She grabbed her bag and ran out of the door, not even taking a moment to leave a note for Matthew. She got to the office at quarter to six with a sinking feeling. There was no way an official could retrieve the information she needed in such a short time. Still, tomorrow would be Saturday, so she had to try.

The receptionist spoke good English and directed her to the relevant office. Beatrice knocked several times but the lights were off and there was no reply. She returned to the reception desk and asked if there were any electronic means of gaining the information she needed. The woman went to lift her glasses and focus on the computer screen, but stopped and looked into Beatrice's eyes. She had a kindly smile and crows' feet at the corners of her eyes.

"It will probably take me an hour or two to find the information you need. But there is another way. If I want to learn something about Deià, I ask Maria José. She lives two doors away from the bakery and she sits outside her house all day every day. She knows everything about everyone. I'm leaving now and I walk past the bakery on my way home. Would you like to come with me and I will translate your questions for her? She's very old; I don't know how old, but her memory is more useful than every computer in this building. My name is Juana." She held out a hand.

"Thank you, Juana. That would be extremely kind."

The old woman on the bench in a flowery pinafore seemed completely unruffled on meeting an English private detective who had questions about property ownership. Her wiry grey hair was pulled back above her temples by two sparkly butterfly clips, better suited to a twelve-year-old. She wore black socks and furry slippers, despite the heat, and evaluated Beatrice through thick plastic-rimmed glasses. Her eyes were bright and her curiosity still brighter.

The first two minutes of their conversation passed with questions from Maria José and answers from Beatrice Stubbs, rather than the other way around. Finally, Juana turned the conversation to land ownership of the three villas in question and pulled out her laptop. Maria José lifted her veiny hands and tapped her fingertips together as she thought. Then she broke into a long voluble speech, enumerating on her fingers.

Beatrice waited without any impatience, intrigued by this fascinating woman whose memory exceeded anything they could produce at County Hall. Juana typed as fast as she could, occasionally adding encouragement or asking a question, until the old lady had run out of steam. An impulse prodded Beatrice to give the woman something, but she had no chocolate or flowers and money would be crass. Instead, she rifled in her handbag and found a postcard she had intended to send to a friend in London. It depicted a classic Devon village, with a central green and rustic cottages. She handed it to Maria José with one of the few Spanish phrases she knew. *Muchas gracias.*

The woman's wrinkled face creased into a broad smile and she pressed the postcard to her chest and returned the favour. "God save the Queen," she said with a cackle.

Beatrice and Juana said their goodbyes and strolled further up the street to sit outside a pavement café. Juana ordered for them both, a glass of Hierbas, which tasted rather like Pernod or some other aniseed drink. There was no doubt it contained alcohol, but Beatrice had no objection. After all, it was Friday. Juana opened her laptop and began relating Maria José's memories.

"I have to translate her words directly. I hope you don't mind, but it's too complicated to put this all in reported speech. Okay, here we go. The Whistler man. He is very new, only two years in that place. Before, it was owned by a pizza restaurant millionaire called Ghiardelli. He was never there. Why he had the place, I don't know. Very selfish to own a property that beautiful and never live there. The Whistler man is here a lot and I wish he wasn't. He wants to knock the whole place down and build apartments. He says he doesn't but I read his lying eyes, the son of a ... well, I don't need to translate that bit.

"Next door, the artists, they've been here eight years and two months. I don't know exactly what he paints, other than mostly naked women, but he makes a lot of money and he spends it here, in Deià. His wife is a nice person. She comes into town every day, says hello, talks to people and speaks Spanish with a Mallorcan accent. I'm not a big fan of her dogs but she is a nice person." Juana looked up. "I'll skip the next bit because she just talks about dogs for a few minutes."

"That's fine," said Beatrice. "If you've got time that is, I'd like to hear everything. By the way, this drink is absolutely delicious. I will have to prevail upon your kindness one more time and ask you to write down the name of the thing before we leave. Sorry, do carry on."

Juana took a sip of her drink and smiled. "It's very refreshing, the perfect thing for a Friday evening after work. So after the dogs, Maria José talked about the previous owners of the Moffatt villa. A family with four kids. Lovely people. Mallorcans from Palma, and she commuted to work in the hospital. She was a surgeon, something to do with eyes, I seem to remember. He stayed home with the children, very creditable in such a young man, and taught English in the evenings at the new place above the leather shop." Juana mugged an apologetic face. "Sometimes it's hard to get to the facts with Maria José."

Beatrice leant forward. "You are doing me an enormous favour and I thank you for taking the time. When I'm speaking to a potential witness I listen to everything they say. Sometimes the truth is hidden in the irrelevancies. Please carry on."

Juana smiled back. "You're the expert. When I asked her

about the villa owned by Señora Navarro, she said this. That woman has had so many face lifts, I'm surprised she doesn't have a beard. What does she think she looks like? She's been there around ten years, I'd say. Rich widow, you know, from Madrid. Her husband made his money in fridges but died young and she moved here. Probably hoping to find herself a replacement and that's why all the surgery. She employs that Garcia couple from behind the church, the ones who can't have kids. She bought the villa from the Palliser family before they went up in the world and got that huge estate near Port de Sóller. That was when they used to live on the island but now they spend all their time in the Caribbean or something similar to that. What has the Caribbean got that we haven't? I'll tell you. No taxes. I think it's disgraceful. These people make their money here! We buy their products and then they take their money somewhere else and no longer contribute to our lives. They should be ashamed. He's a banker and the older son drives racing cars. What kind of social benefit do they make to the world? I'll tell you, none. Yes, they built that property, twenty-five years ago. Those ginger kids grew up there and they do speak Spanish. Badly, but they do speak Spanish. I ask you though, what kind of contribution do they make to the world, to this island? Yoga lessons? Another celebrity bar?

"One thing I can tell you is that I've met a lot of celebrities in my time and no one comes close to Robbie Williams. Charm? He's overflowing with it. Whereas that Nat Palliser is an arrogant idiot with no respect. Racing cars, what a spoilt brat's hobby. Anyway, does she know who killed the girl yet?"

Juana closed her laptop. "After that there was nothing useful at all. I'm sorry, I'm not used to asking the right questions in this situation."

Beatrice looked up from her notes, her focus intense. "Are you telling me the Palliser family lived in the villa next door to the Moffatts' place?"

"That's what she said. Except it wasn't the Moffatts' place then. The Palliser kids grew up there until the family moved north to their estate near Port de Sóller. Sometime later, the parents relocated to the Caribbean. Is that important?"

"As yet, Juana, I have no idea, but this could be a very interesting lead. I'm so grateful to you for your time and patience, particularly on a Friday night. I insist on buying the drinks. Maria José is truly a remarkable woman."

"She really is. There are no secrets from Maria José." Juana rolled her shoulders and gave Beatrice a shy smile. "You know, when I was little, I wanted to be a private detective."

"Do it. I retired from the police force with every intention of growing courgettes and doing some knitting. But if you have a curious mind, the right kind of resources and access to either technology or better still, a Maria José, you should go for it." Her mobile buzzed in her pocket. She checked the display and saw it was Theo. "I have to take this, it's my assistant. I'll get the bill. Thank you so much and have a lovely weekend."

"You too, Beatrice, nice to meet you." Juana put her laptop in her bag. With a grin and a wave, she left the café terrace. Beatrice took her drink and her phone to look out over the flower gardens below.

"Theo? How did it go with Misery-guts Quintana?"

"Better than expected, actually. His focus is no longer on Philly. He's now taking a different tack."

"Let me guess. He's going after Hoagy."

"That's what I thought. But it seems Raf Beaufort has been a little bit economical with the truth. As far as you and I knew, he flew from London on Thursday to be at Hoagy and Philly's side. Detective Quintana told me today that he has been on the island of Mallorca since Sunday morning, staying in an exclusive resort outside Palma. Quintana wants to know why he's been lying and frankly, so do I."

Beatrice stared out across the verdant landscape, her brain

racing to catch up. "Is Quintana going to interview him? If so, when?"

"I don't know," said Theo. "But I had the impression they're not going to do much until Monday."

"They might not do much until Monday, but you and I are going flat out. See you back at the cottage. I have news, too."

In the early evening, once they had exchanged notes, Beatrice suggested Theo attend a church service at Nirvana. She apologised for putting him through such an experience, but he expressed genuine eagerness and loped off down the hill to arrive a little early.

Raf Beaufort was not at the Moffatts' villa and had returned to Palma. Philly gave Beatrice his number and left her to mooch around the garden while she made the call. Raf agreed to make himself available to Beatrice on Saturday morning and suggested they chat while browsing the market in Sóller. On the phone, he sounded completely relaxed and unconcerned at her interest in speaking to him.

The point at which Beatrice had seen Hoagy's studio from the other side of the wall was not difficult to find. She examined the area carefully for any signs of recent activity, droplets of blood or any markers the killer might have left behind. The police would surely have swept the area surrounding the studio, but were unlikely to have paid more attention to this spot than any other.

Her search turned up nothing at all. She refused the offer of an aperitif, keen to get back to the cottage and Matthew. She'd hardly seen him over the last couple of days. If she wasn't careful, she might forget what he looked like.

Chapter 16

Raf had a vintage Jaguar. Of course he did. It was in British racing green, with cracked red leather seats, a wooden steering wheel and retractable roof.

"I bought the old girl at auction, nigh on twenty years ago. The trouble is, I can only drive her three months of the year in Britain. She is not what you call a wet weather vehicle. That is why, at enormous expense, I transported her to her natural home. I spend around half the year in Mallorca so why not have the perfect vehicle to drive the coastal roads?"

Beatrice could see his point. The car suited the landscape so perfectly it could almost be a travel poster from the 1950s.

Philly came outside, brandishing a large silk paisley-print square. "You'll need a scarf, Beatrice. Raf's Jag is a fabulous way to travel but it does play hell with one's coiffure. Here's one of mine. It's not Hermès, probably Marks & Spencer, but it will certainly keep your hair out of your eyes. Have fun, you two! Will you be back for lunch?"

Beatrice took it. "That's very kind. I'm afraid I can't make lunch. I must make full use of the little time I have left. But thank you for the offer."

"That's a damned shame," said Raf. "But I hope you won't say no to a spot of breakfast when we get to Sóller. Philly, what say I pick up a selection of tapas at the market, to save you the bother of cooking lunch for us?" He dropped his voice. "How is the old boy?"

"Depressed, I'd say. I don't mean he's feeling a little blue or down in the dumps, I'm talking about clinical depression. Most of the day he sleeps and when he is awake, he's drinking. If there is no improvement over the weekend, I shall call his doctor first thing on Monday."

Raf reached inside his jacket, pulled out some sort of chewed stick and began gnawing on it. "Poor old bugger. Let's see how the land lies over lunch. It could be as simple as the fact he needs new inspiration. We'll talk later but now I must escort Ms Stubbs to one of the finest markets on the island. Come this way, madame."

Beatrice knotted the scarf around her head, feeling rather like the Queen, and noted that the label was not Marks & Spencer's, but Liberty London.

The journey through the rolling landscape was breathtakingly lovely, especially when one had all the accoutrements of Grace Kelly. Raf pointed out features of interest and Beatrice admired them, resisting the temptation to do a royal wave at the heads turning to stare as the vehicle purred past shops, squares, café bars and out onto the open road.

There was something about Raf which said 'normal rules do not apply to me'. On arrival in the town of Sóller, he left his vehicle at a rakish angle in the parking area, clearly not a designated spot. He did not buy a ticket, simply sauntering off in the direction of Plaça des Mercat. In his crumpled blue suit and shock of white hair, he had the air of someone famous. People did a double take, evidently trying to place him. His confidence and air of entitlement forged a path ahead of them, rather like an icebreaker in a frozen sea.

"We'll circle anticlockwise. Not simply because I'm a rebel but because we can pick up the lighter things first. I need half a dozen leather handbags, some snacks for lunch, a case of craft beer and more of my liquorice sticks. Then we will stop for coffee at somewhere only I know." He tapped his nose. "After that, we'll pick up the wine and the prints before we head back to Deià. Does that suit?"

It was abundantly clear that whether it suited or not, that was the way the morning would unfold. "I don't mind following you around as you do your chores," said Beatrice. "However, I'm not here to shop, but to ask you some questions."

Raf held out an arm to stop an approaching motorcyclist and guided Beatrice across the road. There was no zebra crossing. "And so you shall, PI Beatrice Stubbs. I'm at your disposal. We can walk, talk, sample the wares of this particularly lovely outdoor market and enjoy each other's company, all at the same time. I love Saturday mornings, don't you? This way."

Her frustration at his lack of focus soon gave way due to the lack of hers. Beatrice adored markets. There was something of the treasure hunt about them, the expectation of finding that little undiscovered gem, a secret you would share with no one apart from your nearest and dearest and everyone else that you wanted to impress. She followed Raf's impressive figure up and down the alleyways, underneath umbrellas and along pavements. While he socialised and shopped, she pottered from stall to stall, gazing at a pyramid of cheeses, inhaling the aromas of a herb stall, purchasing a pair of espadrilles for herself and a beautiful little bracelet for Tanya. The market was overwhelming for the senses. The heat increased as the sun rose and more bodies packed into the square. Music, voices and the clatter of magpies in the trees filled her ears, while her eyes ranged over a vegetable stall, a rainbow of aubergine, courgette, peppers, tomatoes, bulbs of garlic and strings of onion. Beatrice took a moment to stop and stare. The sun glinting off this array of fresh vegetables made them sparkle like jewels.

Behind her was a stall selling leather goods. She stroked the furry underside of a satchel and ran her hand over a goatskin rug, inhaling the spicy sandalwood scent of curing. She bought a little wallet for Luke, complete with Mallorcan stitching, and remembered she should also bring something home for Marianne.

"Having fun? This place is a delight, you have to agree. One more stop for my artisanal beers and then I'll take you to my extra special café. That might be a good time for you to ask your questions. The beer fellow has a permanent shop, just over there. I'll conduct my transaction and come and find you. Insider tip, that woman on the end sells pearls at around a fifty percent discount compared to the factories. She's the real deal, I guarantee it. Back in a jiffy."

He sailed off through the crowds, his height and presence creating a natural parting. People simply stood back and watched, convinced they must know him from somewhere. Beatrice moved towards the stall he had mentioned, optimistic of finding the perfect gift for her goddaughter.

Ten minutes later, she was placing three packages containing a pearl bracelet, black pearl earrings and a solitary black pearl necklace into her handbag when Raf appeared at her shoulder.

"Did you find something you liked? *Hola,* Graça. My stomach requires some toast and my brain demands some sugar. Come this way, Beatrice. I really should blindfold you as no one else should know the way to Café Umberto."

Beatrice had met enough upper-class pretenders in her time not to be particularly impressed when they invited her into the inner circle. Her cynicism melted away as she entered Café Umberto. Up a tiny alley and one flight of nondescript stairs, Raf opened a door into a different century. She could have been on the Left Bank in Paris, or in a Viennese discreet establishment, or in a top-class restaurant overlooking Milan's Duomo. At the end of the room, a wrought iron gate led out into a classic atrium. A string quartet played on a raised podium towards her left and on the right stood a long brass bar with coffee machines from the Italy of *Roman Holiday* and *La Dolce Vita* bubbling and hissing like a scientist's laboratory.

A waiter, in his more mature years, shook Raf's hand with great enthusiasm, guided them to a table and presented Beatrice with a menu.

"No need for that, my friend. We will have the full Umberto special. With all the trimmings!" His voice carried a loaded message. The waiter clearly understood, bowed and retreated behind the extraordinary bar.

Raf fixed her with his bright blue eyes. "It's quite something, don't you agree?"

"It is." Beatrice looked around at the black and white tiles on the floor, the chandeliers above her head, the waiters dressed in formal attire, the modern art on the walls and the Art Deco glass of the windows. Each table was of a different design and not a single chair in the room matched. Yet every single piece of furniture was achingly elegant. The quartet came to a conclusion and a light patter of applause echoed off the walls.

"I'm grateful for your introduction to such an unusual establishment. Quite a discovery. That said, the reason we are here is to further the investigation into what happened to Romy Palliser."

His Teflon-style confidence cracked and his head dropped, his gaze on the table. "Yes. I understand that. What you want to know?"

Beatrice looked at the top of his white hair, his manicured nails, his white cuffs, tailored suit and Omega wristwatch. "Several things, actually. How come Hoagy believed he was summoning you from London when you had been in Mallorca since Sunday? How come it took you a full day to join the Moffatts when you were no more than an hour away? What kind of relationship did you have with Romy Palliser? You behave as if you are a member of Hoagy's family and yet you profit directly from his work. Where do you draw the line between the professional and the personal? To your knowledge, was the relationship between Romy and Hoagy sexual? Had you yourself ever become intimate with the girl? I'm sorry to be crude but it is essential that I know the dynamics of your unusual circumstances."

A waiter arrived with a large tray containing two wide cups of hot chocolate, a selection of pastries, two mini bowls of fruit salad and a pair of shot glasses containing a clear liquid. "Enjoy, Mr Beaufort. Enjoy, madam."

Raf lifted his head as if it was extremely heavy. "I will answer your questions as truthfully as I am able. Let us break our fast. The hot chocolate here is the best I've ever had outside a particular establishment in Bruges. Help yourself to pastries. The ensaïmadas are my favourite. You asked about Hoagy summoning me from London. In his mind, I sit in a gloomy office in a rainy city all year round, because that's where he remembers meeting me. The truth is, when I'm in Britain I spend around ten percent of my time in London. The rest I'm at my home in West Sussex. Generally speaking, I winter in Mallorca, but also travel here frequently during the summer months to support my various artists. Do take sugar?"

"No, thank you." Beatrice helped herself to something that looked like an apple turnover. "So if you were in the country when Hoagy called you in a panic, why didn't you arrive immediately?"

Raf passed her a cup. "I'm a businessman, Beatrice. I have meetings, viewings and negotiations every day. When I received Hoagy's phone call, I rearranged all my appointments for Thursday so that I could come to his assistance. To cancel my diary on Wednesday would have been impossible and extremely bad manners. In short, I came as soon as I could."

The chocolate was sublime. Beatrice gave herself a moment to enjoy the pure sensory pleasure of a perfect cup. Then she returned to the over-confident, faux-humble man opposite.

"Do carry on."

"You asked about Romy. I wish you had met her, Beatrice. It would be easier to comprehend the beguiling nature of the girl. Everyone fell in love with her on sight. She was ethereal, delicate, graceful and unattainable. A forest nymph as painted by Rossetti. No, I was never 'intimate' with that gossamer creature, merely transfixed by her loveliness. I've known her since she was tiny, because I was close friends with her parents. Charming people, the Pallisers, with excellent taste in art."

"How did they feel about the situation with Hoagy?"

"I don't know if they knew much about it. They live in Bermuda these days and have enough trouble with Nat. That boy's a bit of a hellraiser, much like his dad. Now, regarding Hoagy and Romy's relationship, I cannot be sure. Based on a comment Hoagy made the last time I stayed at their house, my belief is that they were not sleeping together. It was late March, Philly had gone to bed and Romy was drinking Laccao with Cointreau. Horribly sweet mess but she lapped it up. She got quite tipsy and wandered off to her quarters in the middle of a conversation. Hoagy and I gazed after her, slaves worshipping a goddess. Once she'd vanished into the night, he said, 'Can you imagine what it would be like not just to look, but to touch?' in such a wistful tone, it took me by surprise. I said something about not breaking the spell and continuing the magic, but his hunger was tangible. As was mine, I imagine."

Two sixty-plus men drooling over a twenty-something girl did not strike Beatrice as particularly romantic, but she held her tongue. "You've been Hoagy's agent for ..."

"Ever. I'm the longest relationship the man has maintained in his life. I've known all his wives and muses, but Philly's the sort to last the distance. By God, that woman is tough. I did wonder if she'd scarper after *Flamenco* sold for over a million. Perfect time to claim her share of his cash and run, but she stayed with him and for that, let us give thanks. He would never cope without her."

He dipped one of the churros into his hot chocolate. This whole sticking-food-in-drinks business was not something Beatrice approved of, but here, the two seemed designed to go together. She picked up the liquor glass.

"I assume this is not dry sherry?" she asked, with a cautious sniff.

"It's *Aguardiente de Caña Rossa*. A strong spirit distilled from raw sugar cane. Careful, though, it packs quite a punch." He was enjoying himself again, Beatrice could tell.

She took a tiny sip which burned its way down her gullet. Not that she'd ever admit it to Raf Beaufort, but this was a wonderful way to start a weekend. She wished Matthew was here.

At that moment in time, Matthew was enjoying a buffet breakfast at Hotel Residencia. Theo had extended the invitation on hearing Beatrice's early morning plans. He found Matthew great company, full of anecdotes and snippets of information, so that conversation was no effort whatsoever. Small talk sometimes made Theo feel shallow and uncomfortable. Talk with Matthew was anything but small. Over a plate of bacon and eggs, Theo explored ideas, history, languages and culture with an eccentric but expert guide.

"They only spent a few months here in 1838, but it was a visit the island did not forget. Can you imagine? A woman who took a man's name, smoked cigarettes, wore trousers and cohabited with a man not her husband? George Sand and her affair with Chopin was shocking to Paris, let alone Mallorca. She brought him here to recover from TB, and despite the fact the climate worsened his condition, he was incredibly productive. So was she, come to that. Three years later, she published *Un hiver à Majorque*. I can't recall the exact quote but it goes along these lines. 'Mallorca is the El Dorado of places, the green of

Switzerland, the sky of Calabria, the solemnity and silence of the Orient'. Can't you just see exactly what she meant?"

Theo absorbed the landscape around them, hearing Matthew's words echo in his mind. There was a solemnity about this place, as if it gave them permission to stop and soak in its goodness. "That's beautiful. For me, there's something other than the visuals, although they are striking. There's a spirituality, a sense of balance."

"Well put. It takes a particular kind of openness to recognise that and I'm not surprised you are the one to put your finger on the concept. Even I, a crusty old academic, feel an impulse to express myself. In watercolours, on the piano, perhaps even in words far shabbier than those of George Sand. Did you know Parisian women had to apply for permission to wear trousers in those days? I say, these *huevos rancheros* hit the spot. Part of my five a day, no?" He placed his knife and fork together on his empty plate, his smile all the brighter in his lightly tanned face.

"Have you had a good time, Matthew, despite Beatrice disappearing from morning to night?" Theo asked, aware of a growing affection for the erudite and affable older man.

"Oh, I'm used to that after all these years. My only regret is for Tanya and Gabriel. A violent murder and babysitting her father should not be part of the girl's honeymoon. That's why I told them to go off by themselves today. They're flying home tomorrow, you know. I will happily potter around Deià and might even stroll down to the coast if the sun's not too strong. What are your plans?"

"Yeah, my plans. Returning to Nirvana." Theo wrinkled his nose. "That's a lot less enticing than it sounds. More interviews with the church leaders when I'd much rather mooch about the coast with you. Still, got to keep focused. Catch you later for Tanya and Gabriel's goodbye dinner?"

"Most certainly. Shall we hail that chap so we can pay the bill?"

"It's on my room, Matthew. No charge to you because I stay here."

Matthew stared at Theo over his glasses. "I could have sworn you lived in London. How very odd."

"I've lived in London all my life," Theo smiled. "In Mallorca, I fancied a nice hotel and this fulfils all my requirements." Matthew's gaze over his shoulder seemed distant. "You all right there? Matthew?"

Matthew drew his attention back to Theo as if surprised to see him. "Ah, I see. The joys of linguistic difference. Beatrice never mentioned you were Scottish. Thank you for buying my breakfast, I thoroughly enjoyed it. What's the betting PI Stubbs had a greasy omelette on the road whilst we enjoyed a protein-packed platter of perfection? I should leave you get on with your duties and make my way to the museum. Permission to wear trousers, can you imagine?" He placed his napkin on his plate, scraped back his chair and tipped his hat. "Jolly good company, hope to do it again. See you later and all best wishes for your sleuthing."

"See you later. Have fun." Theo watched his progress through the maze of tables and asked himself why he had an urge to run after his boss's partner.

Chapter 17

It was a good job Will got them up and out of the house early. On arrival at the car park at ten to nine on Saturday morning, parking spaces were already sparse. All along the beach, families were already setting up their pitch for the day, so Will selected a spot near to some rocks, rationalising that other people would be less likely to crowd them. He and Luke dumped their bags, stripped off to their swimming costumes and raced each other to the sea. Adrian watched as they splashed their way into the water, laughing and shrieking with delight. He spread three towels on the sand and arranged cold box, sun cream, books, frisbee, badminton rackets and shuttlecock as sort of territorial markers around their camp.

The sun was strong, even at that hour, and Adrian made a note to ensure Luke was wearing waterproof factor 50+ at all times. He stabbed the base of the beach umbrella deeply into the sand until he judged it secure, then opened it to create a pool of shade. He slipped off his shorts and shirt, folded them neatly into a pile and put on his sunglasses to stretch out on the beach. Beatrice may well be in Mallorca under Spanish skies, but Adrian wished himself nowhere else in the world but on this particular towel on this particular day with these particular people in Exmouth's Sandy Bay.

Voices approached and Adrian sat up, prepared for the fact

that Will and Luke would both find it hilarious to shake their wet hair and spatter him with cold droplets. Will was striding in his direction, Luke trotting at his side holding something in his hand.

"What have you found?" asked Adrian. "Don't you be bringing any dead crabs over here!"

"It's not a crab! It's an ammonite. A fossil. Look!" Luke held out a hand to show a rock with some grey markings which looked rather like bits of a caterpillar.

"Wow, that is really cool. Did you find it in the sea?"

Luke shook his head, scattering droplets on Adrian but more through clumsiness than intent. "It was on the beach. We were skimming stones and I found this one and I was just about to chuck it into the sea when Will asked to have a look. I thought he was trying to nick my good skimmer but he saw these patterns. I saw stuff like this in the museum, you know."

"May I?" Adrian took the rock between his thumb and forefinger, examining it in the light. He wasn't convinced it was a fossil but it had pretty markings and Luke was thrilled with it. "It's a beauty. Why don't you put it somewhere safe to show your mum when she gets home?" He handed it over and smiled up at Will who was towelling his hair dry. "Thank goodness for your sharp eyes, DS Quinn. Luke, dry yourself off and then I want you to apply sun cream and wear your hat. There's no way your mother is coming home to a child who looks like a peeled prawn. Do you want a drink of water?"

Luke did as he was told, swallowed a good half bottle of mineral water and plonked himself on the middle towel. The three of them lay side by side, soaking up the warmth, the light and the promise of a full day with nothing to do but enjoy themselves. They stayed that way for all of twenty minutes. Adrian read three chapters of his Maria Callas biography lying on his back, while Will and Luke turned over, fidgeted, sat up and looked around the beach for something to do. The pair of them had a game of badminton, clambered over the rocks to look for pools, wandered up to the lifeguard hut and came back with three ice creams. When they'd finished the choc ices, Will began his campaign to get Adrian in the sea.

A quarter of an hour of botherment was more than enough. He was hot, sweaty and ready to do anything to shut those two up. Adrian put his book in his bag, slipped his feet into flip-flops and followed his two excitable companions into the water. It was bracingly cold to begin with, but when he got started, swimming against the constant swell was exhilarating and somehow primal. He struck out towards the horizon and floated for a while gazing at infinite blue sky. His ears sank beneath the water and he relished the peace before powering back to the shallows.

For a seven-year-old, Luke swam with great confidence, body surfing, doing an admirable crawl and, under Will's guidance, attempting the butterfly stroke. More and more people crowded into the sea and Adrian waded up to the shore, dodging squealing children. Luke and Will were attempting underwater handstands, so Adrian returned to base. He dried himself and noticed how full the beach had become, with barely an area of sand unoccupied by a couple, group or family.

He lay on his front, reading about the opera singer's return to Greece when a splatter of wet drops hit his back. He jumped and shouted, as was expected, and made as if to chase Luke into the sea. He gave up sooner than he normally would as he could see it was only a matter of time before Luke stumbled right through the middle of somebody else's picnic. Talking of which, he was rather peckish himself.

"I'll get you later!" he yelled. "Now let's eat. It's picnic time!"

Luke skidded to a halt, sending sand all over some poor lady's recently oiled thigh, and ran with equal enthusiasm in the opposite direction. "Great! I'm starving! What have we got?"

Adrian was unable to answer the question as Will had got up and prepared the picnic while Adrian and Luke dozed in their beds. The one thing he could be sure of was that it would be absolutely delicious. He wasn't wrong.

Three cheeses, grapes and apples and cherry tomatoes, a French stick, smoked salmon scotch eggs, a quiche, a flask of gazpacho and home-made lemonade all laid out on one of Beatrice's checked tablecloths looked good enough for a photo shoot. Adrian snapped the display from several angles and realises something was missing. He opened his mouth to ask Will the obvious question and saw his husband withdrawing a half bottle of wine from a chilling sleeve in the cold box. He'd even brought two chunky green glass tumblers.

"The man who thinks of everything," said Adrian. "Right, let's tuck in. Luke, what have you done with your hat? Yes, I know you think I'm nagging, but I don't care. Put your hat on and a towel over your shoulders otherwise all you're getting for lunch is whatever you can drag out of one of those manky rock pools."

They ate in the shade of the umbrella, brushing away flies and grazing on far longer than was necessary. Luke decided that smoked salmon scotch eggs were far superior to the sausage meat kind and enthused about Gabriel's cooking.

"Mum's usually in a rush, so we often have beans on toast or something out of the freezer. But Gabriel makes fresh things like salads and soups and stir fries. He does stuff like you, Will, you know, old favourites but different. Like Marmite in the sausage roll. Can I have some quiche?"

"Help yourself, mate. We'll need to have a rest after lunch because we don't want to get cramp in the sea. I suggest a walk up to the headland if you fancy coming?" said Will.

"Yeah! Oh, I wish we could have brought Huggy Bear. She loves running about up there because there are rabbits. Granddad has to keep her on the lead because he's worried she might run right off the cliff."

Adrian topped up his wine glass and offered the bottle to

Will, who shook his head. "Huggy Bear will be having the time of her life with all the other dogs at Mrs Shaw's house. It wouldn't be fair to bring her to the beach on a Saturday, when it's this hot and with so many people around. Plus the fact, when we pick her up, Will and I are going to look at her rescue dogs to see if we can adopt one."

"You're going to get a dog? Brilliant! One like Huggy Bear or a big one like Poldark?"

Will grinned at Adrian. "We don't know yet. We just going to have a look, but you can come with us and give us your opinion."

"Yes!" Luke pulled down his fist in a gesture of triumph. "I'm good with dogs."

The intrepid explorers got dressed and set off towards the path leading up to the headland. Adrian cleared up the mess left after lunch and placed all the leftovers in the cold box. By the time he had shaken out the tablecloth, tidied the towels and settled back down with Maria Callas, Will and Luke were merely specks at the top of the beach. If it hadn't been for Luke's red baseball cap, Adrian couldn't have identified them. He read another chapter, or tried to. His attention wandered constantly. Eventually, he replaced his bookmark and focused on what was bothering him.

Will was happy. A blind man galloping by a horse could see that. He adored playing Dad and Luke would follow him anywhere, even off a cliff. Adrian sighed. Will wanted to be a father and what was more, he would excel at the part. He was patient, enthusiastic, energetic and an extraordinary role model for any child. If he was a kid again, he'd want a dad exactly like Will. A thought he pushed away quickly due to worrying implications. His own father was a remote, vague man who had always done his best to create as much distance between himself and Adrian as possible. Having a son or daughter would fulfil Will completely, making him whole. The problem was that he was married to Adrian, to whom children were a deal breaker.

He stood up, hoping movement would break the mental impasse of this impossible situation, and wandered down towards the surf, watching the waves bubble over his toes as he buried them into the sand. The conundrum was insoluble. When Will first proposed on holiday in Portugal, Adrian had accepted without hesitation. He and Will were perfect together, he knew that. They were two halves of the scales, improving the best bits and toning down the negative sides of both personalities. They'd had the conversation more than once about their hopes and dreams for the future and Adrian drew his red line. No kids. Under no circumstances did he want children.

They agreed. The five-year plan was for Will to become a detective inspector, for Adrian to build his business, and then, if possible, to relocate somewhere in the countryside. Will could take a senior position in a less stressful force than the London Met, Adrian could establish a wine shop anywhere in the world and they could spend more time doing the things they loved. Like going to lovely restaurants, exploring the countryside, joining choirs or kickboxing classes, each doing their own thing. They were good at spending time alone and together because some of Adrian's hobbies did not entice Will and vice versa.

He paced up and down the shoreline, barely noticing the sea creeping over his feet only to retreat once again. A dog would be Adrian's dream. A point of focus for them as a couple while the responsibility lay with Adrian. But a child? That was a whole different question. He stopped and looked up at the path above the cliffs but couldn't see the red baseball cap. His foot kicked out at the sea as if resenting its constant caress and he turned back to their little oasis on the beach. Maria Callas lay neglected on his towel as he hugged his knees to his chest and thought about how to reconcile two opposing desires.

He had a godson. What if they offered to babysit Alejandro once a month? Will had a niece and nephew. They could visit them on occasion to satisfy Will's need to be around little people.

They could even donate to a refugee program or something like virtual adoption rather than bring a small human being home to disrupt their lives. In terms of a partnership, Will and Adrian were operating like a well-oiled machine. A child would be a spanner … His phone rang. It was Will.

"Hello, Dr Livingstone. How far into the jungle did you get?"

"Stand up! Give Maria Callas a break and look up. We are waving at you!"

Adrian emerged from the shade of the umbrella, his hand shielding his brow as he stared up to the top of the cliff face. Two tiny dots were waving at him and he waved back as if for all the world he knew semaphore. He got his camera from his bag and took a shot of the two of them, zooming in just to record that moment. "I took a picture. Are you coming back down now or going farther?"

In the background, Adrian could hear Will and Luke conversing. "Going as far as the point. We'll be back in an hour or so. Luke reckons he'll probably be hungry again."

Adrian laughed, ended the call and plunged his chin into his hands.

Chapter 18

Church was cancelled, to Theo's surprise. There was a handwritten note stuck to the door with a piece of Sellotape over each corner, explaining that due to family circumstances Greg Palliser was unable to guide his followers this evening.

Theo walked on down the street, his middle finger massaging the point between his brows. Why now? The yoga studio had operated as normal since the discovery of Romy's death on Tuesday. The classes, the church meetings and meditations still took place all week but now the place was closed. Theo stood outside a shop selling Mallorcan art and gazed into the window, seeing nothing at all.

The funeral. Romy was due to be cremated and her ashes scattered on Monday. Perhaps Greg and Miranda had taken the weekend off to prepare for such an emotional event. Theo asked himself if that was plausible and the answer came back negative. He wandered up the street with the intention of talking to a few of Nirvana's neighbours. He started at the café but had only just ordered a coffee when he saw a young curly-haired woman carrying a yoga mat approaching the door of Nirvana. He could have stood up and said something but she was perfectly capable of reading the notice Sellotaped to the door as it was in English and Spanish. To his surprise, she read the notice, shook her head, opened the door and continued up the stairs. Theo drank his coffee and watched the building. Nothing happened. He asked the waiter about the business operating on the other side of the street but the guy simply shrugged.

"Hippie shit. Stuff for bored tourists."

"Do you know the owner, Miranda Flynn?"

"By sight. They come in here most evenings after dinner."

"I don't suppose you'd remember if they were here on Monday night?"

The waiter scratched his chin. "Monday night? Yes, they were. They were pissed off because all the tables were taken with people watching the match. I said they could sit at the bar but it was pretty noisy so they left again. That must have been around ten o'clock."

Theo thanked him, paid his bill and crossed the street. He stood looking at the vegetables on the greengrocer's stall until an altercation between a moped driver and a pedestrian drew everyone's attention. That was his moment to slip inside the door and ascend the stairs to Nirvana. On the landing, he took off his shoes and padded in socked feet to the studio itself. There was no music, no voices, only silence. He waited inside the hallway for a full five minutes, listening and absorbing the atmosphere of the place. Finally he eased open the door to see the young woman dancing with abandon. Whatever beat she moved to must have been inside her head. She was dancing like no one was watching, except someone was. Theo closed the door and knocked, giving her a moment to compose herself.

A moment later, the door slid open and a young, fresh-faced woman looked into his eyes. "Can I help you? Classes and church are cancelled this weekend, I'm afraid."

Theo's whole body froze into stillness. This woman was ordinary but exceptional. Her curly white-blonde hair was escaping its knot, her green eyes, freckled face and a light sheen of sweat from her recent exertions made her appear like a naiad emerging from the water.

"Oh, right, sorry. I wanted to talk to Miranda and Greg, but maybe I should go upstairs and check the apartment."

"They're not at the apartment. Greg's gone home to his family and Miranda went with him. Are you a friend of theirs? Because if you're a student or one of the church followers, you will have to wait a week." She took a pace backwards and stared at him. "Have you been here before? I don't recognise you."

"No, I've not seen you before either. My name is Theo Wolfe and I'm a private investigator. I came here yesterday to attend a church service and talk to Greg about the death of his sister. What's your name?"

She tilted her head to one side and pushed the door open wide. "Come in, Theo Wolfe. I'll make some tea. My name is Fae."

They sat cross-legged on yoga mats and drank camomile tea out of chunky IKEA cups.

"Like I said, Greg and Miranda are with the Pallisers. Romy's funeral is on Monday and I think they wanted some family time together. It was pretty last minute – I got an email yesterday evening telling me all classes were cancelled."

"How come you turned up anyway?"

"In case any students didn't get the information. I hate to think of someone standing outside all on their own. Then I saw the note on the door and thought I could use the room to practise my dance routine. It's rare for me to get time and space to work alone."

"Then I interrupted." Theo gave her an apologetic grin.

"That's OK. I didn't bring my music so couldn't have a full rehearsal. I was just going through the steps. You're investigating Romy's death?"

Theo found it hard to meet Fae's eyes. She seemed strangely familiar even though they'd never met. He cleared his throat and stared into his tea. "Yeah, my boss and I are working the case. Did you know Romy?"

She waggled her head from side to side. "I knew of her, but only met her once. She was part of the Sa Fonda crowd, glamorous party people where everyone knows everyone else. She was beautiful and rich with those Jessica Rabbit locks and always had gorgeous men at her side."

A twinge of jealousy stung Theo at the thought of Fae describing Juan Carlos as gorgeous. He *was* a great-looking guy. Even Beatrice had come over all fluttery, but someone like Fae should be above all that. As she recollected her impressions, she looked out of the window, giving Theo the opportunity to gaze at her. Her neck reminded him of a china vase, so delicate were its lines. Afternoon light shone through her platinum curls to create a halo, glinting as if fireflies dwelt within. He sat upright, mirroring her graceful posture.

She spoke again. "Her older brother was famous on the car-racing scene and they were a particular kind of people. Expensive hobbies, fashionable clothes, they don't speak proper Spanish and they are patronising towards the locals. A lot of people envied her lifestyle. Not me."

"You said you met her only once. When was that?"

She turned her face towards him, her green eyes focused on his. "A few weeks ago. We had a meeting here." She pointed at the floor. "I was supposed to take over her classes. The usual way one yogi hands over to another is by giving a class. She didn't have time for that. I got the impression she would have just walked out, but Miranda insisted she sit with me and explain her style." She exhaled sharply. "Such as it was."

"Not impressed?" he asked.

Her eyes darkened as she lifted her chin. "Theo, I've studied yoga my whole life. I understand it as a holistic discipline. I didn't browse a few online videos and 'invent' my own system. I know a fake when I see it. What Romy had was a presence and the confidence to present a random assemblage of moves as a philosophy. If I had attended any of her classes, I'd have called bullshit."

Theo took a risk. "Kinda like Greg's church?"

Her smile started slowly but lifted her whole face. "Kinda like Greg's church, yes. Listen, I just work here. I don't buy into the whole fakery. I rent a room, I run my classes and I go home. That's it. What Miranda and Romy and Greg have here is nothing to do with me and I do not push any of their esoteric extras along with my yoga sessions. I can't because I don't believe in them. I don't think they believe it themselves. This is strictly between you and me, okay?"

Transfixed as he was by this elven beauty, Theo saw a lead. "They don't believe it themselves? Why do you say that?"

Fae clasped her hands together and rested her chin on her fingers as she looked at the floor. She took several long breaths and then raised her gaze to look into Theo's face. In one fluid movement, she got to her feet and bounced light-footed towards the door. She went out into the porch and locked the door. When she returned, she adopted the same position as before and looked directly at him.

"Romy told me how she runs her classes, the phrases she uses and how she underlines her, as she would say, 'message'. She was completely cynical about the whole exercise. I didn't challenge her, why would I? I was about to take over and apply some ethics to the whole process. I just thanked her and I left, assuring Miranda I would be there the next day to start work. I went downstairs and crossed the street before realising I was still barefoot. My head was so full of the task in front of me, I'd forgotten to put on my shoes."

She reached out a hand and rested it on his knee. "Listening to my own words, I can see why you might consider me a ditzy hippie. I'm not. I was totally amazed at how Romy openly faked her insight and all I could think about was how I could turn that around." Her hand snaked back to rest on her own thigh and the place where she had touched him seemed to glow.

Theo knew this was his opportunity to ask the question but for some reason, he found himself completely tongue-tied, staring at her bare feet.

She gave him a moment but when he did not speak, she continued. "I'm a dancer. I'm light on my feet and I make very little noise when I move. When I opened the door to the hallway, changing area, whatever you want to call it, I heard angry voices. That wall," she indicated the plywood barrier between the practice room and the entrance, "is incredibly thin. I could hear every word of the argument going on inside between Romy and Miranda. It's not an honourable thing to do, eavesdropping, and I'm ashamed of myself. I can't excuse it. All I can say is that I felt I'd just been at a job interview and sensed they might be debating my value as a partner." She opened her mouth to speak again and then closed it.

Finally, Theo found his tongue. "Was that what they were debating? Or did you overhear something else?"

She shook her head with some emphasis, her curls flicking from side to side. "I'm doing it again. Being naïve, locking myself in here with a strange man, ready to tell him my secrets. I didn't ask you for ID, I have no idea who you are and could potentially incriminate my business partner with some idle gossip." She puffed air from her bottom lip, which lifted her fringe, exposing more freckles.

"That's my fault, not yours. A private detective should identify himself the moment he makes contact. I'm sorry and in the spirit of full disclosure, I was sitting in the café opposite, wondering how to get more information on the people who run Nirvana. I saw you go into the building with your yoga mat and I followed you upstairs. I waited in the hallway for a while, then sneaked open the door to see what was happening inside. You were dancing, beautifully if I may say so, but it felt like an intrusion into your privacy. I closed the door, knocked and introduced myself. I forgot to give you my card. Here it is, Theo

Wolfe, assistant to the Beatrice Stubbs private investigation agency. If you feel uncomfortable about being locked inside this room with me, we could always take the conversation to the café over the road. I don't want you to feel uncomfortable, Fae. All I want is to find the person who killed Romy Palliser."

She placed her hands over her eyes and shook her head. "I locked the door, not you." She looked up, her green eyes searching his face. "Sorry, I'm being stupid because I'm freaked by this situation. I don't know why I said that, because I trust you, Theo Wolfe."

Theo bowed his head. "Thank you. I promise you I appreciate that. Tell me what happened when you came back for your shoes. Please."

Fae steepled her fingers across her nose. "Romy and Miranda were screaming at each other. I mean screaming. So loudly they never heard me pick up my shoes in the hallway. I stopped and listened. I'm not proud of my behaviour but that's what I did. Miranda was shouting at Romy, saying she let her down, the business was a dream they had realised together, a labour of love built on faith and trust. Romy shouted that it was not her dream, but Miranda's and Greg's. She said her involvement was only to support them, in the spirit of loyalty. Miranda laughed. It wasn't a nice sound. Her response was that Romy had no loyalty to friends, lovers or even family. That's when Romy snapped. She screeched at Miranda. Her exact words were, 'My family? My loyalty to my family will always come first'. Then she said something that shocked Miranda into silence. She said 'So what if I tell Greg what you did, Miranda? Yes, I know and I'll never tell you how I know. My brother is a firm believer in the sanctity of life. One of the key tenets of his church, I believe. How much is my silence worth?' That's when it all went quiet."

A long exhale escaped Theo as he absorbed the ramifications. "I guess you couldn't leave at that point. Because any sound you'd make would let them know they'd been overheard."

She gave him a look of such melting gratitude, a glow spread from his solar plexus.

"Exactly. I stood like a tree, breathing so quietly and waiting for my moment to leave. Miranda swore at Romy, a really violent curse. Then she stamped across the room to the office. I could hear her pulling open drawers or cupboards or something and then she came back. She gave something to Romy and said something weird like 'this is how much it's worth and there is no more where that came from'. Romy said something in reply but at that moment, the church bells rang and I took my chance to sneak out."

Several minutes ticked by as Theo retreated inside himself to think. Fae's presence was incredibly distracting and he found himself trying to find a fresh angle to keep her talking. He recognised his habits and unfolded himself to a standing position. "You shone a light on this case, thank you. I'd like to talk to you again, if you don't mind. Maybe about something other than murder." His attempt at a casual tone flopped due to his breathlessness. Her proximity made him light-headed and he felt like a schoolboy asking a girl to his first disco.

"I'm free this evening, if you feel like a drink?" she said, her smile lifting.

Theo winced. "I have to report to the boss tonight. But how about tomorrow? I should be able to manage a night off."

"Sure. Why don't you take my number and let me know?" She wrote it on the reverse of one of the many church leaflets sitting on the windowsill, adding her name. Fae.

"Oh, right. Fay with an E. Not seen that before."

"It's an old word for fairy. Lots of fun at Starbucks," she laughed up at him, and he said his goodbyes before he could fall on his knees and propose.

Miranda and Greg had visited the café around ten o'clock on Monday night, when Romy was still alive and well, eating dessert on the Moffatts' patio. He glanced at his watch. He was due to have dinner with Beatrice et al at eight, as a farewell dinner for Tanya and Gabriel. Which meant he had time to try an experiment. He walked at a fair pace from the yoga studio up the hill to the Moffatts' villa. It took him twenty-five minutes. Add on another five to enter next door's garden, creep behind the shrubs and climb the wall and yes, it was perfectly feasible for someone to get up here, do the deed and get back in just over an hour.

He returned to the hotel and changed, his mind on how he could ask Beatrice for tomorrow night off without seeming unprofessional. Perhaps if he mentioned the possibility of a date, she might agree. She was inordinately curious about his love life. From his hotel window, he saw Gabriel and Tanya already sitting on the terrace at the same table he and Matthew had occupied earlier that day. He picked up his wallet and went to join them.

Despite the intrusion into their honeymoon, the happy couple looked relaxed and tanned, just as they should do after a week's holiday. He gave them a wide grin.

"Where are Beatrice and Matthew?" he asked.

"Still getting ready, I suppose. Dad went AWOL this afternoon and forgot the time. He only turned up half an hour ago so Beatrice is probably reading him the riot act. We ordered a bottle of cava, unless you'd prefer something else?"

"Cava's good. Matthew mentioned he might walk down to the cove when we had breakfast together. It's easy to underestimate how long it takes."

Tanya gave a Gabriel a meaningful look. "Theo, have you noticed anything different about my father lately? Gabe thinks I'm imagining things."

Theo thought about it. "I don't know him all that well, so it's hard for me to say, but ... how can I put this? His eccentricity seems to be more pronounced than usual. I had the weirdest feeling when he left here this morning. As if I shouldn't let him go off on his own."

"See!" Tanya turned to Gabriel. "Beatrice keeps going on about how the sun and warmth is doing him good, but she's missing a lot because her attention is on the case. He's getting forgetful and making very un-Dadlike mistakes, such as ordering me a sweet white wine. I hate sweet wine! He knows that. And the other day in the car, he asked ..."

"Ssh now. Here they come," Gabriel said in a low voice.

"Sorry we're late, everyone. My fault. Took a wrong turn on the way back from the cove and ended up Lord knows where. I had to get a taxi home. Completely lost my bearings."

"Completely lost your marbles, more like," said Beatrice. "Ooh, are we having cava? Good idea. Have you seen a menu yet? I'm ferociously hungry. How did it go at the studio, Theo?"

They drank cava, ordered food and shared the latest findings. Beatrice was fascinated by the argument overheard by Fae.

"Do you suppose that 'sanctity of life' comment referred to a termination?" she asked.

"I'm not sure. It's hard to know when you're hearing it second-hand. But if they had a screaming row recently which ended with Romy threatening to spill Miranda's secret, I'd say that makes Ms Miranda Flynn a person of interest. Her alibi was that she was in bed with Greg. What if she sneaked out while he was asleep, killed his sister and was back in bed before he woke up?"

"He'd have to be a jolly deep sleeper," said Matthew.

Beatrice was shaking her head. "I don't buy that. If she killed Romy to protect her secret, what was her motivation for destroying the paintings?"

The food arrived while Theo was trying to find an answer to that. The waitress placed a huge plate of seafood in the centre of the table, along with finger bowls and a basket of bread. Tanya ordered another bottle of cava and they tucked in.

Gabriel spoke. "What if the person who destroyed the

paintings is not the same person who killed Romy?"

"That's a bit of a leap," said Beatrice, picking up some calamari rings. "Two separate crimes on consecutive nights? Although it would speak for two different motivations."

"Unless whoever killed her wrecked the pictures to throw suspicion on someone else," Tanya suggested. "Dad, these prawns are in garlic butter. You'd love them."

"Garlic butter? Yes, please. Pop a couple on my plate, would you? I shouldn't mind a bread roll either."

Beatrice handed him the basket. "Yes, that's a thought. In fact, Miranda Flynn suggested the motive might be jealousy and pointed the finger at Nuria Quintana. Who in turn, pointed her finger back at Miranda. There are two sticking points for me. How would a person manage to get out of bed, walk to the Moffatts', murder someone, dispose of the weapon and presumably the clothes she was wearing, walk back and get into bed without her partner's knowledge? Secondly, she doesn't appear on CCTV, so must have climbed over the wall. How would she know about the hand holds and that Señora Navarro leaves her gate open?"

Theo swallowed a sardine. "Greg would have known. He and Romy grew up in that house. Maybe he told her."

Beatrice wrinkled her nose. "That's a long shot in my view. Anyway, I spent the morning with Raf Beaufort as arranged and quizzed him on his whereabouts. He gave me precise timings and locations, most of which I was able to check with a few phone calls. He was indeed in Palma on Monday, Tuesday and Wednesday. He answered my questions regarding Romy and both the lecherous old gits, sorry to disrespect your godfather, Gabriel, had the hots for the girl, but I can't see him killing the sacred calf."

Beatrice's dismissal of Theo's findings stung him. Especially as she had come up with nothing better. "Couldn't we at least talk to Miranda and Romy's brother again? The family estate isn't far."

"After the funeral, perhaps, but we don't want to intrude on family grief at the moment. Let's wait till Monday."

Matthew dabbed at the oily mess on his plate with a piece of bread. "Are we staying another week, then?"

"I shouldn't think this will require another week." Beatrice took a sip of cava. "But as I have no idea how long it's going to take, it might be a good idea if you return home with Tanya and Gabriel tomorrow to mind the animals. Theo and I will follow just as soon as we are able."

To Theo's amazement, Matthew didn't argue but gave her a bewildered look and said, "Oh, very well, if you think that's best."

"I do think it's best. Tanya would you pass me some of that dressed crab?"

"No." Tanya's voice was firm. "I don't think it's best at all. Dad should stay here with you until you're ready to come home. He deserves a holiday. Gabriel and I are perfectly capable of looking after the animals. Plus the fact, Dad should not be at home on his own."

Beatrice and Matthew blinked at her unexpected statement and stopped eating.

"Steady on, my love, I can look after myself, you know."

"I know you can, most of the time. I just think you and Beatrice should stay together. Yes, sorry, here's the crab." Tanya passed the plate across the table.

Beatrice took it but continued to stare at Tanya. "Why would you think your father is better off here than at home in his own bed?"

Theo put down his cutlery, intrigued by the battle of wills. It was the first time he could remember seeing someone standing up to Beatrice.

"I don't know whether you've noticed, Beatrice, because you have obviously been very busy working on a case I asked you to take on. But Dad is getting occasionally forgetful and I don't think it's right for him to be at home alone when he could stay here with you."

Beatrice's voice was icy cold. "Perhaps rather than you deciding what's right for him, you might consult him as to his own preferences." She turned to Matthew. "What would you choose to do? Stay here and be left to your own devices while Theo and I try to solve this case? Or return home to Huggy Bear and Dumpling and Luke?"

Matthew seemed oblivious to the tension between the two women, winkling a whelk out of its shell. "Well, all things considered, I'd quite like to explore a little more of Deià. I won't get underfoot, I promise. And if Tanya and Gabriel are willing to look after our creatures, then no one is inconvenienced. Eat up, Theo, you're letting the side down. Have you tried one of those oysters? I don't recall having something quite as flavoursome outside Ireland."

Tanya reached for the bottle of cava, topping up each glass. "That's settled then. We'll fly home tomorrow, collect Luke from Will and Adrian and take your animals back to our house." Her eyes widened. "Oh! You do realise it is Saturday night?" She looked at her watch. "Right about now, Marianne will be on her date with DS Perowne. I can't wait to hear how it went!"

Beatrice lifted her glass. "A toast! To Marianne and Jago. May they have the perfect first date!"

Everyone raised their glasses and repeated her words. Theo reached for an oyster and realised he'd just observed a masterclass in how to stand up to Beatrice Stubbs.

Chapter 19

In the wee hours of Sunday morning, a thunderstorm broke over the town. Flashes of lightning lit up the room, cracks of thunder rent the peace as if the ceiling was splitting apart and the roof of Beatrice and Matthew's cottage joined in the cacophony with a constant backbeat of drumming rain. Beatrice found it impossible to sleep in such conditions, although Matthew seemed unaffected. She threw back the duvet and reached for her dressing gown. Another almighty boom followed seconds after the strobe of lightning. This time, it was loud enough to stir Matthew.

"What on earth?" he mumbled.

"It's a storm, my love. Nothing to worry about. I'm going to make some tea."

"A storm? Damn shame I didn't mow the lawn. Grass will be wet tomorrow." He rolled over and went back to sleep.

Beatrice sat there for several seconds as his snores deepened, puzzling over his remark. The cold air crept up her ankles and she put his nonsense down to a liminal state of consciousness. Raindrops pelted against the window as if something tiny and angry was trying to get in. She put the light on in the kitchen and a pan of water on to boil. The storm wasn't the only thing keeping her awake. Her subconscious was nudging her, whispering that she'd overlooked something, but refused to tell her what it was.

She made tea and sat on the sofa with the curtains open so she could see the full drama of a Mallorcan storm. After a while, the display grew less impressive and she pulled out her notes to consider the case one more time. There were more motives than she could shake a stick at; jealousy, acquisitiveness, money, revenge, silencing and envy. She'd spoken to every suspect and none of them had showed a liar's tic. Either they were all innocent and the murderer was a random stranger who returned the following night to destroy all available images of the girl, or one of the interviewees was a better liar than she thought. Beatrice had been in this job for decades and knew how to interview a witness. Or at least she used to.

Therefore, it was reasonable to assume that only the people she had not interrogated personally were the ones with something to hide. It made sense. Theo had been the one to speak to Nuria Quintana on the subject of Romy Palliser's death. As Hoagy's previous muse, she had spent some months in the room above his studio. She might easily have looked over the wall and spotted the rungs below. It was perfectly feasible that she had bided her time, committed the crime and returned the following day to slash the canvases. Perhaps with superior knowledge of Hoagy's working patterns, she had hidden in the foliage, waiting for him to arrive and watched as he entered the code into the keypad. Only to access it later when he and Philly had retired for the night. As for suspicion falling upon herself, she was confident that her uncle would protect her.

Beatrice dunked the teabag one more time and laid it on the saucer. The other question was that huge ceremonial sword in the tourist office. That was exactly the kind of weapon which could all but decapitate a person. Details floated across her mind: Nuria's manicure, her quick temper evidenced by the changing expressions she had seen in those few minutes Theo had engaged her in conversation. Her slight dancer's frame. This was the kind of woman capable of a furious overreaction or crime of passion but was she the coolly calculating sociopath who would return to the scene of a bloody murder in order to ruin all the images of her nemesis?

There was one way to find out. Tomorrow, she and Theo would interview her together, Beatrice guiding the line of questioning. Theo would be the interlocutor and Beatrice would be the observer. By the time the conversation was over, Beatrice would have a gut feeling. She would know and if what she suspected were true, she would need to take her evidence to a higher authority than the girl's uncle.

She drank tea, aware of the lessening rain on the roof. Depending on how things went the following day, or rather later today, she might have this all wrapped up by Monday. A frown twitched across her brow, recalling how Tanya had alluded to Matthew's scattiness as part of a deeper problem. She resolved to take the girl aside once she had returned to Devon and express in the strongest terms how insulting and patronising that kind of language was towards her father.

On the horizon, the sky lightened to an ashen yellow and Beatrice decided it was time to return to bed. She swallowed her cold tea in three gulps, threw off her dressing gown and snuggled under the duvet, drawing warmth from Matthew's body.

For a change, Matthew was up before her. That was not surprising as she had spent two hours sitting on the sofa, cogitating until the storm blew itself out. She sat up in bed, listening to him singing in the kitchen. If only Tanya could hear him now, performing '*Non son più re, son dio*' from the opera *Nabucco* not only in Italian, but also in a fine baritone. Hardly a sign of senility.

When she got out of the shower, the singing had stopped and in its place, she could hear conversation. Theo was here to take her wherever she needed, in order to pursue this investigation. At the dining table, they were each eating a plate of tomato and eggs. The smell of coffee filled the air and sun shone a spotlight on a jug of freshly squeezed orange juice.

"Good morning. Sorry to be the last one at the table, but the storm kept me awake last night. Did you hear it, Theo?" She poured herself some juice.

"It kept the whole town awake. The hotel restaurant this morning was practically empty when I got up. Everyone was sleeping in. I tried doing some relaxation exercises at about four in the morning, but I couldn't concentrate. I went for a run instead."

Beatrice stared at him, appalled. "In that weather? Are you mad?"

Theo sipped his coffee. "Not outside. In the hotel gym. I did seven kilometres before breakfast, which is why I was ready for seconds when I got here. Running is also a good way to think. We really should speak to Miranda Flynn again. I get your point about not intruding on the family's grief but we need some answers from that woman."

"Would you like some breakfast, Old Thing? Eggs sunny side up and a slice of fresh bread?"

"Thank you, Matthew, that would be lovely. Do you think I could have tea rather than coffee this morning? I wanted a hot brew last night but got distracted thinking about the case and let my mug get cold. Theo, as I said last night, we will talk to Miranda Flynn tomorrow, after the funeral. Today I want to interview Nuria Quintana again, even at the risk of annoying her uncle. I want you to ask the questions so I can be the observer. I will tell you what to say, don't worry."

Matthew placed a cup in front of Beatrice. "One cup of coffee, splash of milk, no sugar. Theo, would you like another?"

"No, thanks. Really enjoyed breakfast, though. Beatrice, I'm fine with interviewing Nuria Quintana again but I really don't understand why we can't talk to Miranda Flynn. It's not like she's a member of the family or anything. I want to get to the bottom of that row she had with Romy. When I spoke to them after church, Greg wouldn't leave her side. I think we should try to get her on her own."

Coffee rather than tea, an argumentative assistant, and lack of sleep made Beatrice irritable. She drank juice and looked out of the window at cloudy skies.

"Tanya and Gabriel will be in the air by now," she said. "Luke will be over the moon to see them."

"Beatrice? We could do both." Theo rested his elbows on the table. "Nuria Quintana speaks English so you can talk to her. I could take the car and drive to the Palliser estate, see if I can get Miranda alone."

"No. Definitely not. We're not splitting up. Whatever interviews we do now, we do together. Think about it, Theo. If either of these women is potentially guilty, they could be extremely dangerous to a single individual. You're keen to follow the angle you found, but I must ask you to trust my experience. I know the way to handle an interviewee. We'll talk to Nuria today and Miranda tomorrow, asking questions as a team. Because that's what we are. Oh, that looks exactly what the doctor ordered." She looked down at the plate Matthew had placed in front of her and gave him a grateful smile. He really was a wonderful man.

To Beatrice's intense annoyance, Nuria Quintana did not work at the tourist information centre on Sundays. She didn't answer her mobile when Theo called either. He found her home address, but she wasn't there or wasn't answering the doorbell. Why would she be at home on a sunny Sunday morning? She could be anywhere, shopping, on the beach, visiting her uncle, who knew? Hot and frustrated, Beatrice got back into the car and instructed Theo to drive to the beach.

"You think you're going to find the woman in a crowd of semi-naked bodies? I don't fancy our chances." Theo indicated and pulled away from the parking spot.

Beatrice did not reply, massaging her forehead.

"You realise how crowded it's going to be? Everyone's going to be on the sand making the most of a fresh, post-storm sea," he added.

He was really getting on her nerves today. "Yes, yes, I know. We are looking for an eagle in the haystack. But we've been to her house, to her work and even poked our heads in a couple of nearby cafés. There's a chance she's on the beach and while we are there, we could take the opportunity of speaking to Juan Carlos again. Just putting out some feelers regarding the relationship between Romy and Miranda."

Theo drove without speaking until they parked at the beach. It was not a companionable silence and Beatrice could feel a sense of judgement emanating from her assistant. Sooner or later, she was going to have to address this attitude. They walked down the weathered boards to where bronzed bodies reclined, swam, played and chatted, making the most of a glorious Sunday morning. Beatrice instructed Theo to take the left hand of the beach while she took the right, soon regretting her choice of sunglasses instead of a hat.

She slipped off her shoes and scrunched away through the sand, scanning all the faces she passed to see if any resembled Nuria Quintana. Since she'd only seen the woman once, fully dressed and in uniform, the likelihood she would recognise the girl was close to zero. She searched the beach until the heat became oppressive and made her way to the palm tree umbrellas where they had interviewed Juan Carlos. She couldn't see Theo anywhere and waited in the shade until he returned. It took twenty minutes before she saw his familiar figure heading in her direction, a muscled man in swimming trunks by his side. Juan Carlos. She blushed, now grateful for the sunglasses.

"Hello, Beatrice! Nice to see you again." He held out a hand and Beatrice shook it.

"Same to you. We came here looking for Nuria Quintana but I'm glad to have a chance of talking to you again."

Theo placed his notebook on the shelf between them. "We just had a chat and Juan Carlos shed a little light on the 'sanctity of life' situation. His cousin works at a private clinic. She let slip that Miranda Flynn had attended an appointment to terminate a pregnancy in April this year. Juan Carlos told Romy in passing, without realising the significance of that information. Juan Carlos?"

Juan Carlos nodded with so much emphasis, he reminded Beatrice of a headbanging parrot. "As I told you, Romy and I mixed in different circles. Her friends are not my friends. I don't know her brother or his church or his beliefs or anything. I met Miranda on a couple of occasions but I can't say I liked her. That crowd, the rich players, are not my kind of people. They're not Mallorca's kind of people, but the one thing they are good for is gossip. What they do, where they are seen, who they meet and what they wearing is the subject of a lot of conversation. So my cousin at the private clinic recognised Miranda Flynn and in confidence, told me what operation she had. My cousin is a good person, but she doesn't earn much. That sort of information is, how do you say it, a kind of status. She told me a secret and I told Romy. I don't even know why." His eyes were distant, gazing past Beatrice at the dunes. "Maybe it was a pathetic attempt to level the field. They have more money, contacts, style and fame, but they're still human. Their bodies are the same as everybody else's and an unwanted pregnancy reduces the rich bitch to the same place as her cleaning woman. I'm not proud of telling her that. In fact, I'm ashamed. That was a cheap trick to gain some respect in her eyes."

Beatrice studied the young man and admired him. Not in the physical sense, although his body was hard to ignore, but more for his sense of self-knowledge and capacity to learn from his mistakes.

"I want to thank you for sharing this information, Juan Carlos. It's never easy to reveal something about yourself which makes you look worse rather than better. But what you have told us today will enable us to close the net on whoever killed Romy Palliser. Do you think your cousin would be willing to talk to us?"

"I guess. You want me to call her?"

"That would be marvellous. Here's my card. Would you let me know what she says? Sorry to have disturbed you and I wish you a lovely Sunday."

A pounding headache took hold and Beatrice could tell it was not going to abate in a hurry. What's more, if they couldn't locate the Quintana woman, the best use of their time would be to interview Miranda Flynn. Which meant apologising to Theo.

"Shall I try Nuria's mobile again?" he asked as they drove away from the beach.

"Not while you're driving. Let's stop at a café somewhere. I need to get some water and take a painkiller."

"What's wrong?" Theo glanced at her in concern.

"Headache. Lack of sleep, wandering about in the sun and worried about Matthew." The words escaped her before she'd even formed the thought.

Theo didn't reply as he navigated the narrow streets, passing several cafés that would have done the trick.

"Where are you going?" Beatrice demanded.

"To your cottage. Let's check in on Matthew, get you a drink of water and I'll make some calls. He said he was going to sit on the veranda this morning, so he should be fine."

Beatrice considered his words. He hadn't asked why she would be worried about Matthew, just took it as if there were good reason to be concerned. He parked in the street opposite

176

and Beatrice hurried across the road, suddenly fearful. She opened the door and saw the place was empty, all the washing-up done and table tidied. She ran out to the garden but could see it was unoccupied.

"Matthew?" she shouted, opening the bedroom door.

"Yes?" His voice came from the bathroom.

"Is everything all right?"

"Yes. I'm on the throne, as a matter of fact. You're back early."

"I know. Bit of a headache. We're just going to have a cold drink."

"Righty ho. I'll be out shortly."

She returned to the living room to see Theo adding ice to two glasses of water.

"Is he OK?"

Beatrice dug around in her handbag for paracetamol. "He's fine, in the toilet, otherwise engaged. Thank you for this." She took two tablets and washed them down with a slug of cold water. "Why don't you find the address for the Palliser family and we can take a drive out there?"

It wasn't an apology, but an acknowledgement that he was right, and that would have to do.

"I already have the address. I checked it out this morning." Theo's tone was gentle, a tacit acceptance that he'd won. "Should we call ahead or just turn up?"

Beatrice had to smile. Even though she was in the wrong, he was still asking her opinion, respecting her as his boss. "Forewarned is forearmed. I think we should just turn up."

The bedroom door opened and Matthew emerged. "Are you two off again so soon? Not sticking around for a spot of lunch?"

An idea occurred to Beatrice. They could drive to the family estate, wangle an interview with Miranda Flynn and return via Café Umberto. Matthew would adore the place, she was quite sure. However, when she suggested the jaunt, Matthew had made other plans.

"It sounds like the most extraordinary place, I must say. I should certainly like to visit before we leave the island. Nevertheless, today I must demur. My plan was for a guided tour on the subject of Robert Graves. Do you know his poetry at all, Theo?"

"I remember studying some of his stuff in school, but I tend to get him mixed up with Sassoon and Owen and other wartime poets. What are his best ones?"

Matthew sat down to lace up his shoes. "Well, that is a highly subjective question. Are you dining with us this evening? If so, we might discuss some of his more complex works."

Theo shifted a pace backwards. "Actually, unless Beatrice has other plans for me, I thought I might ask the yoga teacher out for a drink. I mean, on a date, rather than an interview. But obviously, work takes priority."

Beatrice beamed. For the first time since she met him, Theo Wolfe was showing an interest in someone romantically. "About bloody time! Of course you can have the evening off to go on a date. Is that the Fae you mentioned? Sorry, sorry, none of my business. Keep your ears open, that's all. Matthew, enjoy your guided tour and will see you back here around teatime. Do look after yourself, you old coot."

"Of course I shall, my love. Off you go to your sleuthing and I wish you all the very best of luck." He stood up and peered out at the sky. "I say, it's a bit dark over Bill's mother's. I hope we're not due another storm."

Chapter 20

Huggy Bear must have the hearing of a bat. Adrian was listening to Radio 4 while washing up the lunch things. Outside, Will and Luke were practising some kind of martial art in the garden. At some signal inaudible to Adrian, the dog started scratching and barking excitedly at the front door. Adrian dried his hands and went to see what all the fuss was about.

On opening the door, he saw the brake lights of Gabriel's Land Rover switch off. He released his hold on Huggy Bear's collar and the terrier raced to greet the new arrivals. At the same time, the garden gate swung open and Luke tore across the gravel to meet his mother. The reunion was emotional and Adrian swallowed several times, watching the young boy's joy not only at seeing Tanya, but also Gabriel.

They both looked wonderful. Mallorcan sun had worked its magic. Gabriel's hair was lighter, Tanya's skin was darker and if anything, their love for Luke was stronger than ever.

Adrian guided them all into the garden, Tanya distributed gifts and Gabriel asked questions about their holiday, while Luke interrupted constantly to tell him every last detail of what happened since they had left. Will went inside to make lemonade and fetch biscuits, and for the first time, Luke did not follow.

Adrian asked about Beatrice's role, using euphemistic

language in front of Luke.

"It doesn't look like she and Theo have made any progress," Tanya said, her expression pessimistic. "So we still don't know when they're likely to come home. We'll take Huggy Bear and Dumpling to our place until they return. But I don't think they are any closer to finding whoever... I mean, cracking the case."

"At least Matthew can enjoy a holiday even if they don't find out whodunit." Adrian got up to help Will, whose hands were full with a tray of lemonades.

Tanya glanced at Luke. "Why don't you put on your new T-shirt? I want to see if it fits."

"Okay!" Luke started to pull his T-shirt over his head.

"Do it upstairs and put the dirty one in the laundry basket. Maybe you can even take a photo and send it to Beatrice and Granddad. You know how to do that, don't you?"

"Course I do!" Luke raced away inside the cottage.

Adrian could spot a ruse a mile off. "What is it?" he asked, his voice low.

Without warning, Tanya's eyes filled with tears. "It's Dad. I seriously think I can see the signs of dementia, Alzheimer's or some other degenerative disease. He's often been scatty and forgetful and academic and eccentric and sometimes all of those things at once, but this is different. What I don't understand is why Beatrice is missing all the signals. I've tried to drop hints but she's either ignoring them or refusing to face facts. Gabriel thinks I'm overreacting, but even Theo can see it. There's something wrong, I know it."

"Hello! Welcome home, you two." Marianne came through the garden gate, carrying a bunch of flowers. She embraced her sister and her brother-in-law, and blew a kiss to Will and Adrian. "Tell me everything! The food, the weather, the murder! Where is Luke?"

Will handed her a glass of lemonade. "Inside, trying on his present from his mum." He looked at the flowers. "Those for him too?" His tone was bright and his smile friendly but Adrian could sense an undertone of hostility.

"No, they certainly are not. These are for me. Hand delivered by DS Jago Perowne this very morning. So I think we can say, the first date was a success!" She flashed a smile at them all, waiting for their congratulations.

Tanya and Gabriel seemed lost for words, but Will managed to speak. "Wow, so we can celebrate a successful first date as well as an exceptional honeymoon. The Bailey sisters are on a roll! Tanya, you look like somebody just emerging from the surf at Bondi Beach. The sun-kissed look suits both of you. Gabriel, how is your godfather? That must have been such a nasty shock for everyone. I'm really sorry."

But that particular moment, Adrian loved Will with such ferocity he could not even express it. Without any aggression or dismissiveness, his husband had taken the spotlight from Marianne and turned it back to the returning honeymooners.

"Thanks, Will. It was pretty nasty, yeah, but Hoagy has now got Beatrice on his side. That helps." Gabriel put an arm around Tanya's shoulders. "My amazing wife coped with the whole situation like a trouper. It wasn't the honeymoon we hoped for, admittedly, but I believe it brought us closer together."

Tanya dabbed at her eyes with one hand and stroked Gabriel's arm with the other. She was spared the obligation of responding by the arrival of Luke, sporting his new T-shirt.

"It fits! I like it. Can I wear it to school tomorrow?" He addressed the question to Will.

"You'd better ask your mum."

Luke turned to Tanya, opened his mouth and closed it again. "Why are you crying?"

"Because I'm so happy!" she sniffed. "Best husband, best honeymoon and best son in the world." She opened her arms and Luke obediently leant into her embrace. "Yes, you can wear it to school if you take it off this minute. Go on then, we want to hear all about Auntie Marianne's date."

And they did, at length, until Will cut the second retelling short by looking at his watch and announcing it was time to leave.

Saying goodbye hurt far more than Adrian expected. He choked up while stroking Dumpling, hugged Huggy Bear and actually cried when Luke flung his arms around Adrian's neck. Will handled their departure with far more dignity, but a pulse in his jawline told Adrian he was keeping his emotions in check. The family came to stand in the driveway to wave them off.

The weather was beautiful, but Will kept the roof up as they began the journey back to London. Motorways and cabriolets were not a great match. Neither man spoke for the first hour, both absorbed in their own thoughts. Recollections of Luke, Huggy Bear and even the tatty old cat threatened to make Adrian tearful, so he focused on the negative. Marianne was such a selfish cow. To crash Gabriel and Tanya's return, trying to make it all about herself and even showing off a bouquet of flowers was appallingly rude. Worse still, she listened to a few anecdotes of the holiday and then launched into a blow-by-blow retelling of the previous night's date. Narcissism was a quality Adrian had previously associated more with men than women. But Marianne ticked every box on the list.

How was it possible that Tanya could have such passion and empathy and sense of honour, while her sister lacked all those qualities? Will took the junction to join the M4 and Adrian settled back for the long boring drive back to London. Then Will spoke.

"Can we talk?"

"Sure. Sorry, I wasn't being sulky or anything. Just feeling a bit sad about leaving them all. And I'm still shaking my head at Marianne's me-me-me behaviour. You handled her very well, I have to say. Sometimes it's hard to believe they are sisters, they're so different in personality."

Will overtook a lorry and steered the car into the left-hand lane. "Yeah, that was pretty crass of her to steal their thunder. What did you think about Tanya's theory?"

"Matthew, you mean? I can't say I've noticed anything out of the ordinary, but then again, I don't know him like she does."

"I've noticed. While Beatrice was away in Finland before the wedding. You remember Tanya asked me to help Matthew write his speech? I spent a couple of hours with him, writing it and rehearsing it, and I could see then his faculties aren't what they used to be. Whether it's dementia or not, I can't say. I did give Beatrice a talking to on the way back from the airport, not mentioning any specifics but telling her she really needed to be more present. I can see what Tanya means about her missing the signs. For a detective, she can be remarkably unobservant about what's happening right under her nose."

"How old is he? I know he's got a few years on Beatrice but I wouldn't have said he is dementia age."

"Dementia can strike at any time of life, although the incidence increases greatly after the age of sixty-five. When we get home, I'm going to do some research and point Tanya in the direction of some resources. But first things first, somebody needs to talk to Beatrice. It's possible that she has noticed what's happening but doesn't want to acknowledge it. If even Theo has spotted there's a problem, it must be pretty obvious."

Adrian stared out of the window, the sadness at leaving Upton St Nicholas now transformed into a weight of melancholy in his chest. "Poor Matthew. Poor Beatrice. Life can be horribly unfair."

Will made a noise of agreement. They drove for several miles without speaking until Adrian remembered that Will had wanted to talk.

"Is that what you wanted to discuss? Matthew?"

Will's eyes flicked to the rear view mirror and he indicated to overtake a caravan. "No. I wanted to talk about something else. This holiday has done me a lot of good. It's also opened my eyes to something I hadn't realised before now. I loved looking after Luke. The animals too. I'm glad we decided to get a rescue dog."

"Me too. Maybe we can go into Battersea Dogs' Home next weekend. We really should choose together, even though I've got my heart set on a Schnauzer."

"Yeah, why not? Give them a call tomorrow and make an appointment. I know having a dog is going to make you happy and I'm willing to give it a go. I just wondered if you would be willing to do something for me."

Adrian's heart seemed to grow heavy and cold. He knew what was coming. "What would you like me to do?"

"When we first moved in together, even before I proposed to you, we talked about our hopes and plans for the future. We agreed on several things, such as aiming to move to the country once I've attained the rank of detective inspector. We also agreed that we didn't want kids. But that was a few years ago and things have changed. I still want to move to the country after I become a DI. The thing is, I now feel differently about the issue of children. What I would like you to do is think about it. My relationship with you is the most important thing in the world and I would do nothing to jeopardise that. That said, I want to express how I believe having a child would enhance our marriage. We would make wonderful parents. I watched you with Luke and I could have burst with love. You don't patronise him or exclude him from adult conversation, but treat him like a small person. I love that about you, the way you're so natural with kids and animals. It's why my niece and nephew like you so much. I know this is moving the goalposts after we had a full and frank discussion on the subject. So all I'm asking is if you're prepared to consider it. You don't need to answer right now."

The countryside flashed past, horses grazing in a field, a bird of prey gliding in lazy circles, a farmhouse with a duck pond like something out of Constable painting. Adrian gazed at the bucolic scenes, so carefree and uplifting, which was precisely the opposite of how he felt inside. As he had said about half an hour ago, life can be so horribly unfair. That speech was rehearsed. *I want to express how I believe having a child would enhance our marriage.* He had put a lot of effort into wording it for maximum effect.

After years of failed relationships and a growing conviction that he would remain single for the rest of his life, Adrian had met Mr Right. They complemented each other perfectly and when Will popped the question in Portugal, Adrian had accepted joyfully without a second thought. He loved Will to his bones, even when he came home bad-tempered after a shitty day at the Met, even when he blathered on incessantly about this bloody car, even when he micro-managed the simplest of their leisure activities. Everything about their life was perfect. They were both happy in their jobs, they had a lovely flat, tastefully decorated by Adrian himself, they enjoyed good food and decent wine, and had enough interests in common to make their weekends endlessly entertaining. Why would they want to wreck all that by bringing in a child?

There was no possible way this situation could end positively. Adrian was already hurt that he wasn't enough to fulfil Will's life. If he agreed to think it over, only to reiterate his objection to parenthood, Will would be resentful. And if he gave in and they adopted a kid ... no. That would never happen. Some people don't have that nurturing urge and Adrian was one of them. He examined the situation from all angles but couldn't see a way out.

Rather than offering false hope by promising to think about it, he would have to point out the practical difficulties and suggest they spend time with other people's children as a compromise. If Will was desperate to have a child of his own, maybe it would be better if Adrian offered him a divorce so he could find someone else, someone who wanted the same things he did. In a simple either/or scenario, singledom was preferable to fatherhood.

Traffic grew heavier and they found themselves stopping and starting along the Great West Road. While they waited at some lights in Hammersmith, Will shot him a sideways glance.

"What shall we do about dinner? Seeing as we've been super healthy all week, we could let our hair down tonight and have a takeaway. Do you fancy a Thai curry or even fish and chips from the Polish place?"

"I'm not hungry right now. Let's see how we feel when we get home."

"Are you sulking?"

Adrian gave him a cold glare until a horn honking alerted Will to the fact the lights had changed. He raised a hand in apology to the driver behind and drove off.

"No, Will, I'm not sulking. I'm trying to find a way of handling this depth charge you just threw into our marriage. You've asked me to reconsider the one thing I've always been adamant about. If I refuse to even think about it, I'm a selfish git. I could tell you that I will give it some serious thought, but that would be a lie. The more serious thought I apply to the question, the more I will convince myself of my original answer. I do not want children in my life and I've always been honest about that. Fair enough, you've changed your mind. I haven't. Where does that leave us?"

The car rolled through Knightsbridge and into Mayfair before Will spoke. "I'm sorry I said you were sulking. That belittles your behaviour and it's unfair. What I'm asking you to do is look at the situation with an open mind, that's all. You've convinced yourself you don't want to be a father and locked the door to that particular room. You've never re-examined that decision in the light of changed circumstances and that's what I'm asking you to do. Imagine how much richer our lives would be and maybe your conviction will be less strong. Just think about it, Adrian, but not from 'these are all the reasons why it's a bad idea' perspective. If we want something badly enough, we'll overcome all the practical difficulties."

A white heat swelled from Adrian's solar plexus to inflame his head. "I'm sorry? 'We'? There is no 'we' who want something badly enough. And I'll thank you not to patronise me, William Quinn. When Catinca decided to become vegetarian, did you say anything along the lines of 'you've convinced yourself you don't want to eat meat. Maybe you should rethink your decision with an open mind'? No, you accepted that as a grown adult, she is capable of making her own decisions about what she does and doesn't want in her life. As for convincing myself I don't want to be a father, it didn't take much. I don't want to be a father, or a mother for that matter. Because that's what it would mean. You're ambitious, you want to be a detective inspector, you are committed to your work. So who gets lumped with the lion's share of childcare? That's like me saying 'let's have a dog, but you can feed it, walk it and pick up all its shit because I've got other things to do'. Will, we've always been honest with each other. As far as I'm concerned, I'm happy and fulfilled and in love with you. I don't want a child and no amount of focused, open-minded thinking is going to change that. If you feel there is a hole in your life, perhaps you married the wrong person."

Neither spoke the whole way through Clerkenwell until Will pulled up outside the flat on Boot Street. He didn't turn off the engine.

"Why don't you take your bag and go inside? I need some time to think."

Adrian got out, removed his suitcase and the bag of tourist trinkets they had assimilated, closed the door and walked around to the driver's side window to say goodbye. Before he got there, Will drove away.

He stood there and watched until the Audi turned the corner.

Then he unlocked the front door and took his bags inside. His neighbour on the opposite side stuck his head out of his flat, dressed, as always, in grey sweatpants and a Star Wars T-shirt.

"All right, Adrian? How was your holiday?"

"Hello, Saul. It was very relaxing, thanks. Everything OK here?"

"Yeah, nothing to report. I picked up all your post and watered the plants twice a week. One of your African violets is looking very peaky. I moved it into the living room where it's warmer. Where's Will?"

"Gone to get us fish and chips. There is nothing in the fridge. Here, we brought you a present. Some genuine Devon ale and a tub of clotted cream. I wouldn't recommend having them together."

Saul grinned as Adrian handed over the six-pack and the plastic container, his bald patch glowing red. "That's very decent of you, mate. No need, because neighbours look after each other, right? Talking of which, how is Beatrice?"

"PI Stubbs is in Mallorca investigating a murder. Old habits die hard." He pulled out his keys from his pocket. "Thank you for holding the fort while we were gone. Maybe we can go down the road for a pie and a pint next week?"

"Won't say no to that. Enjoy your fish and chips, see ya later."

The flat smelt musty and stale after their two-week absence. Adrian dumped the suitcase in the hallway, took the perishables into the kitchen and opened a bottle of wine. Then he sat on a stool at the breakfast bar and waited for Will to come home.

Chapter 21

The Palliser estate was a huge place with the most astounding views out over the Mediterranean. At the end of the drive, their path was blocked by two solid-looking electronic gates. Theo parked, got out and pressed the buzzer for admittance. There was no reply. Beatrice wandered along the lane, peering through the fence. Not a soul to be seen in the neatly kept garden. It must take a small army to maintain something that size, but the Pallisers could probably afford one.

She heard voices at the gate and returned to listen to Theo's conversation.

"No, we don't have an appointment. We just wanted a word with Miranda Flynn, if possible. Is she there?"

The voice from the intercom said nothing for a moment. Theo and Beatrice exchanged a glance.

"What do you want with Miranda? We've told you everything we know."

"Oh right, this is Greg? I didn't recognise your voice. This is Theo Wolfe. I attended your church the other day. We just have a couple more questions for Miranda. It won't take long."

Another long silence stretched out. "Miranda's not here, I'm afraid, and my parents and I are preparing for tomorrow's funeral. Your visit is not convenient at the moment, sorry."

Beatrice bent closer to the microphone. "Can you tell where

we might find her?"

"I have no idea. Must dash. Goodbye."

Beatrice and Theo stood looking at each other for a moment, then got into the car without a word. Once they had closed the doors, Beatrice snorted. "He's a bloody liar. Let's go to the yoga studio and try her apartment again. But if she's there, I'll eat my cat. I bet you anything she's hiding in there somewhere. But why won't he cooperate with us? We're trying to find out who killed his sister, for crying out loud!"

Theo reversed out of the driveway and turned the car in the direction of Deià. "Way I see it, you're right. She's not coming out and we have no authority to insist. But Quintana does. There must be a way of informing him, even if he does take weekends off."

"You didn't get his mobile number?

Theo shook his head. "I asked, but he said to contact him via the station. That's why I have the feeling Detective Pedro Quintana is a nine-to-five kind of guy."

Beatrice had to agree with that. "Right, here's the plan. We'll go to Nirvana and check her apartment. She won't be there, but we have to go through the motions. After that, we'll go to the police station and ask whoever is on duty to contact Quintana on our behalf. Then when we have handed over all the information we know, I'll find Matthew and you can go and get ready for your date. I assume that's still on?"

"It's on. I sent a message while we were at your place. It's just a drink."

"That's what they all say," Beatrice said, with a knowing smile.

There was no answer at Miranda's apartment and the yoga studio was still closed. Beatrice sent Theo across the street to ask the waiter if he had seen her in the last couple of days and the response came back negative. When he returned, Beatrice donned gloves, eased a credit card into the lock and opened the apartment. Inside, they stood and listened for a full sixty seconds. Beatrice looked up at Theo, who shook his head.

"There's no one here. I can feel it."

They examined each room together, finding little of interest anywhere except the bedroom. There was a clear his and hers side to the bed. On Greg's side, the drawer opened to reveal a packet of condoms, lubricant, and a pair of handcuffs. Theo lifted them up with his gloved hands and showed them to Beatrice. On the side closer to the window, Beatrice opened the drawer to find enough medication to start a pharmacy. Headache tablets, vitamin pills, allergy medication, sleeping tablets, antiseptic cream, sex toys, eye drops, supplements and antidepressants. She recognised one package as the mood stabilisers she herself used to take, until James prescribed something with a lower dosage. There was a small turquoise box at the back. Inside, there was a ring with a solitaire diamond.

Theo came over for a closer look and whistled. "Jewellery from Tiffany's? Yoga teaching must be more lucrative than I thought."

"Not just any old jewellery, either. This is an engagement ring."

"Is it? Well, if they're engaged, why isn't she wearing it?"

"Good question." Beatrice took out her phone and snapped pictures of everything.

They drove to the police station immediately, even though Beatrice had moved from peckish to absolutely starving. The duty officer seemed almost pleased to see them, as if she was bored out of her mind. She took a statement from Theo and asked several questions, including a request for both Fae's and Theo's mobile numbers. After the interview, she assured them she would impart the information to Detective Quintana as soon as possible.

As soon as possible was a vague sort of term. Beatrice wasn't keen on vague and asked Theo to press the point. The woman glanced at her watch and with a gentle smile promised them she would do it before she went off duty at six. There was nothing more to be done, so Beatrice and Theo thanked the lady and walked outside to the afternoon sunshine.

"I'll walk back, it's not far. If Matthew is not home, I'll find out where he is and go and meet him. You enjoy your date. Tomorrow morning, we should attend the funeral. I'll find out the details and send you a message. I don't suppose you have a black suit, do you?"

"Not black, but dark grey. I've read *The Accidental Tourist*. Okay, I'll see you in the morning. Thank you for giving me the night off."

"You're welcome. Good luck." She gave him the thumbs up and walked in the direction they had come. He drove off with a wave and she softened, remembering the day he turned up on her doorstep and announced he was her new assistant. She was very lucky to have him, she knew it.

At the cottage, she checked all the rooms, including the smallest one, but there was no sign of Matthew. Most likely he was still on his walking tour. She raided the fridge for a slice of tortilla and some tomato salad with a side of pan Catalan, taking it out into the garden with a glass of rosé. While eating, she opened her laptop and searched for the details of the Palliser family funeral the following day. Eleven o'clock in the village nearest to their estate. Now that Quintana had all the facts, she and Theo could merely attend in the background and report back to the Moffatts. With a quick message to Theo containing all the details, she was officially finished for the day. She checked her watch again and decided to call Matthew and find out where he was.

A second after the ring tone began in her ear, it reverberated from their bedroom. She went inside and sure enough, Matthew's mobile was lying on the bedside table, lit up and vibrating, announcing her call. He was the most exasperating man. After all these years she spent trying to convince him to get a smartphone, he either ignored it, left it behind or accidentally called her, Tanya, the delicatessen or one of his friends in Rome. She lost count of the number of times her mobile had rung, showing his name as the caller. When she picked up, alarmed, wondering what the emergency might be she could only hear a muffled rustling from inside his pocket.

No matter, she knew where he was going. She could simply follow in his footsteps. She cleaned up her crockery after her late lunch, found her hat and went out once more into the streets of Deià.

The place all guided tours began from was Deià's tourist office, housed in the same building as the council. Unlike the tourist bureau in Port de Sóller where Nuria Quintana worked, this place had already closed. Maybe they didn't even open on Sunday. Beatrice frowned and looked at the offerings pasted in the window. She saw it almost immediately.

Walking tour on the trail of Robert Graves. Spanish/English speaking guide, duration two hours. Assemble outside this office at 14.00. Cost: 20€ (including entry to museum).

Two hours? It was now twenty to six. Matthew should have been home an hour and a half ago. She pulled up the map on her phone and located the Robert Graves Museum. It was a short walk from the town but Beatrice noted from the website that it closed at five o'clock. Perhaps he'd got chatting to someone on the tour and gone for a drink and some tapas. She followed the directions, checking the patrons of cafés and bars to see if she could spot his distinctive fedora. By the time she had walked all the way to the Graves house and back again, the clocks were striking six.

Where would he have gone? Did he forget Theo's date and go to the hotel, expecting dinner? No, Matthew always changed for dinner if they were going out or had guests. There was always the possibility he had got lost again, although the distance to the tourist office from their cottage was only a touch longer than the stroll to the bakery. If only the bloody man had taken his mobile. Beatrice stood in the doorway of the cottage looking out at the street, at a loss as to what to do next. She was tempted to call Theo, but decided against it, giving the man a genuine night off.

Finally, she realised it was pointless to wander about the streets in search of him and returned to the cottage. She sat in the garden with another glass of wine, waiting for him to come home.

Chapter 22

Beatrice jerked awake at the sound of her mobile. The sky was growing dusky and when she picked up her device, she saw it was already ten to eight. Philly's name was on Caller Display.

"Hello, Philly?"

"Beatrice! My dear girl. Am I interrupting you in something dreadfully important? It's just I thought you should know that Matthew is here. He, Raf and Hoagy had a few drinks this afternoon and I'm sorry to say they are rather the worse for wear. I thought I might feed them something stodgy in the hope of sobering them up. I don't want to interrupt whatever it is you're doing, but if you are free, would you like to join us? Do bring your fabulous assistant; he's awfully easy on the eye."

Beatrice sat up, rubbing her face. "Matthew is with you? I've been sitting here waiting for him. Philly, we don't need to impose on you for dinner. I'll come and fetch him and take him down the road to the place that does the whitebait."

"Oh my God, they're cracking open the brandy. Beatrice, I have to put a stop to this. Come up here and we can decide whether to cook or break up the party. Frankly, a strong female hand is required and you and I are both up to the challenge. See you in a bit. Bring Theo!"

What the hell was he doing getting drunk with Hoagy and Raf when he should have been exploring the stomping grounds of a twentieth-century poet? Beatrice brushed her hair, washed her face and headed up the hill towards the Moffatts' villa.

The dogs greeted her as the gate opened and the sound of raucous, drunken male laughter echoed from the patio. Her molars pressed together, helping her control a growing anger. She walked straight past the three men, ignoring their calls of greeting, and found Philly in the kitchen, boiling a huge vat of pasta.

"You angel! I couldn't cope with those old farts on my own but I daren't leave them because they'll crack open the spirits and things will get extremely messy. Thank you so much for coming. I thought carbs might be the order of the day, you know, soak up all that alcohol. It's really nothing special but if you and Matthew would like to join us, your company would be most welcome."

The dogs paced around Beatrice as if protecting her. "Philly, you're extremely kind but I really think I should take him home. To be honest, he's incredibly starstruck around Hoagy and Raf too, for that matter. Whatever either of them suggests, he will follow. In addition to that, it's incredibly rude to turn up at your house expecting dinner. It's better if I take him home."

A huge cloud of steam engulfed Philly's head as she drained a pan of spaghetti. "It's ready now. Let's eat, then I'll kick Raf out, insist Hoagy goes to bed and you can drag Matthew home by the scruff. This is over and above the call of duty, my dear, but I really would appreciate your help in managing those three drunken sots. Sorry, one of them is your other half."

"He is indeed. Both my other half and an easily influenced old sot. Do you have any sauce to go with this?"

"In the microwave. It's out of the jar but who gives a monkey's? Certainly not those three. Let's feed them and if we can get a word in edgeways, perhaps we can have a chat. There's a packet of Parmesan in the fridge. Where's Theo?"

"He's ... still gathering information. Shall I bring the

peppermill?"

The bowls of pasta were received warmly and all three men fell on their plates as if ravenous. Philly rolled her eyes at Beatrice and asked her about the progress of the case. Beatrice gave vague yet positive replies. Even if Hoagy was picking up the bill for her work, there were limits as to what she was prepared to share.

"Theo and I are going to the funeral tomorrow. I hope to speak to a couple of people and after that, I'm going to write up a full report. Depending on what the police choose to do with our information, it's possible my task is complete. At this point, and I know it sounds coy, I'd rather say no more for fear of appearing unprofessional."

"Funeral?" asked Matthew. "Whose funeral? Was I invited?"

Beatrice looked at him, flecks of tomato sauce all over his white shirt, hair mussed, eyes glazed, and resolved to remove him the minute he had finished what was on his plate.

"Of course you're invited," Raf said, placing a hand on Matthew's shoulder. "We're all going to pay our reshpects to Romy and her family." Raf's usual clipped diction was blurred around the edges.

A sudden clatter made everyone turn. Hoagy had dropped his fork and was shaking his head. "Not me. I'm not going, I can't face it. Her family, all those memories of the girl, I simply cannot do it. Top me up there, Philly?"

With practised nonchalance, Philly poured water into Hoagy's wine glass while distracting his attention with a question. "I perfectly understand why you don't want to go, but would you have any objection to my attending the ceremony? Do eat, Hoagy, I hate making food for people who leave it. Eat!"

Hoagy stabbed at some pasta with his fork. "Is that what you want? I mean, you'll have the worst, most hostile reception from the family, locals and media. There is no way on God's earth I would attend the ceremony for exactly those reasons, but you are made of sterner stuff. Not only that, but you'll have Raf, Matthew and Beatrice by your side. Are you any closer, Beatrice? Do you have a clue who killed my lovely muse?" He took a long draught from his glass, apparently unaware it was eighty percent water.

Matthew's eyes were drooping and Beatrice could take no more. "I'll tell you all about it tomorrow, after the funeral. Philly, that was a lovely meal and exactly what we needed. Thank you so much for cooking and hosting tonight's dinner. As I said earlier, I will deliver my report once I have consulted with the police. Now, I would like to take Matthew home so we can rest and recuperate before the big event. Goodnight, Raf, goodnight, Hoagy and goodnight, Philly." She looked directly into the other woman's eyes. "You are very kind."

"I'll walk you to the gates," said Philly. Hoagy got up and staggered into the house with an apparent urgency. Beatrice suspected his goal was the bathroom. Raf tucked his arm under Matthew's and helped him to his feet. The dogs at their heels, they made slow progress towards the gates.

Philly lowered her voice. "I won't press you, but do you think you know who did it?"

"I'm an ex-detective with the London Met. I will point no fingers until I'm absolutely sure there's a watertight case against whoever I'm accusing. All I have here is a third-hand conversation and no confirmatory proof. This could be nothing at all and you should prepare yourself for that eventuality. Goodnight, Philly, and thank you for managing all this mess."

Raf and Matthew caught up with them. Matthew embraced Philly effusively and chuntered on about the pasta. Beatrice shook Raf's hand and thanked him for his help. To her surprise, Raf drew her closer and placed a kiss on each cheek. He took the opportunity to murmur in her ear.

"I hope I'm not shpeaking out of turn, but here's my doctor's card. He is an expert in treating Alzheimer's patients." He hiccupped. "You may have no need of it, but having seen the shymptoms in my sister, it might be useful. I'm very shorry. Really, so sorry."

Unable to speak, Beatrice took the card, nodded to Raf and Philly, and manoeuvred Matthew out of the gates. Smiles and waves took the place of verbal farewells. They strolled down the hill, arm in arm, Matthew waxing lyrical about the town, the company and the cottage.

"Matthew? Where did you meet Hoagy and Raf? I thought you were doing a guided tour this afternoon."

He rested his head on hers. "So I did! It was marvellous. You would have loved it, Old Thing. The gardens are simply sublime and the whole place, as everyone says, looks like he's just popped out for a few minutes. Perfectly preserved. You could go tomorrow, unless you prefer the beach again?"

She stopped and faced him. "I asked you a question. Where did you meet Raf and Hoagy?"

Matthew gazed at her, his eyes trying to focus. "I can't recall. Oh, wait, yes. They drove past as I was leaving the tourist office and invited me for one of those drinks, what is it? Herbie something, taste of aniseed. Jolly tasty, you should try one. Raf has an old Jag, did you know? Yes, so we had a few drinks, went back to Hoagy's villa and had a few more. Raf gave me a guided tour of Hoagy's studio. Fascinating to see the paintings in the flesh, so to speak. We were just about to round the afternoon off with a brandy when you popped up, which was handy."

Beatrice walked on, leaving Matthew to catch up. When they arrived at the cottage, he crashed headlong onto the bed and immediately began snoring. Normally when he dozed off after a few too many, Beatrice would attempt to wake him up and make him clean his teeth before bed. Tonight she only took off his shoes and flung her half of the duvet over his fully clothed body. Then she took a blanket and went into the living room to think.

Chapter 23

It was three o'clock in the morning when Adrian finally went to bed. He'd finished an entire bottle of wine on his own and fallen asleep on the sofa. When he awoke, he assumed Will must have arrived while he was sleeping. But a glance out of the window showed no sign of the Audi and the bedroom was empty. He washed his face, cleaned his teeth, dropped his clothes into the laundry basket, set his alarm and got under the duvet to stare at the ceiling.

Where the hell was he? Will had a few friends in the force he might have gone to visit, but most of them lived the other side of London in places like Chiswick or Putney. Even if he'd gone to a pub to drown his sorrows, closing time was four hours ago. Unless he'd met a guy in a bar, poured his heart out, said 'my husband doesn't understand me' and gone home with someone willing. Why would he stay out all night if not to worry or hurt Adrian?

He turned over to face the window, feeling sick and furious. They both had to go to work in the morning and he was likely to turn up for his first day at work in two weeks hungover and lacking sleep. A great look for the boss. He squeezed his eyes shut and shook his head. "This is all your fault, William Quinn. This is on you."

At quarter to eight, the alarm woke him from a strange dream about climbing mountains. Will's side of the bed was still empty. Adrian checked his phone and the landline for any messages, but other than 'Hope you got home safely' from Tanya, there was nothing. He went through his morning routine as usual and left the house an hour earlier than usual at half past eight. He considered leaving a note, but what would it say? On the bus to Shoreditch, he allowed himself to consider the worst-case scenario. If he hadn't gone to see a mate or picked up a one-night stand in a bar, perhaps he'd had an accident. The police might be knocking on Adrian's door at this exact moment, looking for next of kin.

He called Will's mobile, which went straight to voicemail. He didn't leave a message. Instead he practised his post-holiday expression for his employees, mentally rehearsing a few anecdotes to give a flavour of their blissful fortnight away.

His team had done a great job. The place looked spotless, Jed's records were up to date and a cursory look over the books showed June had been a very good month for business. Tamsin, who stepped into Catinca's role on the design side, had begun a new promotion, pairing the right wine with the right book. It proved a savvy move, shifting serious numbers of bottles to go with the Booker Prize shortlist. Adrian made a note to give her some sort of bonus. It was busy all morning, which helped distract him, but when the doors opened at eleven, the staff slipped into their usual roles without any need for Adrian's guidance. He had trained them well. So much so, he was superfluous. He went into the office to do what he was supposed to do – strategic thinking – but his concentration was shot. All he could think about was his husband and where he might be. He needed to talk this over with someone with good sense who knew them both. There were two obvious candidates, but one of them was in Mallorca. He picked up the phone to call Catinca.

There was some debate about the lunch venue, but Catinca won, mainly because Adrian could not be bothered to argue. He arrived at The English Restaurant in Spitalfields just after one o'clock and wished he had brought his sunglasses. Catinca was sitting outside, wearing one of her own creations, a pleated neon pink and yellow maxi dress with red Converse trainers. Her hair hung into thick plaits over each shoulder and over one ear sat a blowsy silk flower in shades of pink. She jumped up to hug him.

"I missed you, mate! You wanna sit outside or is it too hot?"

Adrian squeezed tight and stood back to look at her. "I missed you too. Not outside. It's too hot and you're too bright. I feel underdressed sitting opposite you."

Catinca gave him the once over. "You are underdressed. Still in holiday mode, I reckon. Let's go in, I'm hungry."

They found a table underneath the stairs, and ordered food and a bottle of mineral water.

Catinca folded her arms on the table and searched his face. "What is it? Or you just wanna show me your holiday snaps?"

Adrian pressed his fingers to his brow and shook his head, determined to suppress the tears. When he had his emotions under control, he looked into her concerned face. "Will wants kids. After a week of babysitting Luke, he got broody and has asked if we can reconsider. I said no, he drove off and I have no idea where he spent last night. He's not answering his mobile and for all I know he could have hooked up with some butch biker in a gay bar and gone home with him. Or perhaps he went round to an ex-boyfriend and asked if they could try again, bring up a family together, with three kids and a bloody Labrador. I don't know where he is, how he's feeling or even if he's dead in the Regent's Canal. We had a lovely holiday and on the drive home he ruined it and drove off in a strop. Am I being unreasonable? Or is he being unfair?"

Catinca stroked her plait, gazing over his shoulder in thought. "Will went off in a strop? Doesn't sound like him. That's the sort of thing you would do."

A twinge of guilt nudged Adrian. "Yes, I suppose it is. As a matter of fact, I did have a wobbler last week. One afternoon I had a few drinks with some people outside the pub and when Will said I was being unreasonable, I threw my toys out of the pram and went off …"

"… in a strop? That I can believe. He is due at work today, right? Did you call the Met and ask to speak to him?"

"No! Why the hell didn't I think of that? Hold on, I'll do it now." He reached for his phone and then realised Will might see his number and decline the call. He spotted the public phone at the end of the corridor and used that instead.

"Good afternoon, you're through to the London Metropolitan police. How can I help?"

"Oh hello, my name is…" Adrian scanned the room for inspiration. "Samuel Smith. I have some information for Detective Sergeant William Quinn. Could you possibly put me through?"

"One moment, Mr Smith. Do you have a case number?"

"Oh, no, sorry. I must have left it at home." He cringed at his own appalling lie.

"Not to worry. Connecting you now"

The phone rang twice before Will's voice came on the line. "DS Quinn? Hello?"

Adrian put the phone down, breathing heavily.

"Oi! Food is here," called Catinca. "Did you speak to him?"

Adrian returned to the table and sat down, his pulse throbbing in his ears. "No, I didn't say anything, but it was definitely his voice. He's at work. Not dead in the canal."

Catinca bit into a chip. "That's what I thought. Do you want ketchup?" She offered him a sachet and took a slug of wine, leaving a lipstick mark on the glass.

"No, thank you. Just salt and vinegar for me. Actually, bollocks to that, I do want ketchup and in fact, I want a glass of wine."

Catinca looked towards the bar and caught the eye of one of the serving staff. With her catlike smile, she raised her glass and lifted two fingers. The guy got the message and gave her the thumbs up.

"They just fall at your feet, don't they? How is it possible that you're still single?" asked Adrian.

"Sodding hell, you sound like Beatrice! Anyway, who says I'm still single? And why don't the ones I want fall at my feet? Thing is, mate, we were talking about you. What's the deal with you and Will?"

"The deal is that the deal has changed. We got married on the basis of the fact neither of us wanted children. Now he's changed his mind. I can see no way out of this other than offering him a divorce. If I can't give him what he wants, maybe someone else can?"

Catinca gazed at him for a long time while tucking into her fish. Finally she spoke. "You love Will. Will loves you. If you let something like this come between you, you are pair of boneheaded sodding idiots. Intelligent people talk things through, give each other time, listen to opposite points of view and keep an open mind. You don't just chuck in the towel at the first sign of trouble. Can't believe I have to give you relationship advice!"

Adrian dipped a chip into the mushy peas and listened.

"Don't cock it up, mate. Not sure I believe in soul mates, but you and Will are the closest thing I've seen. Sit down together and talk it through. Know your red lines before you start and be prepared to compromise. It's like any other negotiation, innit? Except in this case you both want the same thing. To make each other happy, right?" The barman placed two glasses on the table. "Oh, the wine. Thank you very much, will you put that on the same bill?"

"Yes, no problem. Can I say I really like your dress?" The

expression on the barman's face was as if he was looking at a kitten.

Catinca pulled out a business card from her handbag. "I'm a fashion designer. We haven't got this one in your size but I'm sure I could find you something. Give me a call, yeah?"

He took the card with a blush. "I will, thank you. Enjoy your meal."

As the man walked away, Catinca returned her focus to Adrian, who was giving her a sardonic smile. "Shut up. It's called networking. After lunch, before you get back to Dionysus, call Will again and make arrangements. Tell him you're prepared to talk it through. It may take more than one conversation. Tonight, make nice dinner, put your side forward, listen to his. Agree to think and maybe talk some more. No more stomping off and throwing toys out of pram. Behave like grown-ups. Relationships are like gardens, need constant tending."

Adrian lifted his glass to bump it gently against hers. "To Catinca Radu, fashion designer, relationship counsellor and damn good friend."

She laughed and took a sip of wine. "Reason I'm so good at giving relationship advice is because I'm on the outside. You owe me full-on counselling session, if ever I find myself a boyfriend." She flipped her gaze at the barman who was sneaking glances in her direction. "Never know where you're gonna strike gold, innit?"

On the walk back to Dionysus, Adrian considered Catinca's advice. In his heart, he knew the concept of kids was anathema to him, but perhaps they could be some kind of compromise. If they went into this discussion with the determination to achieve a positive outcome for both, perhaps the marriage would survive.

He pulled out his phone and dialled Will's number.

Chapter 24

Sunrise found Beatrice still awake on the sofa drinking herbal tea. Worrying was a pointless occupation but decision-making was not. It was clear in her mind that Matthew needed to see a doctor, which could only happen when they had returned to their local GP. In the meantime, she had to bring this case to some sort of conclusion before they could fly home. Between now and then, he had to be under supervision at all times. She owed Tanya an apology. Thinking back, Will had flagged this situation over two weeks ago. It could be anything, she told herself. Her own mother had gone completely doolally for a week until the hospice diagnosed a urine infection. It still could be anything, but the priority was to find out the truth.

She gave up on the whole concept of sleep, folded up the blanket and tiptoed into the bedroom. Matthew had thrown off the duvet and was lying on top of it, fully clothed and snoring. Beatrice had a shower, scrubbing herself as if removing a crust, dressed and prepared breakfast for a man with a hangover.

As she scrambled eggs and fried bacon, she forced herself to acknowledge the worst-case scenario. If Matthew had some kind of degenerative illness, she would have to stop work and become a full-time carer. That was not a problem. She would find other things to occupy her mind, but what of his? Her eyes filled with tears and for the first time since she acknowledged the reality, she wept, huge gulping sobs at the injustice of the world. He was a classics professor, a fine mind, with extraordinary intelligence to such a level that he could develop it in others. He was the brains of the outfit, combining intellectual excellence with emotional comprehension. If anyone deserved to rot from the inside, it was her.

The bacon was burning. She took it off the heat and dabbed her eyes with some kitchen towel, sniffing and blowing her nose.

"What is it, Old Thing?" Matthew stood in the kitchen doorway, crumpled and creased, his face wrinkled in concern.

"Ah, there you are! Oh, it's nothing, chopping onions always has the same effect. We are having the full English, as far as I can cobble together the ingredients."

"Yes, that ought to do the trick. I had one tipple too many last night and I can feel it now. Memories of last night are a tad vague, but I hope I didn't do anything too awful."

Beatrice dropped the tissue and embraced him. "You never do anything awful. I love you, Matthew Bailey. Now come and sit down before the bacon goes cold."

He squeezed her tightly, kissed her forehead and pulled out a chair, humming a refrain from *The Pirates of Penzance*.

While he attacked the contents of his plate, a thought occurred to Beatrice. She wished she'd paid more attention to Matthew's waffling last night.

"Do you remember telling me you saw the inside of Hoagy's studio?" she asked, as casually as she could manage.

Matthew stopped chewing and a panicked expression crossed his face. Then his forehead cleared and he swallowed. "I remember very well. Due to the fact I am familiar with his work, it was nothing short of a revelation to see some of the earlier work in progress, as it were. Quite fascinating. On top of that, I had an expert guide by my side. Raf explained the arc of Hoagy's career and some of its significant turning points. I wish you had been there, my love."

"So do I," said Beatrice, with feeling. "Tell me, was Hoagy with you?"

"No, he was in the wine cellar looking for a particular bottle of red, I disremember the name. That's right, Philly was inside the house, Hoagy was in the cellar and Raf and I were discussing some of the elements of the *Flamenco* piece. He offered to show me some of the preliminary sketches. I practically bit his hand off. What an experience, I must say."

"Doesn't Hoagy mind people poking about in his private workspace?" Beatrice asked.

"I imagine he would mind people poking about, but Raf is his agent. He treats the place as if it's his own home. I rather envy him."

"Hmm. Do you want some more toast to mop up those beans?"

"Go on then, you've twisted my arm."

A rap came at the door. "Ah, Theo's here. We have a little job to do before we go to the funeral. Could you clear up and have a shower? We shan't be long, so don't leave the house."

The clinic was halfway up the mountain and boasted the most spectacular views out to sea. The most perfect place to recuperate, she could imagine. Paloma Mendez was waiting for them in the foyer, wearing white trousers and a white tunic. She held a folder in her hand. Theo introduced them in Spanish and at Beatrice's prodding, repeated the assertion that she was under no obligation to speak to them.

She answered him in English. "I understand. It's OK. Can we talk outside?" She glanced over her shoulder at reception.

They followed her into the gardens, past blooming bushes of hibiscus and towards a bench out of sight of the building. Beatrice and Paloma sat down while Theo leaned on a rock opposite.

Paloma's voice was quiet and gentle. "Juan Carlos said you

want to talk about Miranda Flynn, yes?"

"That's correct. This is in relation to the murder of Romy Palliser, so if you tell us something which could be relevant, we may have to share it with the police. I hope you appreciate that."

The young woman nodded. Like her cousin, she had glossy brown hair and olive skin, but her demeanour was less confident. "I understand. I brought her file. I can't give it to you but I will answer your questions. It's not allowed, but ..." She shrugged and opened the pale blue folder, and Beatrice cursed herself for leaving her glasses at the cottage.

"Miranda Flynn, twenty-seven years old, American citizen. Admitted third of May this year for a termination. She was fourteen weeks pregnant."

"As far as I know, a termination in the early stages is a simple procedure and the patient can return home the same day. Was that true of Miranda Flynn?"

The girl shook her head. "It depends on what kind of anaesthetic they have and if there's someone to take care of them. Ms Flynn was alone and she wanted a general anaesthetic. She stayed here overnight and took a taxi home the next day."

"Do you provide counselling for women requiring a termination?"

"Yes, before and afterwards. The initial consultation is mandatory. But follow-up sessions are optional and Ms Flynn refused."

Theo spoke. "An operation plus an overnight stay. That must cost a bit."

She checked the grounds to be sure no one could overhear and spoke in a whisper. "Two thousand and forty Euro. Paid by credit card."

Beatrice looked up at Theo. "That's all very interesting, thank you, Paloma. I'm sure you're very busy, so I just have one last question."

"Go ahead."

Chapter 25

The weather suited the atmosphere of a funeral. A mist rolled in over the island, blocking the sun and draping everywhere with an atmosphere of dampness. Like a veil, it distorted perspective so that the benevolent mountains embracing the town of Deià took on an air of ominous portent. The perfect day to dress in grey. Theo checked himself in the mirror in Beatrice's living room. The suit looked good. Just a shame about the trainers, but at least they were black. He looked sober and a little sad, the exact opposite of how he felt. A secretive smile crept over his face, which he hid as Beatrice came out of the bedroom.

A hurriedly packed bag to travel for an urgent case was unlikely to contain a formal funeral suit. But Beatrice happened to be very fond of dark grey and always had a jacket and a handbag in those colours. Matthew was a completely different proposition. When Theo had seen him at home in Devon, he always wore greens and browns. On holiday, it was all beige, white and ecru. Not that he would ever call it ecru, more sort of off-white. Beatrice improvised by borrowing Theo's leather jacket and a pair of black chinos, and fashioned a black tie from one of her scarves. The end result gave him the air of Keith Richards, especially as he looked hungover and his hair was wild.

"Finally, I think we're ready. Matthew, do brush your hair, for heaven's sake."

"Righty ho." He retreated into the bedroom once again.

"You look smart, Theo. You're like Adrian, grey suits you. Which reminds me, I didn't ask you how it went last night."

"It was good. We had fun."

"Is that it?"

"No, there's more. When I met Fae last night, she'd already had a visit from the police. On Sunday afternoon."

"Ah ha! So Quintana did get the message then."

"Yup."

"And Fae?" Beatrice cocked her head, waiting for more.

"She told him what she told us. Now we've just corroborated her story."

"Yes, but what I meant was ..."

"How's that? Will I do?" Matthew said, looking slightly less rock and roll.

Beatrice sighed. "Yes, you'll do. Come along now, we don't want to be late."

They drove north towards the family estate. Matthew, in the back seat, chatted on about his tour the previous day with great enthusiasm. Theo asked questions and encouraged him to go into detail. Mainly to keep Beatrice quiet. She had tried three times to get more information about last night's date.

The landscape was far less appealing than the previous time they had taken this journey, and it made Theo question whether Mallorca would be a pleasant place to be in the winter.

Before they got anywhere near to the crematorium, it was clear the event was going to be a total bunfight. The small village was heaving with journalists, camera crews, ambulance chasers and a large number of genuine mourners. Theo drove all the way through the village and out the other side. Finally he found a parking spot beside a gate to a field. They left the car there and walked back to the centre.

They could get nowhere near the building itself due to the

crowds, but Theo spotted more than one point of interest. Firstly, two police vehicles at either end of the street. Beatrice saw them at the same time.

"You think they are going to arrest her here?" she asked.

"It certainly looks that way to me."

The second point which drew Theo's attention was the media focus. Camera flashes and shouted questions revolved around a couple of people entering the building. A tall man with white hair was escorting Ophelia Moffatt through the crowd.

"Raf Beaumont," muttered Beatrice, standing on tiptoes.

Trying to get closer would require the skills of an American footballer and she gave up, content to observe. They waited in the grounds as the ceremony began, beamed onto a screen for those shut outside. Greg Palliser gave a eulogy for his sister which was schmaltzy and overwritten, and his delivery was not particularly heartfelt. Next up, racing driver brother Nat delivered a pointed speech directed largely at the police, expressing disappointment that no one had been charged with the murder of his sister. There were a few songs and many more tributes from Romy's friends, all of whom were dressed as glamorously as you could get in black. Miranda Flynn gave an unimaginative poetry reading with a veil covering her face. A veil? Surely that type of gear should be the prerogative of very close family, not somebody who'd had a screaming row with the murder victim shortly before her death.

Theo turned to address Beatrice and realised Matthew was no longer standing behind her.

"Where'd Matthew go?"

Her head snapped from left to right scanning the crowds. Theo could see no sign of him.

"Quick, we have to find that wretched man," she hissed.

Just as they had done on the beach, Theo and Beatrice split up to search the crowds, him left, her right. Many people were weeping, hugging each other and making the sign of the cross.

Mostly those in designer clothes, Theo noted. Halfway up the driveway, beside a rosebush arch, he saw Matthew in conversation with a short bald man.

"Theo! There you are. This is Mike, who works for the *Daily Express*. Comes from Bristol, would you believe? Mike, this is Theo, my wife's assistant."

Theo tried not to show any alarm. "Hello, Mike, what brings you to Mallorca?"

"All right, mate? Covering the Romy Palliser case. What about you?"

"We're on holiday, but one of our party has wandered off. We'd better go and find her. Nice to meet you, Mike. Come on, Matthew, this way."

"Righty ho. Have a safe trip back to Bristol." With a contented smile, he allowed Theo to steer him closer to the crematorium. "It's a charming building, don't you think? Crematoria often are, I find. There she is!"

Red-faced and puffing, Beatrice hurried towards them.

"Where did you get to, you old goat?" she asked.

"Beatrice! We've been looking for you, haven't we, Theo? I just got chatting to a chap from Bristol. A reporter, as it turns out. He's here to cover the funeral. Seems this is international news."

Beatrice checked Theo's expression. He gave an infinitesimal shake of his head. He was pretty sure Matthew had given nothing away. Before she could ask any more questions, the doors opened and the mourners poured out, some red-eyed and sniffling, some hurrying away from the cameras. They stood back and waited, watching as the family departed, protected by some burly individuals in black suits. To Theo's amazement, Greg and his brother Nat were actually laughing together, as if they were coming out of the pub rather than saying a final farewell to their sister.

Beatrice nudged him and nodded towards the street.

Detective Quintana stood beside the family car, his arms folded and his gaze fixed on the approaching party. As they passed, Theo noticed Miranda Flynn was not with them.

Theo had a bad feeling about that. He looked at Beatrice. "Stay here in case she comes out, I'll check the other doors."

Mourners filed past in small, subdued groups. Not one contained Miranda Flynn. The gardens cleared at speed and Theo saw another funeral party entering via the other end of the building. It was pretty much a conveyor belt.

Theo rounded the corner and paced down the side of the building in the shade. He got almost to the end when a movement caught his eye. Miranda Flynn was speed-walking down a slope towards the garden of remembrance, beyond which lay the car park.

"Miranda!" Theo called. "Just a minute!"

She whirled around and saw him, then broke into a run.

Theo launched himself after her without hesitation, heedless of Beatrice's warnings not to tackle anyone alone. She was fit, sure, but she had the impediment of heels, whereas Theo wore running shoes. He gained on her fast and reached out to catch her jacket. As he did so, she let out a piercing scream and two men came running from the gardens towards them. Theo held up his hands in a peaceful gesture but Miranda continued screeching so he could not make himself heard. The two men grabbed an arm each and frog-marched him in the direction he had come.

He kept trying to explain, twisting to see Miranda running towards the car park. They dragged him onwards.

"What on earth is going on?" Beatrice and Matthew stood at the corner of the crematorium,

"Beatrice, call Quintana! She's getting away! She's heading towards the car park! Tell the police!"

Beatrice turned to rush in the opposite direction and collided with Detective Quintana running towards her.

Theo yelled, "*¡La mujer se escapa! ¡Ahí abajo!*"

Quintana bellowed an order to the gardeners, who released Theo, and spoke into his radio. Theo took off at a run, Quintana on his heels. Theo scanned the area for a fleeing female but could see nothing more than trees. She had disappeared.

"Over there!" Beatrice shouted from the top of the slope, pointing at the incoming funeral party. Abruptly, Theo veered right, running directly at the group of mourners. Quintana yelled '*¡Policía!*' and the black-clad crowd parted to allow them through. In the gap, Theo saw his target. Sprinting across the grass, shoes discarded, was Miranda Flynn. People moved out of Theo's path, all gawping at the pursuit. He was closing the gap, near enough to see her handbag bouncing at her side and her veil flying.

Behind him, Quintana shouted for her to stop. Miranda did not heed his warning and ran straight into the road, colliding with a passing car. Fortunately, the car was turning into the crematorium, so only travelling at around five kilometres per hour, but the impact bounced Miranda onto the ground. Just enough time for Theo to catch up. He reached down a hand to help her up and to his horror, she drew a knife from her bag and slashed at him. Theo scrambled away from the blade, giving her time to crab her way into a crouch.

The driver of the car got out and on hearing Quintana roar, instantly got in again. The Spanish detective drew closer, his weapon trained on Flynn.

"*Alléjate de ella*," Quintana told Theo, no longer shouting.

Theo reversed, leaving a space between him and the cornered woman. Two uniformed officers raced over the lawn, both drawing their own weapons as they skidded to a halt. Miranda had nowhere to run. She took a couple of cautious paces until her back pressed against the car. Her left hand reached for the driver's door handle. A shot boomed into the silence, making Theo gasp.

Quintana's aim was true. The front tyre shattered, pieces of rubber flying into the air like a shower of spiders. It was enough. Flynn dropped the knife and raised her hands. Quintana and one other officer kept their guns pointed at her as their colleague kicked away the knife and put her in handcuffs.

Once the police car carrying the would-be fugitive drove away, Quintana strode up the drive to face Theo and Beatrice, his hands on his hips. He shook hands with them both.

Quintana looked at the ground and inhaled deeply. Once he had released his breath, he looked them in the eyes and spoke in English. "We will charge her today. Her behaviour gave us all the evidence we needed. Thank you both for the information and thanks to you, Mr Wolfe, for your help with the arrest."

Theo also switched languages. "You're welcome. Do you need statements from us?"

"If I take statements from you, I don't get the glory." He gave them a wry smile. "You did a good job and I appreciate your help. As a thank you, I'll be in touch to tell you what happens next. Have a good afternoon." He stalked off as if going into battle.

"Detective? Can I have a word?" Beatrice asked. She joined him to walk down the drive, leaving Theo to look for Matthew. He was seated on a bench in the garden of remembrance and smiled as Theo approached.

"What a lovely spot," said Matthew.

"Perfect," Theo agreed and sat beside him to appreciate the shade and the silence.

"I knew it," said Beatrice, when she found them a few minutes later. "That whole I-don't-speak-English shtick when he works as a cop in a tourist town. Oh well, what does it matter now? So long as they have caught Miranda Flynn and can find out exactly what happened, Philly is in the clear. Objective met. I'll write up a report for Hoagy and we can head home."

"This is the frustrating bit," Theo said. "I want to know the whole story. If Greg was in on it, if it was her who spoiled the paintings and most of all, I want to hear her confess."

Beatrice beckoned them and began walking towards the exit. "Come on, let's get out of here. I have a theory about the paintings, and whether Greg was in on it remains to be seen, but we should know soon enough. We'll get a call from Quintana later today. Now what do you say to a spot of lunch before knuckling down to that report?"

Matthew caught up with them and linked his arm in Beatrice's. "Capital plan. I wouldn't say no to dining at that café you mentioned."

"Which café you mentioned?" Theo looked up to see a willowy woman with white-blonde hair standing on the other side of the road. "Hang on. There's someone I need to speak to. Give me five minutes. I'll meet you at the car."

Beatrice's head snapped around to stare. "Is that who I think it is?"

"Five minutes, OK? I'll meet you at the car." Theo raised a hand to wave at Fae. "Matthew, take this woman away."

"Quite right. Come along, Old Thing, I've had more than enough drama for one day."

Chapter 26

The formal discussion was scheduled for seven o'clock. Some elements of their meeting were not yet clear, others had been agreed. Adrian had no idea whether Will would stay the night and if so, in their bed. However, his offer to cook was gratefully received. He was nervous and as always when his mind was agitated, he spent hours on preparation for the evening ahead. He left work early and went to the delicatessen to collect all the ingredients required for a jambalaya. The Creole-style dish was one of Will's favourites and the fact that Adrian was cooking it tonight was a display of consideration Will would not fail to appreciate.

He chose a robust Californian Chenin Blanc to accompany it, along with cornbread and a green salad with slices of avocado. Once the pot was in the oven, he showered, shaved and changed into jeans and white shirt. Will was a big fan of the Waltons look. While he prepared the salad dressing, he ran over his arguments once again, often discarding a particular word for something more accommodating. He repeated his mantra, 'I will not cry' twenty times as he laid the table.

At ten to seven, keys jangled in the apartment door. Adrian went into the corridor to greet his husband and his heart leaped at the sight of that gorgeous man in his work suit. All formality dropped away and in two strides, Adrian took his husband in his arms. They held each other close, Adrian inhaling Will's aftershave.

"I was so worried about you," he murmured into Will's shoulder.

Will placed a hand on the back of his head. "I know and I'm sorry. I just needed some space. I should have called except I was busy being an arrogant idiot." He pulled away and looked into Adrian's eyes, his hands on Adrian's shoulders. "You were the bigger person, calling me to talk things over."

The urge to ask where Will had spent last night grew as insistent as a drumbeat in Adrian's head but he forced himself to ignore it. "I wouldn't call myself the bigger person after my behaviour in the car but I thought it over. We can't let something like this fester and damage our open communication. So I made jambalaya Creole-style, chilled a nice white and thought we could do this like grown-ups."

Will leaned in for a kiss. "I love jambalaya. And I love you."

If it wasn't for the fact that the rice needed fluffing, Adrian would have dragged him into the bedroom there and then. But there was a conversation that needed having before they could consider make-up sex. "I know you do. Right, are you hungry?"

After a few appreciative comments on the food, which Adrian had to admit was one of his best one-pot dishes ever, they turned to the matter at hand.

"I thought about what you said," said Will, "about the fact that you would have to be mother. That made me realise how selfish I was being. Because it's true. When I went to work this morning, I asked myself if I would be prepared to give up this job to be a full-time parent. I wrestled with that all morning and came to the conclusion that no, I wouldn't. So expecting you to give up the business that you built from scratch was unreasonable and unfair. I wanted us to think about it and talk about it in a practical way but I went at the argument from an emotional perspective. I apologise for that."

In Adrian's head, he could hear Catinca's voice. *It's like any other negotiation, innit? Except in this case you both want the same thing. To make each other happy, right?*

"Right," said Adrian. "Apology accepted. I hope you'll accept mine. I flew off the handle when you brought it up in the car because the truth is, I could see it coming. I'd already been making contingency plans, such as babysitting Alejandro or spending time with your sister's kids. But I hadn't thought about it in any other terms than practical. This is important to you, I know that. So let's look at both sides of the question, practical and emotional."

Will grinned and lifted his glass. "We are so damned reasonable it's like an ACAS meeting. Cheers, and risk of being seen a flatterer, this is your best jambalaya yet."

"Cheers," Adrian returned the smile. "I don't see it as flattery at all, because it's the truth. The secret is that chorizo from the deli. Now, you brought up the topic of parenthood and I think it's only fair you should go first. Why don't you explain how you feel about the subject and how you think it might work. I will hear you out without interruption and then give you my perspective on the question. After that, we can discuss each other's assumptions. Does that sound fair?"

Will's grin spread again. "Very fair. That's exactly how I wanted to handle it. OK, I'll start with context. When we met, I had two priorities in my life. One, promotion to detective inspector. Two, meeting a man I could build a life with. That night I interviewed you after that freak made accusations, I fell head over heels in love. You've heard this before, but you thought it was pillow talk. It wasn't, Adrian. That was the night. I broke protocol to return your laptop so I could ask you out on a date. I was younger then, and could only see as far as the next couple of years. Last week showed me a different side of myself. Being an ersatz parent was even more fulfilling than breaking up a gang of gun runners. The idea of shaping a little person's character, teaching them a sense of right and wrong and the feeling of responsibility all thrilled me to my core. I wanted more than a part-time gig. You and I would make… Sorry. I felt that you and I would make great parents. It wasn't just me getting broody. I watched you interact with Luke with such naturalness that I could see us raising a child together." Will's swirled his wine around the glass but did not drink.

"If you let that jambalaya get cold, I will never cook for you again," said Adrian.

They ate for a few moments in silence, Adrian restraining himself from making any comment on Will's previous words. He didn't stare, or sigh, or drum his fingers on the table. He just allowed some time for Will to organise his thoughts.

"In terms of fitting a child into our lives, I guess I thought we could cross that bridge when we came to it. But that's naïve, I know that now. My desire for fatherhood addresses my emotional state and if I'm honest, is a fantasy. We can't do this as a trial run, like experimenting with BDSM or something like that."

Adrian put down his fork, his mind racing. "You want to experiment with BDSM?" He began to think he didn't know his husband at all.

"No! I'm not into that kind of thing, you know that. What I meant was, it's not a game changer to introduce a new sexual preference, redecorate the bedroom or switch roles in a relationship. Because if it doesn't work, you can press the reset button. That is not realistic when it comes to adopting a child. That is the definition of a game changer. I know it would transform our lives. What I'm saying is, it might transform them for the better."

The CD player chose a new track on random select. As if the machine had a sense of irony, it picked 'Clouds' by Joni Mitchell. The lyrics held a particular significance as they finished their food. They listened to the entire track without speaking, occasionally meeting each other's eyes. The poignancy was lost on neither of them. When the final chord faded, Will put down his fork and looked into Adrian's eyes.

"Your turn," he said.

The music had a soothing effect on Adrian's mind and he relaxed into his chair, tasting his wine. "No, it's not my turn. We agreed to express our emotional reactions and address practical concerns. You've only told me half the story."

The second he had spoken, Will's gaze dropped to his empty plate. Adrian recognised that look. Will did not want to talk about the reality of bringing a child into their lives. Instead, his focus was on the sunlit rainbow over a vision of their future. The silence dragged on and Adrian took several patient breaths. Somewhere in the back of his mind, a small yappy dog was barking questions.

Do we have to move? This flat has one bedroom and an office. Where would we put a child and all its accessories? Who is responsible for taking him or her to school and picking them up afterwards? Who handles all the nappy changing/teenage tantrums/talks about the birds and the bees? Who is the primary carer? What happens if it doesn't work out?

"Practicalities, yeah." Will heaved in a breath. "All right, my dream was that we would adopt a child aged around two years old, maybe a bit older. If you didn't want to stop work, we could afford day care. This place is probably too small, I know that. We might need to move further out and I would have a longer commute. The likelihood is that I will get promoted to a DI position if not this year, the next. Then I would want to do the job to the best of my ability for a couple of years, before taking early retirement. And moving to the countryside with you, our dog and our son. I don't think that sounds like a nightmare scenario."

A red mist clouded Adrian's vision. He took the plates into

the kitchen and went to the bathroom to wash his face, battling with his rage. Will's entitled attitude angered him to the point where he could not even speak. *If you didn't want to stop work. I would have a longer commute. I don't think that sounds like a nightmare scenario. Our son?*

He stayed in the bathroom for a full five minutes, controlling his temper. Then he returned to the living room to deliver his side of the story.

"So you want us to adopt a child because you think it will be fulfilling for you, at least that is when you spend an hour with said child after a twelve-hour day. Who takes care of the rest? Why would I want to give up work? Sure, we probably could afford day care, but what would be the point? Will, I'm sorry to say this, but that scenario you just presented is that of a hobby parent. Basically, your life would carry on as normal, except you'd have a child to play with at weekends. Whereas I would have another full-time job on top of the one I've got. To be quite frank, I don't want another full-time job. I'm busy enough with the one I've got. In addition to juggling my hours to fit around the school or kindergarten timetable, I would have to give up Gay Men's choir, say goodbye to spontaneous drinks with friends and leave the foreign-language cinema club in order to stay home and help our child with his or her homework. Is there any part of you that sees that as fair? Don't answer yet. That is only the practical side."

He topped up both the glasses and took a large swig of white wine. "I completely appreciate what you say about how much you loved spending time with Luke. You're brilliant with him and he hero-worships you. The thing is, do you remember your tennis phase? Correct me if I'm wrong, but we had a doubles game with Mick and Hussein one afternoon and you were by far the best player on the court. You saw tennis as something you were good at, and you bought all the kit, took lessons and spent most weekends at the tennis club. You were good at it and you improved. And then you got bored. The tennis kit gathered dust in the cupboard under the stairs and you moved on to training for the London Marathon. Can you see why I'm reluctant to upturn both our lives for an experiment that you think you might be good at?"

"This is different ..."

"Please do me the courtesy of letting me finish. The other factor on the emotional side is that I don't want to be a parent. My father was as emotionally distant as you can get while still being physically present. My mother overcompensated, almost smothering me with affection and love. I overheard them one night, talking in the living room. She was lecturing him, criticising his lack of interest in me and asking him to make an effort. He said, and I still recall his calm tone of voice, 'That would be a lie. I can't demonstrate my love for him because it isn't there. It's not his fault, I just don't like children'. He was right to say it would have been a lie. Children see through fakery better than adults sometimes. Still, growing up knowing my father wished I'd never been born was incredibly painful. I can't put another child in that position."

He reached for his glass and realised he was trembling. Will stretched a hand across the table but Adrian moved out of reach, holding up a hand for patience.

"You never told me that before," said Will, his voice gentle. "Of course something like that makes a difference. I'm sorry. It must have hurt."

Adrian replaced his glass and looked directly at Will. "Where did you spend last night? Tell me the truth."

Will tilted his head to the left, his habitual confused expression, as if he were a dog trying to understand human language. "On Catinca's sofa. I called around to her place to get it off my chest, but instead, I got off my face on some dodgy Russian vodka. There was no way could drive home, so I crashed on her sofa."

Adrian narrowed his eyes. "Odd that she didn't mention that when I had lunch with her today. Be honest with me, Will. Where did you spend last night?"

"At Catinca's! I swear. Come on, stop looking at me like that. If I was going to lie to you about where I was, why would I choose one of our closest friends who'd tell you the truth in a second? In fact, give her a call right now. Go on."

Adrian didn't move, still staring at Will. What he said made sense and Adrian did not want to look like a suspicious spouse by checking up on him.

"Okay, I'll do it." Will pulled his phone from his suit jacket and pressed the screen. He held Adrian's gaze as he listened for a response. "Hi, Catinca. Sorry to disturb you, but Adrian wants a word." He thrust the phone at Adrian, who took it with some reluctance.

"Hello, Catinca."

"All right, Adrian? How is it going? You're not ringing me to be sodding referee, are you?"

"No, not exactly. It's just that Will said he spent last night on your sofa. I'm wondering, if that's true, why you didn't mention it at lunch today."

"None of my business. I didn't tell him I had lunch with you either. It's up to you two to be honest with each other. Tell him I'm sorry about the vodka. I was pretty rough this morning an' all. Right, anything else? Because I've got a date with that barman in half an hour."

Adrian wished her luck and ended the call. He met Will's smug gaze. "I thought you'd gone to some rough club and picked up a hairy biker."

Will gave him a sardonic look. "Which of the two of us in the past week has spent the most time in the company of hairy bikers?"

Adrian got to his feet. "Sod the washing up. Let's go to bed."

In one movement, Will drained his glass, stood up and came

to stand in front of Adrian. "That's a very good idea. What about … the subject under discussion?"

Adrian snaked a hand around Will's neck. "Nobody said we had to come to a conclusion tonight. Let's give ourselves another twenty-four hours thinking time now that we've both heard each other out. At the moment, I'm tired of conversation and in the mood for some action."

"Is this the time for me to do my Elvis impression?"

"Maybe later."

Chapter 27

It came as no real surprise to Beatrice when Theo asked permission to take a holiday. He said he would like to stay in Mallorca for a couple more days. Beatrice agreed readily, as she had cut into his week's leave, so he could most definitely stay on. She was itching to ask questions but reminded herself that while she might be his boss, she had no right to pry into his private life. Once they had completed their full report, she apologised to Theo for being a bully and released him from all official duties for the rest of the week.

She gave herself a reward of a post-prandial nap and a wander with Matthew down to the cove, and booked their flights to Exeter. They would be home early afternoon, which meant she could attend her counselling session from her own office. The sound of James's reassuring voice was exactly what she needed at the moment. She had just finished sending a message to Tanya, with their arrival times, when her mobile rang.

"Beatrice, dear girl, Philly here. We just had a visit from Quintana. We have news and much to celebrate. Can you join us for dinner? Any time after seven. We'll manage something slightly more sophisticated than last night's improvisation. Do please bring Matthew and Theo, if you can."

"Do you know, that would be most welcome. I have your

report which I intended to deliver today and we are flying home tomorrow. Theo has other plans but Matthew and I will be there. Can I bring anything?"

"Certainly not. Hoagy has raided our cellar and we shall be cracking open a few bottles of cava. See you in a short while."

She mooched into the bedroom to see how Matthew was getting on with the packing. He had folded everything into neat piles and placed them on the bed. He looked up as she came in and gave her a puzzled frown.

"Beatrice, thank goodness you're here. I'm afraid I need your help. I have everything organised, but for the life of me I cannot find our suitcase. Did you put it in one of your secret hidey holes?"

"They're in the wardrobe. You must have seen them while you were taking out the clothes." She walked past him, opened the wardrobe door and pulled out the two wheelie cases.

"No, no, those aren't ours. Far too small. Ours is made of leather and at least half the size of this bed. You remember, we bought it in Marrakesh that year when you went over the top in one of the markets. Cost an arm and a leg, but lasted forever."

She did indeed remember that suitcase and how long it lasted. From 1993 through to sometime in 2009. They'd thrown it out over ten years ago.

"Marrakesh. You're right, I did go over the top. So many bargains, I couldn't resist. We may have left that suitcase at home this time. In fact, yes, I remember as I bent down to put on my slippers, I saw it underneath our bed. We brought two little ones with wheels instead. These do belong to us, I promise you. By the way, we've been invited to dinner at the Moffatts' tonight, so leave out one decent shirt. You'll also need clothes to travel in tomorrow, the flight leaves at twenty past eleven. Have you packed your sponge bag?"

They were walking towards the villa when a horn sounded

behind them. Raf's Jaguar pulled alongside and he offered them a lift for the rest of the way. The gates to the villa swung open to admit his regal vehicle, which he drove cautiously along the drive because of the excitable wolfhounds. Hoagy came outside to meet them, wearing an apron and waving a glass.

"It's all over, *amigos*, and Ophelia is exonerated. Let me get you some cava. My darling wife is in the kitchen making *caldereta* and *pa amb oli*, or as I like to call it, fish stew and garlic bread. Don't tell her I said that because she will call me a barbarian. Beatrice! I hear there was all manner of drama at the funeral this morning. Come inside and tell us all about it."

The party gathered at the dining table, the crockery, cutlery and glassware more sophisticated than on the previous occasions they had dined there. Beatrice told the story of Theo's pursuit twice, from her perspective and from his.

"Those gardeners are utter bastards!" said Raf. "Theo could have a jolly good case for racial discrimination, if he chose to pursue it."

"My mind ran along similar lines," Beatrice replied. "But as Theo himself pointed out, a man running after a screaming woman is cause for concern, regardless of what ethnicity he might be. I can't blame the gardeners for trying to stop him grabbing Miranda Flynn. They weren't to know she was the bad guy. What bothered me more was Theo's philosophical acceptance of the fact that he will always be under suspicion of nefarious activities based on nothing more than his skin colour."

"Very good point, Beatrice. That young man is wise beyond his years," Philly said.

"I think he had to be," said Beatrice. "This *caldereta* is an explosion of taste. I have had some good food since we've been in Mallorca, but this is a meal I will never forget."

"It is absolutely extraordinary," agreed Matthew.

Raf inhaled deeply over his bowl. "You excelled yourself this time, Philly. I think it's the longer steam. Whatever you changed, it works."

"She's a fabulous cook. Just fabulous," said Hoagy. "No, not a cook, my wife is a chef and I'm lucky to have her."

Philly gave a gracious bow around the table and turned her attention to Beatrice. "You mentioned a report. Hoagy and I would be very interested to read that. And I think you would be interested to hear what Detective Quintana had to say."

"Me too!" said Raf. "Was it really that yoga teacher who was seeing Romy's brother? I can't believe anyone could be so angry when a business partner pulls out a joint venture as to kill her? I still have so many questions."

Philly scooped up some stock from the stew. "I should imagine we will all have many questions over the next few days, maybe even weeks. Even Quintana admits he doesn't know it all. The Flynn woman is refusing to cooperate, but forensics will soon tell the police whether or not her knife was the murder weapon. Her arrest was thanks to some excellent detective work on the part of DI Stubbs and her assistant, apparently. Beatrice, put us all out of our misery, would you?"

Beatrice hesitated. "It's all there in my report."

"We're eagerly looking forward to your report," said Hoagy, dipping his bread into his *caldereta*. "But what say you give us an executive summary? I'd like to know how you cracked this in your own words. Here, have another glass of cava."

"Thank you. Are you sure you want to hear this now?"

"Yes!" said Hoagy. "Answers are what we need after all the confusion. What happened and why?"

"Very well. But I can't take credit for cracking this alone, because Theo did the heavy lifting. Let's start with motive. Of all the potential suspects in this case, no one seemed to have sufficient reason to commit such a horrible crime. Thanks to Theo, we discovered Miranda Flynn had more than professional disappointment to motivate her. Miranda is Greg Palliser's girlfriend and his right-hand woman when it comes to his church, 'The One Truth'. The church's teachings are a muddle of tenets from other religions, accessed by expensive online courses, but one of them is the sanctity of life. The right to prematurely end one's existence is expressly forbidden. As is the right to prevent a being from coming into existence. Assisting a suicide or enabling an abortion are both grounds for being excommunicated.

"So when Miranda found herself pregnant by the leader of such a church, she had to be extremely careful. A termination at a private clinic costs a great deal of money but should guarantee discretion. Unfortunately for her, this is a small community where people tend to know each other's business. Romy found out about Miranda's operation and when the row blew up over her leaving the yoga business, she used it as a threat to blackmail her ex-business partner."

Hoagy laid down his cutlery. "Blackmail? Romy? She would not be capable of such a thing!"

"Oh, I think she might," said Philly. "Please continue, Beatrice."

Beatrice took a sip of wine to allow the couple a moment. After Hoagy chose not to press the point, she continued.

"However, I believe Romy made a fatal mistake. She threatened Miranda, thinking her brother didn't know about the abortion. When I saw Miranda's drawer with the expensive medication, I wondered where the money came from and how she could afford a termination in a private clinic. Considerably more than a yoga teacher would earn, I am sure. This morning, Theo and I visited the clinic, where we confirmed my suspicions. The operation was charged to Greg Palliser's credit card. Greg not only knew about the termination, he paid for it. Which led me to ..."

Her phone rang, interrupting her flow. She scowled at the device until she saw the name on the screen.

"I'm sorry, I have to take this." She stood up and walked a

little way into the gardens. "Detective Quintana, thanks for calling me back."

She listened intently to the detective's words. "And did he have it on him? I had a feeling he would! Has she said anything yet? Ah ha, so that loosened her tongue. I appreciate the call, detective. Thank you for letting me know. Not at all, you're most welcome. Good luck."

Beatrice returned to the table and the circle of expectant faces. "That was the police. They just provided the last piece of the puzzle. Where was I? Romy threatened to tell her brother about the termination and extorted money from Miranda to keep the secret. But of course, Greg already knew, because the hypocritical bastard stumped up the cash. Miranda must have told him of Romy's threat and I suspect that triggered a plan in his mind. The threat to his church business was simply too great. Somehow, he convinced Miranda that Romy had to go and she should be the one to do the deed. She appears strong in a physical sense, but I have reason to believe she's a good deal more vulnerable in mind. The kind of person who can be talked into a state of paranoia.

"I believe they wanted to frame Nuria Quintana. They knew the girl had a motive and they also knew she was in Deià on Monday night because they had been at the same bar. What they didn't know, because they take so little interest in the life of the town, is that the police detective in charge of the investigation was Nuria's uncle. On Monday, after a few drinks in the bar, where Miranda saw Nuria Quintana, she and Greg went to the café opposite to drink an espresso. It was crowded with people watching football so they went home for their nightcap."

All eyes were on Beatrice, and her fish stew was going cold. She took another mouthful and savoured the taste.

"I don't know for sure, but this is what I believe happened. Miranda left the apartment between two and five in the morning, which is when the streetlights are switched off. She entered Señora Navarro's garden, climbed up the wall via the handholds Greg told her about and did the deed. Miranda is muscular in comparison to what I know of Romy, and since seeing the weapon she brandished this morning, it would have taken one stroke. I'm sorry, I know we're eating, but you did ask. I would guess Miranda wore black so that any bloodstains would be hard to spot and enable her to move through the shadows without being seen."

No one spoke for a few moments and Beatrice used the opportunity to eat some more food.

Philly asked, "But how can you be sure it was Greg's idea? And if he was the mastermind, why didn't the police take him in?"

"Private detectives sometimes use methods the police cannot. Theo and I entered Miranda's apartment when we were unable to secure a second interview. While examining Miranda's belongings, I found a very expensive ring in a box among some heavy medication. The kind of ring you receive in combination with an important question."

"Greg and Miranda wanted to get married?"

"I think he proposed to her – maybe as an incentive to follow through with his plan. Anyway, when she reacted so badly to seeing the police at the funeral, all eyes were on her. She committed the crime, I have no doubt, but as to his role? My instinct told me Greg would make a run for it as soon as he could manage. At my suggestion, Detective Quintana agreed to station officers at the airport, particularly the private jet terminal. They have just picked him up, about to board a flight to Bermuda. In his possession was ..."

"Her ring!" Philly exclaimed. "But how will they prove it was his idea?"

"I cannot say. Apparently, his arrest after attempting to flee the country has made Ms Flynn reconsider her silence and she is making a statement as we speak. Looks like he planned to run his church and online courses from a beach house with a sea view, abandoning her to rot away in a Mallorcan jail. Charming chap. He's a slick performer and made sure the crime could not be attached to him. Yet with the payment record and the fact Miranda couldn't have known about the ladder on your neighbour's wall, he'll have a hard time claiming complete innocence. He'll see the inside of a Spanish prison, as he deserves."

"His own sister," said Hoagy, staring into his flute.

"Beggars belief," added Raf.

"Delicious, absolutely delicious," said Beatrice as she placed her knife and fork together in the empty bowl. "Thank you, Philly. Yes, Miranda had a watertight alibi in Greg, an alternative suspect and despite a thorough search, Theo and I found no potential weapon. She must have had a hiding place we didn't discover or she kept it on her, in her handbag, for example."

"Must have been a sizeable handbag," said Matthew. "I saw the size of that knife while she was threatening Theo. It was the length of ... of... of a smoked salmon."

Philly and Raf burst into laughter, but Hoagy looked puzzled.

"Why on earth would she hang on to the murder weapon?" asked Hoagy. "She really must have a confused mind. I suppose that's the same hunting knife she used to slash my paintings. Brutal." He shook his head, his expression grief-stricken.

Beatrice had been looking forward to this. She took a long draught of cava and faced Raf Beaumont. "No, I'm afraid to say it was not the same weapon, was it, Raf? I couldn't possibly guess what you used to destroy your client's work, but I suspect it was something slightly more precise. You knew perfectly well that the few paintings in your possession of the murdered girl would skyrocket in value. Especially if the remaining canvases had been damaged or destroyed. A million for *Flamenco* would seem like peanuts in comparison to the only remaining renditions of Romy Palliser. Hoagy believes he is the only one to have the code to his studio, but that's not true, is it? Hoagy changes it regularly but always uses the same system. A system Raf Beaumont knows very well. With a few too many beers under his belt, he demonstrated he can access the building independently."

"Oh dear," said Matthew.

Raf said nothing, his gaze fixed on his plate.

"Rather than rushing to the defence of your star client and his wife, you waited and planned how to make maximum profit from the tragedy. You withdrew the three paintings you had on display in London, citing 'out of respect' on your press release. People searching for those images online were unable to find them because you refused permission. Therefore, the pictures had a mysterious allure, exciting private collectors and museums into a frenzy. Each one of the artworks in your possession could probably reach a seven-figure sum at auction. The one thing that could drive the price still higher would be the destruction of the remaining canvases."

No one was eating or drinking anymore. Even the wolfhounds came to sit at Beatrice's feet, as if spellbound by her words.

"Raf timed it well," said Beatrice, her gaze meeting each pair of eyes. "He gave Hoagy to understand that he was en route from London, while in fact he was forty-five minutes away in Palma. He let Philly stew in the police station all Tuesday and arrived like a saviour on Thursday. That was not his first trip to Deià. He drove here in the dead of night on Wednesday. He parked down the road, entered the gardens of Señora Navarro and climbed over the wall. How did he know those hand and foot holds were there? Because he had been friends with the Palliser family for decades. He entered the garden, and opened the studio door in the full knowledge Hoagy would be unconscious and Philly wearing earplugs. The police referred to the canvases as slashed, as if in anger, but that's actually not the case. Each painting had been cut with a fine blade, such as a Stanley knife.

This means the pieces would be irreparable."

"Good God!" Hoagy spluttered. "You ruined my paintings of Romy just to push up the profits? Those were not currency, they were art!"

Raf continued to stare at his plate and the only sound in the garden came from the cicadas. Wafts of garlic and fish danced across the table as the heat of the day rose from the patio stones.

Finally Raf lifted his head to address Beatrice. "You're better than I thought," he said. "You and your assistant make a good team." He swivelled his torso to address Hoagy and Philly.

"I did take a knife to the canvases, that much is true. But you're wrong if you think this was purely a financial move. I could not say this before but those paintings … exposed Romy and I found that quite insufferable. The three I took to London demonstrate her grace, her beauty, her exceptionalism. They will make you and me a great deal of money. The ones I cut are the ones I would not want to sell. They're too intimate. After she was killed, I considered how valuable those canvases would be and how much I would hate to sell them. Then I understood there was a different narrative. The person who killed her had also destroyed her image. My dilemma could be resolved. I would damage the remaining renditions of the girl, thereby pushing up the price of the only existing paintings on the market, and make those prurient pictures unsaleable. I apologise, Hoagy, and I want you to know I did this as an act of love. Love for you, and love for Romy."

In the silence, Beatrice sensed a heat emanating from Philly. Raf appeared to sense the same thing.

"Philly, you have every right to hate me. I have been devious and untruthful with the sole aim of protecting your, and my, livelihoods. Perhaps I should go now and we could talk after we've all had time to think. Thank you for dinner, thank you, Beatrice, for doing an extremely thorough job and thank you, Matthew, for your erudite conversation. Good night, one and all,

I'll be in touch."

No one spoke as the tall man shambled in the direction of his vintage car. Beatrice stood up and cupped a hand around her mouth. "Raf? Confess to the police."

He saluted. "Yes, ma'am."

The gates swung open and Raf reversed into the street.

Beatrice stood up. "Philly, Hoagy, that meal was divine, but now I think Matthew and I should leave you in peace. You have a lot to take in. We're leaving tomorrow, first thing in the morning. So here is the report, including all the detail, and thank you for the opportunity to investigate this case."

Hoagy looked up, his expression plaintive, and said, "Must you go?"

Before Matthew could open his mouth, Beatrice snatched up his hand. "Yes, I'm afraid we must. Thank you and good night."

Philly walked them to the gates. "I wish you could stay. Not just tonight but always. It would be wonderful to have you both as neighbours. Beatrice, I think you and I could be jolly good pals. This is ridiculous, of course, as I've only known you a matter of days, but I shall miss you. Please know this: the cottage we loaned to Tanya and Gabriel is at your disposal whenever you wish to use it. Safe trip home, my dears."

She embraced them both, then turned to walk back to the villa, sniffing.

Chapter 28

For a change, returning home to Devon from a Mediterranean island was not the depressing comedown it might have been. The skies were cloudless and if a slightly paler blue than the heavens above Mallorca, filled with the sounds of birdsong and insects. Gabriel helped them unload their suitcases, hindered by an excitable Border Terrier.

"I've got a job to do over at Shobrooke Park this afternoon. A beech tree came down in the storm. When I finished clearing that, I'll bring Dumpling over. I don't suppose you feel like cooking tonight, so should we come over with a takeaway?" he said, standing in the doorway.

Beatrice inhaled the scent of home. "That's a very good idea. I want to talk to Tanya and can't wait to see Luke. I'd better invite Marianne too because I want to hear about her date."

Gabriel rolled his eyes. "She can't talk about anything else. The woman's smitten. Right, I'm off. There's fresh bread and milk in the kitchen if you feel like a cuppa. See you later."

"Gabriel, you're very kind."

"I'll second that," said Matthew. "Very decent of you to collect us from the airport. The curries are on me tonight, I insist."

The Land Rover crunched its way out of the drive and with a toot of the horn, he was gone.

"What say you to a cup of tea and a slice of bread with

blackcurrant jam, followed by a light stroll in the forest with Huggy Bear?" Matthew rubbed his hands together.

"Tea and bread and jam, certainly. But perhaps you'll excuse me walking duties as I have a session booked with James for this afternoon."

"Tip top." Matthew looked down at the dog. "Looks like it's just you and me, scruff. I'll put the kettle on."

Conversations with James were predictable only in the sense that they never went how Beatrice expected. When she felt confident about her mental health and the way she was coping with whatever stresses she might be under, she ended up crumbling into a weeping heap. When she sensed she was losing her grip or worried about something to the extent that she could not sleep, their conversation was measured and calm. However, that was when she was talking about herself. On this occasion, she would be talking about the man she loved. She fully expected to be a sobbing mess. To which end, she prepared herself.

She drew the curtains on the June sunshine so that her face was only partially visible on the computer's camera. She prepared a box of tissues, the same brand James kept in his consultancy. For a person well versed in the quirks of human behaviour, Beatrice could be strangely superstitious. Finally, she poured herself a glass of warm water and squeezed half a lemon into it. She was ready to tell James her worst fear.

The tissues and lemon water turned out to be superfluous to requirements. Beatrice read out the notes she had prepared and added some extra detail when James asked questions. Seeing it all written down, she didn't really know why she was asking for his help. It was perfectly obvious that Matthew was suffering from some kind of mental degeneration. She attempted to explain.

"It's not that I'm expecting some kind of remote diagnosis from you, James. That would be ridiculous. I'm not even sure why am telling you all this, apart from the fact that it will obviously have an impact on me, but I don't mean that in a selfish way. It's just you're the only person I know with any expertise on mental health. How would you handle this?"

James lifted his eyes from his notes to look at the computer. "Let's frame this in a different way. If Matthew was demonstrating symptoms of physical discomfort, I don't know, back pain or digestive problems, what would be your course of action?"

"I'd insist he saw a doctor. Perhaps if it was something minor, he could go to his GP. If something potentially serious, I'd advise a specialist in that area. But this isn't something treatable that can be cured with a course of antibiotics. This could potentially affect our entire lives."

James rested his cheek in his hand. "A specialist in that area? If you think Matthew is suffering from some form of dementia, what kind of specialist might we be considering?"

She pressed her fingers to her temples and looked into his patient, sympathetic eyes. "I'm doing it again, aren't I? Failing to address the issue and floundering about for some snake oil. You don't need to unpack this one for me, James, I've been there before. In my mind, you fixed me. No, I'm not fixed, I'm still a work in progress. The thing is, because our sessions have been the cornerstone of my recovery, I want to use you as some kind of panacea for everyone else. That's like asking a dentist to treat athlete's foot."

"Thank you. We've taken one step closer to addressing the reason for today's session. I appreciate the fact you reflected on your behaviour with very little prompting from me. Yet I have to say, there's still a way to go. Take a moment, Beatrice, and consider the aim of this video call, or any of our video calls. How would you define our relationship?"

Beatrice stared over the monitor at the other end of the room. "You are my counsellor and we entered into a contract whereby you help me realign my thought processes. Together we break down patterns of behaviour which can prove negative or harmful. Our sessions are an opportunity for me to reflect on my reactions and interactions without judgement. There was probably more, but I can't remember what it was."

"That will suffice for now. I am your counsellor and as you say we work together to manage external and internal events which may have an effect on your equilibrium. So now I ask you again, what is the purpose of today's call?"

Beatrice looked at the lemon water, the tissues and the semi-closed curtains. "I think I wanted to feel sorry for myself and dressed it up as concern for Matthew. I am concerned and frightened and furious at the injustice of it all, but I don't want to face that just yet. What I wanted from you this afternoon was nothing more than a 'poor you'. How is it possible for one person to be so egotistical and self-interested without spontaneously combusting in shame?"

"If that was the natural consequence of egotism and self-interest, the planet would be a pile of ashes. Human beings are designed – I won't use the phrase wired because that suggests it can be rewired – to analyse their environment from a standpoint of self. Everything that happens around us is, and logically should be, evaluated as to personal impact. It is entirely natural to feel anxiety when someone close to you shows symptoms of illness. With such a breadth of scientific and even cultural references to such conditions as Alzheimer's, senile dementia and other forms of mental deterioration, you can imagine what's over the horizon. Which leads us in a circle. I do not know and refuse to guess what Matthew's symptoms might mean. That is a task for a qualified neurologist. My job is to support you throughout whatever you're facing. Until we know what that is, I will not say 'poor you'. What I will say is, whatever you face, I will be here to support you. Always."

Beatrice closed her eyes. Not to suppress tears, but out of a sense of gratitude. "Thank you, James. It stings a bit, when you tear off a mask. That said, I'd rather deal with it barefaced and honestly. You prod me into doing that and in the process, I hate your guts."

James laughed, throwing back his head to look at the ceiling. It was the first time in their relationship Beatrice had ever seen him do that. She found herself smiling.

"That's very honest of you, Beatrice. Do you feel ready to move on to the practicalities?"

"Mood stabilisers? Check. Diary has been a bit neglected of late, but I did find it useful when I was on this Mallorcan job. It's an observation thing. It even helped with the case. I'll keep it up more religiously now. Not just for me, but also for Matthew."

"I'm very pleased to hear that. Now, would you like to summarise today's call before we end?"

Beatrice got up from the desk and opened the curtains. Then she sat down in front of her computer screen and faced James. "Yes, I would."

Plates warmed, table set and French windows wide open, the garden was ready for guests. Matthew was pottering around in the kitchen preparing some sort of yoghurt dip when the sound of the Land Rover attracted Beatrice's attention. Before she could even wash her hands, Luke came through the garden gate with uncharacteristic solemnity, carrying a cat basket. His expression was so serious, Beatrice feared the worst.

"Is Dumpling all right?" she asked.

Luke set the basket on the grass and opened the hatch. "He's a very old man and needs to be handled gently," he said. Tanya and Gabriel came through the gate and watched as Dumpling sniffed his way out of the basket, padded daintily across the grass and entered the kitchen.

"You're so good to look after them for us," said Beatrice embracing the happy couple and turning her attention to Luke.

"Who gave you permission to grow so fast since we've been gone?"

Luke grinned and ran into the kitchen to find his grandfather.

"The table looks lovely," Tanya exclaimed. "I should take a photo of this, it's so pretty. Marianne has picked up the curry and she should be here in about ten minutes." She snapped a picture of the table setting and showed it to Beatrice. "Gorgeous!"

"Gorgeous," Beatrice agreed. "Gabriel, would you be so good as to help Matthew with the poppadoms? He always gets distracted and burns the delicate little things."

"Sure. Nothing worse than burnt poppadoms."

Beatrice took Tanya's hand and they walked together down to the stream.

"I've made an appointment with a senior neurologist at Exeter hospital for next Monday morning. You were right. There's something wrong and it might be nothing or it could be something. The fact is, we need to know. I want to apologise for wilfully ignoring not only the signs but also your advice."

Tanya teared up and she embraced Beatrice with a sigh of relief. "Thank you. If this is what I think it is, we need to work together. Does he know he's going to the doctors?"

Beatrice released her and looked into her watery eyes. "Not yet. I need to find a way of persuading him it's just a precaution. I'll get him there, I promise you that, even if I tell him it's a check-up for both of us. But I want him to understand, while he's still lucid, the reality of the situation. It could be a minor blip, but if it isn't, there are a lot of drugs that can help slow the progression of the disease. What about telling Marianne? She should know."

"Can we wait until he has seen the neurologist?" Tanya asked. "Just a few more days. Then maybe we can have lunch together, the three of us, and make a plan."

"Mum! Auntie Marianne's here with the Indian food! Come on!"

Beatrice and Tanya returned to the house, slapping on upbeat expressions and exchanging a glance of complicity as they took their places at the table.

By the time they had finished the poppadoms, Beatrice was heartily sick of the name Jago. Jago had reserved them a window seat at Chez Bruno and pre-ordered champagne. Jago had collected her in his Mazda MX-5 and opened her door when they arrived at the restaurant. Jago had paid her compliments and the bill, then after a chaste kiss on the cheek, hand-delivered flowers the next morning. Jago Perowne was the most chivalrous, considerate, charming man on the planet and Marianne couldn't thank Beatrice enough for the introduction. Jago had suggested a picnic on Saturday, so they could get to know each other better. Jago was good-looking, fit, financially stable with his own home. What, Marianne demanded, was not to love?

"Well, he sounds absolutely charming," said Matthew. "When do we get to meet him?"

"Don't be daft, Dad. You met him last Tuesday. One of the nicest things about Jago..."

Luke interrupted. "Is it time for the curry now? I'm really hungry."

"I'll get it," said Gabriel, Tanya and Beatrice all at the same time.

Beatrice sank down in her seat and allowed Tanya and Gabriel a momentary escape. Luke ran after them. She couldn't blame him.

"Marianne, would you like some wine? Do the honours, Matthew, my glass is running low. Did Tanya and Gabriel show you any photographs of Mallorca? It is the most extraordinary place, as I'm sure they told you."

Marianne held out her glass for Matthew to refill. "No, they haven't shared any pictures, thank God. They know holiday pictures are only interesting for the people who were on holiday. I remember all those boring slideshows we suffered as kids. Mum and Dad in Cornwall. Mum and Dad on the Scilly Isles. Mum and Dad in Scotland. So very, very dull. I have an aversion to other people's photographs and an even stronger aversion to the explanations that go along with them. Yawn."

Neither Beatrice nor Matthew spoke for a moment and Marianne seem to pick up on the atmosphere.

"Sorry, I didn't mean... yay! Here's the food!" Beatrice watched as Luke distributed the takeaway cartons under Tanya's supervision. She found herself wondering why someone should not be able to choose godparenthood. Similarly, why shouldn't a child decide for themselves who their godparent should be? An adoptive godparent, for example. To Beatrice that seemed like a far more satisfactory state of affairs. Because if she could choose, she'd swap Marianne for Tanya in a heartbeat. She shook her head at herself. That was a churlish thought she would not be sharing with Matthew.

Chapter 29

Due to a stock-take, it was later than usual when Adrian got home on Tuesday evening. The whole bus journey to Old Street his mind had been occupied with what to make for dinner. He thought of calling Will and suggesting fish and chips, but that seemed somehow flippant in light of the fact they were yet to finish their conversation about parenthood. Instead, he swung by Marks & Spencer where he picked up three different kinds of salad and some focaccia.

He got home to Boot Street, picked up the post and was just putting the food into the fridge when he heard the front door open. A strange panting sound made him freeze. Claws rattled across the parquet floor and Will's voice said, "Wait, take it slowly." He emerged from the kitchen to see a small black hairy dog with a moustache straining at the end of the lead.

He stared at the animal and up at Will. "What's this?"

"This is Molly, part Schnauzer, part something else. What the something else is, the woman at the dogs' home wasn't sure, but she suspects some kind of spaniel."

Adrian got to his haunches and reached out a hand. The dog's tail wagged madly and she stretched forward to lick him. "Hello. You're a sweet little thing, aren't you?"

"I haven't officially adopted her, don't worry. But I made enquiries at one of the rescue centres we use and got permission to bring her home on a trial run. If we decide to keep her, we have to go back and fill in the forms tomorrow." He unclipped the lead, releasing the dog to explore their apartment.

Tail wagging constantly, she sniffed her way around the kitchen, returned to jump up at Adrian, then scampered off into the living room. Will and Adrian followed, both wide-eyed with delight. Molly completed two circuits of the living room and came to sit at Will's feet, her tongue lolling out. Adrian fetched a bowl of water and she immediately started lapping.

"She's two years old and was given to the rescue centre for re-homing when her owner went into a hospice. She's had all her jabs and is very healthy. Because she's young, she'll need regular exercise and continued training. I asked the woman if it would be a problem to rename her, if you didn't like the name Molly, and she said not at her age."

Adrian stroked the dog's silky fur. "I don't mind the name Molly. It suits her. She's a pretty little pooch. Friendly too. What are we going to give her to eat?"

"I bought a packet of kibble and a bowl from the rescue centre, but I left them in the car. More to the point, what are we going to eat? I quite fancy something quick and dirty. Shall we take her for a walk down the road and get some fish and chips? Then we can all eat when we get home."

"Good idea! Molly? Do you want to go for a walk? Oh, look at her, Will. She's so excited."

He clipped her lead on and they left the flat to walk down to the Polish fish shop, stopping at every lamppost and tree for Molly to sniff or pee. Adrian couldn't stop grinning with pride. Normally, Londoners walked right past without making eye contact, but with a dog in the equation, people smiled at them and even said hello.

While Will was inside the shop getting cod and chips twice, Adrian fell into conversation with an old man who stopped to stroke Molly and tell him all about his own Jack Russell who had died earlier that year. It was as if the city had transformed into friendlier place now they had a dog. Will emerged with a delicious-smelling paper bag and they said goodbye to the elderly gentleman to make their way back to Boot Street.

Will fed Molly her kibble, which she devoured with enthusiasm while they sat at the dining table, eating the fish and chips. Once she had checked the bowl a further fifteen times, she drank some more water and then came to flop at Adrian's feet.

Adrian beamed at Will. "I knew I would like having a dog, but I didn't expect to like it this much. I think I'm in love."

"Me too. So shall we go back tomorrow and fill in the forms for an official adoption?"

"Definitely. Miss Molly belongs here. Talking of adoption, what about the other topic we've been discussing? I think she's rather distracted us."

Will didn't speak for a moment, adding more vinegar to his chips. "At the moment, I think we should just enjoy life as the three of us. You, me and Molly. I could be pretty contented with that, I reckon."

"Would you? Really? You're not going to feel frustrated or that you're missing out?"

Will shook his head and met Adrian's gaze. "You were right. I do tend to get all enthusiastic about a subject and go the whole hog. After two days back at work, the idea of us having a child has lost some of its charm, if I'm honest. That's why I went to the rescue centre. Being a dog parent is a lot less complicated and something we *both* want."

Relief bubbled up in Adrian as if he'd been drinking champagne. "I love you, William Quinn. I feel like we've weathered a storm together. With the help of Catinca, of course. Ooh, I can't wait to show her Molly. Are we going to stick with her name? I always thought if I had a dog, I'd like to call her Dorothy."

Will rolled his eyes. "You're such a walking cliché. How about we compromise and call her Dolly. Not too big a change for her and you still get your Wizard of Oz reference."

"Brilliant idea!" Adrian exclaimed, looking down at the ball of black fur. "Hello, Dolly."

Chapter 30

For the August bank holiday weekend, Beatrice prepared to receive guests. Will and Adrian were driving to Upton St Nicholas with two female companions. One, a highly successful Romanian fashion designer and the other, a part-Schnauzer rescue dog called Dolly.

The problem with living in such a beautiful part of the world was that the whole country seemed to descend on Devon whenever there was more than one consecutive day of sunshine. Will's method for avoiding snarl-ups on the A303 was to leave before dawn. Beatrice could only imagine the moaning and protestations from Adrian and Catinca when forced out of their beds before it was light. However, their journey took no longer than usual and the party arrived just before lunchtime on Saturday.

Even though she had been dragged out of bed in the wee hours, Catinca looked amazing, in a halter-neck gold-coloured dress and sparkly Converse trainers. "Very Marilyn Monroe," said Beatrice approvingly as she welcomed them in.

"Thought about doing the hair too, but blonde don't suit me. Suited you though."

"Don't start that again. I am perfectly happy with patches of grey. Adrian, you look very tanned."

"Walks in the park with Dolly." He kissed her on the cheek.

"And where is she?"

"Will took her straight into the garden. She probably needs a wee."

Huggy Bear and Dolly were both sociable dogs and played in the garden from the minute Dolly burst through the garden gate. After greeting the humans, Matthew crouched down to introduce himself to the new arrival. She was a dear little creature, all wriggly and eager to please, rolling over to let Matthew tickle her tummy.

"Her hair is so soft!" he said. "Huggy Bear feels like a Brillo pad in comparison. Although Dumpling is like a powderpuff. Might be a species kind of thing."

"Talking of the cat," said Beatrice. "Close the French windows. We're not sure how feline-friendly Dolly is. I don't want her to get a scratched nose from a bad-tempered old tomcat. Let's take your suitcases upstairs through the front door."

She showed her guests to their rooms and left them to unpack while she finished making lunch, keeping half an eye on Matthew as he laid the garden table. Adrian was the first to come downstairs. He stood beside her, looking out of the window.

"How's he doing?" he asked. "How are you doing?"

Beatrice rinsed the radishes and shook them into a paper towel. "As you might imagine, he has good days and he has bad days. The medication is definitely making a difference but it's impossible to predict when he's going to have one of his, I don't know what to call it, moments. The odd thing is, when he's himself, it's almost worse. He understands what's happening and can do nothing to fight it. A very cruel disease, if you think about it."

Adrian put his arm around her shoulders and pulled her close, resting his head on hers. He smelt of lemony aftershave, a scent Beatrice always associated with her ex-neighbour.

"I have thought about it and it is. Not just for him, but for you. It's one of the reasons we wondered if we should stay at The Angel instead of imposing on you as house guests. But if, as you say, familiar faces cheer him up, then here we are, reporting for duty."

Beatrice gave him a peck on the cheek and dried the radishes. "Thank you. The key point is not to correct him. If he calls you Luke, answer as Luke. We enter into his world, not drag him back into ours. Is Catinca still vegetarian?"

Her voice came from the doorway. "Definitely! Pretty much vegan these days, but that's when I'm at home. When I'm guest, I'll eat anything except meat. Can I give you a hand?"

With the help of Adrian and Catinca, Beatrice managed to produce a summer buffet to meet all her guests' dietary requirements. Will entertained Matthew with stories of puppy training school and they grazed in the garden until the village clock struck two. After lunch, the party pursued individual activities. Will took the dogs for a walk, Matthew dozed in the conservatory, Catinca set off on foot to visit Tanya, Adrian did the washing up and Beatrice put away the leftovers.

"We were talking about where to go tomorrow," she said, trying to find space in the fridge for yet another piece of Tupperware. "The beaches will be an absolute nightmare, but Gabriel gave us an insider tip. There's a lagoon in the forest where the river expands. Few people know about it, it has shade and sunshine and cool water. As it was Gabriel's suggestion, I obviously invited them and could not leave Marianne out."

Adrian shrugged. "I don't have a problem with that. Is she still seeing that detective sergeant? Because he and Will got on like a house on fire."

"Yes, they're madly in love and rather sweet. She's no less self-absorbed, but what can you do? Is that agreed then, a riverside picnic with dogs and child?"

Adrian dried his hands and held out his arms for a hug. "Do you ever miss the days when the two of us could just wander round a gallery and criticize each other's taste in art?"

She squeezed him tight, resting her head on his chest. "At least I had taste. You were always running after the latest, hottest, brightest young trend you'd seen in *Time Out*."

His chest vibrated with laughter and Beatrice squeezed him once again before letting him go. "The only question now is whether I can keep working. I'm nervous about leaving Matthew for any longer than a couple of hours. Since that Mallorcan murder case when he came with me, I've limited myself to a couple of local jobs and let Theo handle everything else."

"How does Theo feel about that?"

"He's fine with it so far. In fact he's actively seeking out jobs himself. He advertised our services in Mallorca and got two cases already, so he could go back and see his yoga teacher. I wouldn't mind returning myself. Perhaps get a holiday home there. Matthew would love a little *pomme de terre* in Deià."

Adrian snorted with laughter. "How I've missed your Bea-lines. A holiday home is a great idea."

"It is, isn't it? You and Will could use it too, while we dogsit Dolly."

"Ooh, yes! Let's go and browse properties on the Internet right now."

As so often with these affairs the preparation was the most fun. They cooked and chopped and prepared the picnic as a team. Catinca made something that looked like a cowpat which turned out to be an incredibly tasty Iranian stew called *fesenjan*. To much catcalling and laughter, Adrian baked two different kinds of quiche. Beatrice and Matthew took charge of the salads, while Will made his famous smoked salmon Scotch eggs. The atmosphere was excitable and upbeat, which seemed to have a positive effect on Matthew, who laughed and joked and related long Ronnie-Corbett-style anecdotes to everyone's amusement.

Tanya and Gabriel turned up at half past eleven and it

appeared all Luke's Christmases had come at once. He ran around the kitchen twice, hugging everyone, then rushed out into the garden with Will to meet the new dog.

They all piled into the Land Rover, picnic baskets at their feet. In the front, Tanya got on her phone to advise Marianne as to the route. When they arrived at the makeshift car park, Jago's Mazda was already in place. Gabriel led the way through the trees, carrying two camping chairs while the rest of them followed with various bags, cold boxes and blankets. The spot he had chosen, Beatrice had to admit, was quite lovely. A grassy slope, semi-shaded, led down to a broad sunlit pool with slippery rocks and clutches of reeds.

The party of ten plus two canines set up camp under the trees. Will, Luke, Jago and the two dogs couldn't wait and immediately waded into the water. Luke tore off his T-shirt and shorts and flung them towards the bank. They didn't quite make it and flopped into the water. Gabriel jogged down to the water's edge, scooped out the boy's clothes and spread them in the sunshine.

Beatrice and Matthew took off their shoes and walked down to the river. Chilly water rippled over her toes as she balanced on the rocky river bed. Matthew lifted his face to the sun, his visage dappled by the leafy canopy. He was smiling.

On the return to base camp, Tanya began opening all the elements of the picnic. It was quite obvious that they had catered for a party of twenty, rather than ten. Jago threw a tennis ball for Dolly to keep her from trampling over or stealing the food. Adrian enthused about Catinca's walnut and pomegranate stew enough to tempt Beatrice to dip a spoon into the brown mess. It was so delicious she scooped a portion onto her plate.

Matthew leaned forward and pressed a finger to Luke's shoulder. "Too much sun here, I'd say. Pam, did you bring a T-shirt for Marianne? She's awfully pink."

Beatrice sensed the entire party freeze. Tanya unrolled a T-shirt from her backpack and handed it to Luke with a wink. "Yes, I did. Put that on, my love, we don't want you to get burnt."

No one moved for a second. Then Luke dragged on the T-shirt and returned his mother's wink. "OK, no worries."

"Isn't this a lovely spot?" said Marianne.

Everyone made noises of agreement and continued eating.

Acknowledgements

With sincere thanks to Florian Bielmann, Gillian Hamer, Jane Dixon Smith and Julia Gibbs for sterling practical support. Much gratitude to Jim and Gina Prewett for the introduction to Mallorca and Simon Gough for a reminder.

Message from JJ Marsh

I hope you enjoyed *The Woman in the Frame*. I have also written
The Beatrice Stubbs Series, European crime fiction:

BEHIND CLOSED DOORS
RAW MATERIAL
TREAD SOFTLY
COLD PRESSED
HUMAN RITES
BAD APPLES
SNOW ANGEL
HONEY TRAP
BLACK WIDOW
WHITE NIGHT
ALL SOULS' DAY

I have also written standalone novels:

AN EMPTY VESSEL
ODD NUMBERS

And a short-story collection:

APPEARANCES GREETING A POINT OF VIEW

For more information, visit jjmarshauthor.com

For occasional updates, news, deals and a FREE exclusive prequel: *Black Dogs, Yellow Butterflies*, subscribe to my newsletter on jjmarshauthor.com

If you would recommend this book to a friend, please do so by writing a review. Your tip helps other readers discover their next favourite read. It can be short and only takes a minute.

Thank you.

Made in United States
Orlando, FL
17 February 2022

14903389R00161